"Chantal,

She froze and w̶ ̶ ̶ ̶ ̶ ̶ ̶ ̶ ̶ ̶ ̶
Luke in horror. ̶ ̶ ̶ ̶ ̶ ̶ ̶ ̶ ̶ ̶
real name?" She ̶ ̶ ̶ ̶ ̶ ̶ ̶ ̶ ̶ ̶ ̶ ̶ ̶ ̶ ̶ ̶ ̶ake
sure nobody here ̶ ̶ ̶ ̶ ̶ ̶ as anything but
Carol Worth. How long had he known her
real identity? How the devil had he found
out?

He stepped closer, close enough that
she could smell the scent of minty soap
and his spicy cologne. That's one thing
she'd noticed about him – no matter how
disreputable he looked, he always smelled
clean and good.

"Don't worry, your little secret is safe with
me. I'm not worried about where you live
or what's in your bank account. I'm more
worried about the fact that according to
my sources you now have a price on your
head."

Available in October 2007 from Mills & Boon® Intrigue

Secret Alibi
by Lori L Harris

Diamonds Can Be Deadly
by Merline Lovelace

Dakota Meltdown
by Elle James

Rules of Re-Engagement
by Loreth Anne White

Automatic Proposal
by Kelsey Roberts

Haunted Echoes
by Cindy Dees

Look-Alike
by Rita Herron

Hell on Heels
by Carla Cassidy

Hell on Heels
CARLA CASSIDY

MILLS & BOON®
Pure reading pleasure

*First published in Great Britain 2007
by Harlequin Mills & Boon Limited,
Eton House, 18-24 Paradise Road, Richmond, Surrey TW9 1SR*

© Carla Bracale 2006

ISBN: 978 0 263 85760 3

46-1007

*Harlequin Mills & Boon policy is to use papers that are
natural, renewable and recyclable products and made from
wood grown in sustainable forests. The logging and
manufacturing processes conform to the legal environmental
regulations of the country of origin.*

*Printed and bound in Spain
by Litografia Rosés S.A., Barcelona*

To my fellow MARA members, thanks for putting up with my craziness and never telling me to go away! I appreciate all of you.

CARLA CASSIDY

isn't a secret agent or martial arts expert, but she does consider herself a Bombshell kind of woman. She lives a life of love and adventure in the Midwest with her husband, Frank, and has written more than fifty books.

Dear Reader,

I confess, I have a passion for high heels, and my heroine in *Hell on Heels* embodies that passion. Chantal Worthington. I loved her the first time she popped into my head. Young, wealthy, smart and savvy, she's a girl after my own heart. Best of all, she has a fierce loyalty to her friends and a heart the size of the price of the designer clothes she loves.

Of course, Chantal needs a strong counterpart – and crazy Luke Coleman is just the ticket. These two characters are such fun! I hope you enjoy reading their story as much as I loved writing it.

Carla Cassidy

Chapter 1

The fundraiser had been a smashing success. The staff at the exclusive Kansas City Club had worked overtime to ensure that the decor and the service for the two-hundred-dollar-a-plate dinner was impeccable.

Everyone who was anyone had been there, afraid that if they weren't then they'd be fodder for gossip during the evening. Of course if there was one thing the wealthy of Kansas City loved to do more than spend money, it was to talk about one another.

"I could live on this." Belinda Carlyle scooped up a cracker full of caviar and popped it into her mouth.

Chantal Worthington wrinkled her nose at her best friend. "Not me, I can't stand the stuff."

The two women stood next to a buffet table. The

fancy appetizers had been picked over hours earlier. Chantal would have left long ago but her mother had been in charge. Chantal knew her mother would expect her to stay until the last party gasp.

"See the waiter over there? The one with the flashing dark eyes and tight pants? I'm thinking of having him on a cracker later this evening."

"Honestly, Belinda…" Chantal bit back the lecture that sprang to her lips, knowing from past experience that it wouldn't do any good.

Belinda had been on a path of self-destruction for years and Chantal knew there was nothing she could do except be there when her friend fell…which she did often.

"Your mother looks good. Botox?" Belinda asked as she grabbed another cracker.

Chantal looked across the room where her mother stood talking with the mayor. At sixty-five years old Katherine Worthington was still a beautiful woman, thanks to a man named Pepe who was paid an inordinately large amount of money to keep her hair the perfect shade of champagne blond and her skin like that on a baby's butt.

"If she's had it, she'll never admit to it," Chantal replied dryly. "She'll simply say her ageless beauty is the result of good genes."

"I met a guy in the bar earlier whom I would have liked to talk right out of his jeans." When Belinda got no rise from Chantal she changed the subject. "How's the bounty-hunting business?" Belinda shook her head, her highlighted brown curls dancing on her painfully thin shoulders. "I still can't believe my best friend is a bounty hunter."

Chantal grinned. "There are times I can't believe it myself. Mother insists it's a form of late rebellion." Belinda was one of only a few people who knew what Chantal did during her free time.

Belinda raised a perfectly waxed eyebrow. "Is it?"

Chantal didn't answer immediately. "I'm not sure," she admitted. "I was bored, looking to challenge myself with something more than shopping and doing lunch."

"Seems a little extreme," Belinda observed.

"So does taking home waiters you don't know to have meaningless sex," Chantal retorted.

"Darling, don't knock it until you've tried it," Belinda purred. Then she widened her eyes. "Oops, I forgot, you did try it. What was his name? Larry or Harry?"

Chantal laughed and nudged her friend with her elbow. "Gary, and that was definitely a wild, crazy rebellion." Gary Burkett was a poet she'd met at a literacy function.

He'd been intensely handsome with soulful eyes. They'd spent thirty minutes talking at the bookstore then had left and had spent the next two days in bed.

Chantal had begun to believe she'd found Mr. Right, then they'd gotten out of bed. What was it about silk sheets that could make a man irresistible but once the sheets were off transformed him into an asshole?

"I can tell you why you were so bored with your life," Belinda continued. "You don't have enough dysfunction. You're the only person I know who doesn't have a therapist."

"You have two. Me not having one keeps the world in perfect balance."

Belinda picked up her purse from a nearby chair. "On that note, I'm going home. Call me tomorrow?"

"As always," Chantal replied.

Belinda pulled her keys from her purse, then looked at Chantal again, all trace of humor gone from her pretty features. "Did you hear that the case went to the jury late yesterday afternoon?"

Chantal didn't have to ask which case Belinda was referring to. The Willowby rape trial had been one of the most highly publicized cases ever tried in the state of Missouri.

Ten months before, Marcus Willowby, heir to the Willowby Whisky fortune had been arrested on two counts of rape. It was alleged that twenty-eight-year-old Marcus had drugged the victims with GHB, then videotaped himself raping the unconscious young women.

The crimes were brought to the attention of the police by a young woman and her friend who had spent the night at Willowby's condo after a night of dancing and partying at a local club.

According to the young women they had gone to Willowby's place and had a few drinks and neither of them remembered anything after that. They'd awakened the next morning in Willowby's spare bedroom, fully clothed on top of the bed. Willowby had been in the kitchen fixing them all breakfast.

It wasn't until one of the women went to use the bathroom and discovered her underwear inside out that she became suspicious that something had happened that shouldn't have. She and her friend had left Willowby's and gone directly to the nearest police station where rape kits were performed on the two women and traces of semen were found on their underwear and skin.

An investigation had yielded the videotape of the two women being raped by Willowby while they were unconscious. Although the police suspected there were other victims, no other videotapes had been found and no other women had come forward.

It was an ugly case, but there had been very little gossip among Chantal's friends and peers. Willowby was one of their own, but the heinous nature of the crime and the power wielded by Rebecca and Roger Willowby, Marcus's parents, had kept public gossip at a minimum.

But Belinda and Chantal had spent a lot of time talking about Willowby. Ten years ago Marcus had raped Belinda.

"I hope the bastard rots in hell," Belinda now said, her voice husky with suppressed emotion. "I hope somebody kills him in prison."

Chantal placed a hand on her friend's arm. She knew the devastation that single night had wreaked in Belinda's life. She knew the emotional scars had been ripped open again when details of Willowby's arrest had hit the news.

"Belinda, he's not going to get away this time," she said softly. "According to everyone there's no way the jury can come back with a not guilty verdict."

"I know...I just wish..." She shook her head once

again. "I've got to go home. I'm getting one of my head-aches." She leaned forward and kissed Chantal on the cheek, then turned and headed for the banquet-room exit.

Chantal watched her friend go, her heart aching. She and Belinda had been best friends since seventh grade when the two of them had attended an exclusive summer camp and discovered they both had a passion for mint chocolate truffles from the Tenth Street Bakery, *Vogue* magazines and late lunches at the Plaza.

During those early teenage years, they had shared their despair over the fact that high fashion came to Kansas City six months later than every place else on earth and that the grapefruit diet didn't really work.

They'd shared the joy of discovering that Calvin Klein jeans actually made their butts look good and that bitchy Susie Winchester had become a cliché and run off with her family's gardener.

Those had been the most carefree years Chantal had enjoyed, even though, looking back, she recognized that she and Belinda had been totally self-absorbed and shallow as only teenagers can be.

The night of the party at the Willowby mansion had changed everything. They'd been sixteen, and, despite not really hanging out with Marcus and his friends, they hadn't been able to resist a party at the Willowby home.

The house had crawled with teenagers. Drugs and liquor had flowed freely and in the space of the thirty minutes that Belinda and Chantal had been separated, Marcus Willowby had nearly destroyed Belinda's life.

Chantal had tried to talk Belinda into going to the authorities and reporting the crime, but Belinda had been afraid. She'd been afraid of what Marcus might do, what her parents would think, and the gossip that would surround her if she told.

While Chantal and Belinda's friendship had only grown stronger, Belinda had transformed from a happy, carefree teen to a neurotic mess who only occasionally allowed glimpses of the happy girl she had once been.

"Darling, where are you?"

Chantal blinked and realized her mother stood before her. She smiled. "I got lost in my thoughts for a moment." She leaned forward and kissed her mother on the cheek. "The evening was a huge success."

Katherine frowned, a dainty wrinkle forming in the center of her forehead. "The salmon was overcooked and the salad wasn't chilled enough, but the good thing is, according to my best guess, we raised almost twenty thousand dollars for Kansas City Kids."

Kansas City Kids was one of Katherine's pet charities, an organization that provided medical and dental treatment to the underprivileged children in the city.

"That's wonderful, but certainly not a surprise. You're definitely an expert at fundraising."

Katherine smiled. "Your father used to say that if necessary I could raise a million for a family of toads." Her smile grew wistful and Chantal knew she was thinking of Chantal's father, who had died unexpectedly of a heart attack five years before.

"He'd be proud of you," Chantal said softly.

"Yes, I think he would be," she agreed. "So, are you heading straight home?"

"I'm not sure. I'm going to check in with Big Joey and see if anything is happening."

The frown that had disappeared from Katherine's forehead appeared again. "You will be careful?"

"Heavens, why would I want to do that?" Chantal teased. "You know I will be," she added and kissed her mother's cheek once again.

Minutes later she walked out of the lobby and into the sultry mid-June night and waited for the valet to bring her car around. She was glad the fundraiser was over. This had been her third one in the past two weeks. Friends of the Zoo, People for Pets, Save the Whales… everyone needed money and Chantal was on everyone's list as a benefactor.

As she waited for her car she pulled her cell phone from her purse and hit the speed dial for Big Joey's Bail Bonds.

Even though it was after eleven, she knew Joey would be in. Joey was almost always in. He slept, ate and drank his bail-bond business, and that business was never closed.

The phone was answered on the first ring. Monica Hyatt, Big Joey's assistant, barked a hello. "Monica, it's Carol. Is the boss in?"

"Nah, he left about fifteen minutes ago."

"Everything all right?" Chantal asked in surprise.

"Fine, just the slowest Saturday night we've seen in years. Every criminal in the city either went to bed early or decided to take the night off."

"So, there's nothing popping?"

"Absolutely nothing."

"Anyone else around?"

"James and Brian are playing cards and keeping me company, bitching about the slow night."

"Thanks, Monica, I'll check in sometime Monday." Chantal ended the call as the valet arrived with her car.

As she drove away from the hotel she contemplated her options. She could go straight home and get out of the sinfully short, clingy, red Valentino dress and the Gucci heels that made her long legs looks sexy but pinched like hell, or she could swing by Ruby's and see if Wesley Baker was as dumb as his rap sheet implied.

She decided on the latter. She headed toward the west side of town where Ruby's was located. As she drove, her thoughts were scattered, shooting first in one direction, then another.

For the last eight months she'd been living a lifestyle that would please a schizophrenic. Her life as Chantal Worthington revolved around fundraisers and parties, lunch dates and social events.

When she wasn't being socialite Chantal, she was working hard at being Carol Worth, bounty hunter. From the moment Big Joey had hired her she decided the smartest thing to do was keep the two lives as separate as possible.

She was wise enough to understand reverse snobbery, that the men she worked with at Big Joey's wouldn't trust her, wouldn't respect her if they knew where she came from and what her bank account contained. As it was, even after several decent collars she didn't feel as if she'd gained the respect of her co-workers at Big Joey's.

As a bounty hunter she used the name Carol Worth and worked from a post-office box. Only Big Joey knew that in reality she was heir to Worthington Boat Indus-tries and worth a small fortune.

Ruby's was a hole in the wall, a bar that catered to a leather-and-Harley clientele. Chantal parked across the street, shut off her engine and rolled down her car window.

You could always tell how business was at Ruby's by the number of motorcycles parked out front. Tonight there was an even dozen, all chromed and shiny in the illumination from a nearby streetlight.

For the last four nights Chantal had been watching Ruby's, waiting for one Wesley Baker to show up. Baker's latest crime, an attempted robbery using a Slim Jim beef stick as a pretend gun in his pocket had gone bad when the convenience-store clerk had pulled a very real gun on him.

Baker had no known address, unless you counted Ruby's, where on most nights before his arrest he could be found. He'd missed his court date a week ago and Chantal had a feeling it was just a matter of time before he showed up back here.

It was a funny thing about criminals…most of them were stupid.

Closing time was two and she settled back in her car seat to wait and watch. As always, a small kick of adren-aline filled her as she anticipated catching her quarry.

The burst of adrenaline was as addictive as Godiva chocolate.

It had been her personal assistant, Harrah, who had gotten her into the bounty-hunting business. Harrah was a struggling jewelry designer who had come to work for Chantal a year ago as a stepping stone into the society she hoped to cultivate as clients.

Harrah had come up by way of the school of hard knocks. One of four children raised by an alcoholic mother and an absentee father, Harrah had big dreams and a willingness to work for success.

One day while she and Chantal were working together, Harrah confessed that her brother, Jimmy, had a court date in two days and had disappeared.

Harrah had gone through Big Joey's Bail Bonds to secure her brother's bond and was scared to death he didn't intend to show at court and Big Joey would come looking for her.

On a lark, Chantal told Harrah not to worry, that she'd help her find her errant brother. For the next forty-eight hours Chantal and Harrah had pounded pavement, knocked on doors, and had finally located Jimmy two hours before court time.

It had taken every minute to talk him through his fear and convince him that it was in his best interest to show up and take his punishment.

In those forty-eight hours, a couple things happened that had changed Chantal's life. She'd met Big Joey and she'd realized she loved the hunt.

Harrah's brother had gone to prison to serve a three-

year sentence on drug charges and Big Joey's Bail
Bonds had hired Chantal as a bail-enforcement agent.

She sat up straighter as she saw a tall young man approaching the bar. Despite the heat of the night he wore
a jacket, the collar pulled up as if to hide his facial
features from view. Dark hair, a lanky build and suspicious clothing. She had a feeling it was her man.

Adrenaline once again twisted in her gut as she grabbed
her purse from the seat next to her. She peeked inside,
making sure she had both her handcuffs and her pistol.

Even though she'd been watching Ruby's for the
past four nights, she'd never ventured inside. It definitely wasn't the kind of place she'd choose for a night
out.

As she got out of her car she wished she were
wearing black leather instead of Valentino. She had a
feeling she was going to stick out like a bad cubic zir-
conia among a scatter of Harry Winston diamonds.

She approached the entrance, her heels clicking
against the pavement that still radiated the heat from
the day. Raucous music and laughter poured from the
opened doorway. She began her mantra.

"Prada handbags…sunny days…lunch with Mom…
Chloe jeans."

Whenever she was going into what might be a dangerous situation her habit was to list in her head all of
her favorite things. That way she figured if something
went wrong and she was killed, the last thing her mind
would remember was something she loved.

"Facials at Mimi's…sad movies…slumber parties

with Belinda…" She stopped as she walked through the front door of Ruby's.

The smoke was as thick as socialites at a Versace sale. The bar was to her left, a long expanse of scarred wood holding up a handful of drunken men and women. To her right were the biggest, meanest men she'd ever seen playing at two pool tables.

She scanned the people inside and spied Wesley Baker at the far end of the bar. He'd removed his jacket and looked at ease as he nursed a beer.

As she moved toward the empty stool next to him, she consciously made no eye contact with anyone. She didn't want trouble. She just wanted to get Baker outside and into handcuffs.

"Hey, baby, slumming tonight?" a deep voice said from behind her.

"Get lost on the way to the prom?" a woman laughed.

Chantal ignored them and wove her way toward the empty stool, walking as if she was lit like a Christmas tree. She sat on the stool and slumped forward, elbows on the bar. "I think I'm lost," she slurred. She offered Wesley a loopy, but friendly grin.

She knew from all the information she'd gathered on him that Baker considered himself a real ladies' man. Maybe in a worm colony, she thought.

"Where are you supposed to be?" Wesley asked, then raised a finger for the bartender.

Chantal giggled. "I can't remember the address. Maybe a little drink will help." She grinned at the bartender, a bear of a man sporting more tattoos than hair.

"How about a little top-shelf Scotch on the rocks?" She turned to look at Wesley, who had a cheap beer in front of him. "How about a Scotch on me?"

"Now you're talking." He shoved the beer aside as the bartender poured the two Scotches.

For the next few minutes Chantal small-talked with Wesley, who proved to be as charming as a Brazilian wax. Although anyone seeing the two of them interacting would assume her attention was focused solely on Baker, she was conscious of everything going on in the bar around them.

She needed to get Baker outside. There were too many men in the bar who looked as though they walked on the wrong side of the law, and if she tried to take him down inside she had a feeling she'd wind up wearing her own handcuffs, or worse.

She wasn't just worried about the men she could see, but there were others hanging out in the hallway near the bathrooms and in the poolroom. Chantal didn't mind taking risks, but she wasn't suicidal.

"I just remembered where I'm supposed to be," she said, after taking only two tiny sips of her drink. "At the Radisson Hotel."

"Sweetcakes, you're about two freeway exits off. You need to get back up on the interstate and take the Broadway exit."

"Is that left or right?"

He stared at her blankly. "Where are you parked?"

"Out front."

Wesley finished his drink. "What direction are you facing, north or south?"

"North…no, south." Chantal released what she hoped sounded like a half-drunk giggle. "Wow, I'm so turned around I'm not sure."

Wesley slid off his stool. "Come on, I'll walk you out and we'll see where you need to go."

The taste of sweet success filled her mouth. This was going to be a piece of cake. Once she got him outside and away from the crowd, she'd slap the handcuffs on him and take him to Big Joey's. From there he'd be taken to the police station.

The outside air smelled wonderful as they stepped outside of the smoky alcoholic haven. Chantal frowned as she saw a couple of men loitering by the row of motorcycles.

She'd hoped that nobody would be out front. The last thing she wanted was for anyone to try to get involved in her collar.

As they walked across the street, she opened her purse so she could gain access to her handcuffs. "Oh, wow, I can't find my keys," she said and pretended to rummage in the bottom of her purse.

"Maybe you left them in the car." As Wesley reached the driver door he bent down to peer into the window.

Chantal yanked the cuffs from her purse and slapped one on Wesley's wrist. It didn't fasten. "Hey, what the hell?" He attempted to whirl around to face her, but she held his wrist and tried to get the damned handcuff to connect.

"What's going on over there?" a deep voice yelled.

As Chantal and Wesley fell to the pavement, she was

aware of the sound of running feet. It wasn't exactly music to her ears, but she refused to release her death grip on Baker's wrist.

"Everybody back off. This is official business," a deep, familiar voice rang out.

A wave of dread swept through Chantal. Of all the men she wanted to see right now, Crazy Luke Coleman was the last. Just her luck that he would appear at the moment she suspected she was about to get her ass kicked.

With irritating ease, he grabbed Baker, yanked him up and cuffed him, then reached out a hand to help her up off the sidewalk. "Darlin', you're in way over your head," he murmured as he held out her cuffs.

She snatched the cuffs from him and jammed them back in her purse, aware that the group of men who had begun to advance had gone back to the opposite side of the street.

She eyed the tall man who now had control of her prisoner. "I could have managed on my own," she exclaimed.

Luke Coleman, or Crazy Coleman as he was known in the bounty business, looked as if he belonged at a biker bar. His dark hair hung to his shoulders and his jaw was covered with more than a day's dark stubble.

His sleeveless shirt exposed not only bulging biceps but also an intricate tattoo of an eagle. His jeans were worn and fit snugly on his long, muscular legs. He looked edgy, dangerous and more than capable of taking care of himself.

The other bounty hunters who worked for Big Joey

spoke of him as if he was a demigod. In the time Chantal had worked for Joey she'd found Luke Coleman to be arrogant, irritating and unsettling. He was also the most successful bounty hunter in a four-state area.

"Wait! What are you doing?" she asked as he started to lead Wesley Baker away from her car.

"I'm taking my prisoner to my truck," he said, then turned and proceeded to walk away from her.

"Stop!" She hurried after him and grabbed him by the arm. "What do you mean your prisoner? He's my prisoner."

Coleman turned to look at her once again, a glint of amusement in his dark eyes. "My cuffs, my collar."

She watched in outrage as he continued toward his truck, *her* prisoner in tow. "Bastard," she hissed. He had the audacity to turn and salute her.

She remained on the sidewalk, cursing a blue streak as Crazy Luke Coleman drove away with Wesley Baker.

Chapter 2

"That bastard will never take another one of my collars," Chantal exclaimed to her assistant as she gripped her handcuffs in her hand. "Come on, let's try it again. Pretend you're just walking along and I'll grab your wrist and handcuff it."

It was late Monday morning and the two women were in Chantal's living room where, for the past hour, Chantal had been practicing slapping cuffs on Harrah's wrists.

"You don't pay me enough for this," Harrah grumbled.

"Nonsense, I pay you three times what you're worth. Now, come on, just one more time."

"I go home with black-and-blue wrists and Lena will

think I'm seeing somebody who's into bondage," Harrah exclaimed.

"Lena knows you're devoted to her, now stop bitching and walk like a criminal."

With a long-suffering sigh, Harrah walked in front of Chantal. Chantal grabbed one of her wrists and slapped the handcuff over Harrah's smooth mahogany skin. Harrah twisted her wrist and the cuffs dropped to the ground.

"Damn," Chantal muttered. She picked up the cuffs and threw herself onto the overstuffed burgundy sofa. "You know, they make it look easy in the movies, but apparently there's a finesse to handcuffs that I still haven't figured out."

She frowned with irritation as she thought of how easily Coleman had cuffed Baker on Saturday night. "I still can't believe he walked away with my prisoner. He's the most irritating, arrogant man I've ever known."

Harrah didn't have to ask who she was talking about. Her full lips curved into a smile as she sank into the wing chair opposite the sofa. "He might be arrogant, but that bad boy is sexy enough to make *me* rethink my sexual preference." Harrah was a self-proclaimed lipstick lesbian who had been in a relationship with her partner for over five years.

Chantal scowled. "He looks as disreputable as the people he hunts."

"I hate to change the subject while you're nursing a grudge, but I need to get those invitations in the mail today."

"Invitations?" Chantal looked at her blankly.

"You know, the dinner party you promised your mother you're giving next week for Mr. Barnes? They're already going to be sinfully late. I'm going to have to overnight them. I've got Enrique catering and he's also taking care of the cake."

The dinner party was for Jeffrey Barnes, financial advisor and close friend of both Chantal and her mother. Jeffrey was turning sixty next week and Katherine had thought it would be nice if Chantal put together an intimate dinner party as a birthday celebration.

"I've got the list for you in my office. I'll get it so you can get started." Chantal got up and left the living room to go into her office off the kitchen.

The first thing that greeted her was the view, a stunning panorama of an exclusive golf course. Chantal didn't play, but when she'd house-hunted a year ago she'd fallen in love with the four-bedroom, story-and-a-half home and the pleasant surroundings.

Besides, there was nothing better than sitting in her office on a hot summer day and watching sweaty, well-built men swing a golf club.

In addition to the floor-to-ceiling windows across one wall, the room sported a wall of bookcases that held her favorite novels and knickknacks, a massive desk and a computer with all the latest bells and whistles that money could buy.

It was in this room that she did not only her work for various charities and organizations, but also much of her bounty-hunting work. Most people thought bounty hunting was all about bursting through doors and hopping over fences in pursuit of a bail jumper, but that wasn't reality.

Reality was long hours on the phone, using the Internet as a tool, talking to snitches and watching a particular location while fighting off sleep. The rush of a capture was the payoff for all the boring, tedious hours it took to get to that point.

She sat at the desk and opened a drawer to pull out the guest list she'd written out several days earlier. Thank God for Harrah, who managed to keep her life organized.

She leaned back in her chair and smiled as she thought of the day almost a year before when Harrah had shown up to apply for the position of Chantal's personal assistant.

"I'm black, gay and named after my mama's favorite casino, but I'll be the best damned personal assistant you'll ever have," she'd pronounced.

She hadn't lied. There were days Chantal didn't know how she'd functioned before Harrah. Harrah was tall and beautiful and the most efficient person Chantal had ever met. Harrah not only kept track of Chantal's appointments and social engagements, she also kept the house clean and occasionally cooked.

As if conjured up by mere thought, the woman appeared in the office doorway. "Got it?"

Chantal nodded and handed her the list. "Do I have anything on my schedule for today?"

"Nothing," Harrah replied.

"Once you get the invitations mailed off you can take the rest of the day off. I think I'll head to the Plaza and work out in the Gym, then go to Mimi's and get a facial and a massage. I've been tense since Saturday."

Harrah grinned, exposing perfectly straight white teeth. "Kicking his ass would probably do you as much good as a trip to Mimi's."

Chantal laughed. "Yeah, but a trip to Mimi's is a lot less dangerous."

With plans made for the day, Chantal left her office and headed for her bedroom to change clothes. It had been the master suite that had ultimately sold Chantal on the house.

The room was huge with windows that overlooked the ninth hole. She'd chosen melon tones to decorate: lush cantaloupe and cool honeydew colors that she found sexy yet restful.

In the center of the king-size bed, a large gray cat raised its head and hissed as if to protest her very presence in the room.

She'd found the cat six months ago in a box near the Dumpster behind Big Joey's Bail Bonds. It had been a miserably bitter January day with snow in the forecast. Chantal had brought the cat home and named it Sam, after her beloved father.

When she'd first found him she'd entertained fantasies of a warm purring fur ball against her chest, a little creature who would coil affectionately around her legs the minute she got home.

She'd obviously been delusional. Savage Sam, as she liked to refer to her roommate, didn't seem to have an affectionate bone in his body and she had yet to hear him purr.

It took her only minutes to change into workout clothes, pull her shoulder-length blond hair into a ponytail, then grab her gym bag and leave the house. It was a thirty-minute drive to the Plaza, a high-rent, beautiful shopping area of the city.

The gym where Chantal worked out wasn't an exclusive one and catered only to the serious-minded exercise freaks. The Gym was as simple as its name, a place that smelled of sweat. It definitely wasn't a place for social gatherings or chitchat.

Power shopping was as close as Chantal had gotten to exercise before going to work for Big Joey. But she'd realized that if she intended to be a successful bounty hunter, she needed to make sure she was in the best physical shape possible.

She worked out for a little over two hours, until her muscles were limp as linguini, then showered and dressed in clean clothes for a trip to one of her most favorite places in the whole world.

Mimi's was an exclusive club with membership reserved for those people who had the right name, the right connections and the ability to pay exorbitant fees for massages, facials and tanning sessions.

Chantal decided to have a full-body massage. As Mary, the masseuse, worked her magic on her tense muscles, Chantal's thoughts turned to Luke Coleman.

She still couldn't believe what he had done Saturday night and wondered if he had been at Ruby's to score Wesley Baker or if that was one of his usual hangouts?

She knew little about the man, only that he was a

loner. He'd worked for Big Joey for the past five years and in that time had garnered a reputation for being tough and having the best street contacts in the business.

"You are one big bundle of tension," Mary said as she kneaded Chantal's shoulders. "What have you been doing to yourself?"

"The usual stresses. I'm giving a dinner party next week."

"Oh honey, no wonder you're tense. We all know how stressful entertaining can be."

Chantal didn't reply. Entertaining was nothing. Stress was watching a Neanderthal saunter away with the criminal she'd collared. It was as if she were a gold miner and had spent hours, days digging for gold. She'd finally uncovered a nugget and some other prospector had reached over her shoulder and stolen it away.

She didn't care about the fee that she'd have earned for delivering Wesley Baker. Money wasn't the reason she'd gone into this business in the first place. What bothered her more than anything was Luke's assessment that she was in over her head.

By the time Mary had worked her magic, Chantal had managed to put Luke Coleman out of her mind. She left Mimi's feeling rejuvenated. After a fast lunch at a nearby restaurant, she headed for Big Joey's to see whose mug shot had made it to his wall of shame.

Big Joey's Bail Bonds was located in downtown Kansas City, three blocks from the city square that held the court house, the police station and various other government buildings.

On top of the flat, one-story business, a neon sign—as gaudy as that on any Vegas casino—flashed, despite the brightness of the afternoon.

At this time of the day the heat radiated up in fierce waves from the blacktop parking lot, intensifying the scent of motor oil and rotting garbage that permeated the area.

Chaos ruled the front office. Chantal had never been in the place when the desk wasn't littered with mounds of papers and fast-food wrappers, the phones weren't ringing off the hook and the scent of burnt coffee, sweat and fear didn't saturate the place.

A large bulletin board sporting mug shots of the people who had jumped bail and not made their court appearances covered one wall. Skips, as they were referred to in the business, were the people Chantal and her fellow bail-enforcement agents hunted.

Monica Hyatt sat behind the only desk in the room and she waggled two fingers in greeting at Chantal as she continued talking into the phone. As usual, she wasn't the only one in the room.

Two other bounty hunters played cards at a table in the corner and a pizza-delivery boy stood impatiently waiting for somebody to pay him for the pizzas that teetered precariously on the edge of Monica's desk.

"Hey, Carol," James Walker, one of the card players, greeted her. "Heard Coleman trumped you Saturday night." He and Brian Cooke, the other card player, laughed.

"I'm glad you two are so amused," she replied and

walked over to the wall to see if any new photos had been put up since Friday when she'd last been in the office. There were two and she pulled a notepad from her purse and wrote down their names and all the pertinent information about their crimes.

"Honey, I'd never have done anything like that to you," James said.

Chantal raised one of her blond eyebrows to gaze at the older man. "James, you'd cuff your own mother and bring her in if you thought a fee was involved."

She turned back to Monica and motioned toward the inner-office door. "Is he in?" she mouthed. Monica nodded and indicated she should go on in. Chantal knocked on the door, then pushed it open.

Big Joey Barlow stood less than five feet tall and weighed a hundred pounds soaking wet, but he had the attitude, the aggression and the guts of a man four times his size. The biggest mistake people made with Joey was to underestimate him because of his stature.

"Just turn yourself in, Pete," Joey said into the phone as he gestured Chantal into a chair in front of his desk. "If I have to send one of my people after you I can't guarantee things won't get ugly."

As Joey alternately cajoled and threatened whoever was on the receiving end of the call, Chantal sank into the chair opposite the desk and waited.

In the eight months that Chantal had been working for Joey she'd found him to be a generous, kind man unless you crossed him, then all bets were off.

"Just get your ass in here," Joey yelled into the receiver, then slammed it down and grabbed a bottle of antacid tablets from the desktop. He popped two of the chalky tablets into his mouth and chewed feverishly.

"Some days I think I should get out of this business, sell it and spend the rest of my days living on a beach somewhere and sipping drinks with those pretty little umbrellas stuck in them."

Chantal smiled at her boss. "You'd go crazy with boredom within a month and use one of those umbrella toothpicks to put yourself out of your misery."

He laughed. "You're probably right. This business is in my blood." He reared back in his chair and gazed at her with his intelligent brown eyes. "So, you in here to bitch?"

She frowned. "Why would I bitch?"

"Two words. Luke Coleman."

Chantal sighed in exasperation. "What did the man do? Take an ad out in the paper?"

"He came in here Saturday night and explained to me what had happened so I'd have a heads-up if you had a beef."

Chantal bristled with irritation. "I'm not a crybaby or a tattletale. I'd had no intention of even mentioning it to you," she replied.

"If I thought you were either, I wouldn't have hired you," Joey replied.

"I just wanted to check in. I see we've got a couple of new glamour shots on the wall."

"Yeah, mostly penny-ante stuff." Joey pulled a big cigar from his top desk drawer. He stuck it into his mouth, but didn't light it. "I'm much more interested in a phone call I got a little while ago from my source close to the DA's office."

Chantal leaned forward. "About what?"

Joey frowned and his eyes narrowed, giving him a dangerous look that only a fool would fail to see. "According to my source, Marcus Willowby failed to make his noon check-in with the authorities."

Chantal checked her watch. "But that was over an hour ago."

"Nothing official has come down. His lawyer is supposedly on top of it. He's sure it's nothing more than a monitor glitch of some kind."

"You'll let me know what you find out?"

"Honey, if that pervert tries to skip out on me, I'll call in every bounty hunter I know, every marker I'm owed, to see that bastard's balls tied to the highest tree." There was a soft menace in his tone, a menace that made her believe all the rumors she'd heard about him.

Joey leaned back in his chair and his frown deepened. "I didn't feel good about this from the very beginning. I should have told them to go to another bail bondsman."

"Why did they have to use a bail bondsman at all?" she asked. "I thought the Willowbys had more money than Trump."

"Just because you got a lot of money on paper doesn't mean you have a lot of ready cash. Willowby was arrested on a Saturday night and apparently he couldn't get his hands on ready cash right away. He didn't want to spend a minute in jail so he contacted me. And now this." He scowled.

"Has any of this made the local news?" she asked as her thoughts shifted to Belinda. If her friend got wind of this, she'd be beyond distraught.

"I don't know, but I'd doubt it, since nothing official has been announced yet."

Chantal stood. "I've got to run. Let me know as soon as you know anything about Willowby."

"Will do," Joey replied.

Minutes later as Chantal drove toward home, she thought of the man who was her boss. Rumor had it that years ago Joey had been engaged to a beautiful woman. A week before their wedding she was killed by a drunk driver who had half a dozen DUI arrests on his record. Joey went crazy. He hunted the man down and three days later beat him to death with his bare hands.

Joey went to prison for ten years. With his physical stature alone, prison should have been hell for the man, but Joey had not only survived, he'd thrived. He'd come out of prison with a zeal to right the wrongs of his past, and thus Big Joey's Bail Bonds was born.

Before Chantal had gotten into bounty hunting, she, like so many others, had a romanticized view of the business. She'd thought bounty hunters were honorable men fighting for justice and righting the wrongs of an inadequate legal system.

In truth it was a business shadowed with darkness. Perhaps there were some honorable men, but there were also men drawn to bounty hunting by their own propensity for violence and power and control.

By the time she pulled into her driveway her thoughts

were back on Belinda. She knew the emotional invest-
ment Belinda had in seeing Marcus Willowby tried and
convicted for his crimes. She also knew Belinda had no
support system other than Chantal.

Belinda was the cliché of the poor little rich girl. She
had no siblings and her parents had always been more
interested in traveling than in their only daughter. Belinda had been raised by a variety of nannies and had
never connected with the people who had given her life.

Sometimes Chantal thought Belinda had been drawn
to her because of the relationship Chantal had with her
own parents. Katherine and Sam, while he'd been alive,
were loving, caring people who always had time for
their only child.

Belinda had loved spending time at Chantal's house
when they'd been growing up, and she'd mourned the
death of Sam almost as deeply as Chantal and her
mother had.

Chantal and Belinda had spent many hours discussing
the differences between their parents. Belinda insisted
that she thought it was because her parents had been born
wealthy and Chantal's parents had made their money.

Inside the house, Chantal went directly to her office.
She sat behind her desk and turned on the television
with the remote control. She channel-surfed, seeking
any news report on the Willowby trial.

Since the case had gone to the jury late Friday afternoon. Marcus wouldn't have been required to show up
in court today unless a verdict had come down. However, he was required to wear a monitoring device and

check in with the authorities at specific predetermined times during the day and evening.

There could be a hundred innocent reasons why he had missed his noon check-in or there could be one reason why he hadn't…and that was because he'd run.

When she found nothing on the news, she turned on her computer and went to the Web site devoted to the trial. It was run by a group that identified itself only as Women Against Rape and had sprung to life the day after Willowby had been arrested.

The headline across the first page read: Willowby on the Run?

The provocative headline wasn't substantiated by the blurb beside it, which indicated only that Willowby had missed a check-in and his lawyer had assured the authorities it was some sort of technological glitch. She shut down the computer, picked up the phone and dialed Belinda's number.

Margaret, the Carlyles' housekeeper, answered the phone on the second ring. "Hi, Margaret, it's Chantal. Is Belinda there?"

"Ms. Belinda is resting."

It wasn't unusual for Belinda to nap during the day, but Chantal needed to speak to her friend, needed to find out if Belinda had gotten word about Willowby. "Could you get her on the phone? I really need to speak with her."

"Just a moment."

Chantal tapped her sculptured nails on the top of her desk as she waited for Belinda, hoping that her friend hadn't seen the Web site, had no idea that there was even the most remote possibility that Willowby had fled the jurisdiction.

"Ms. Chantal, I can't get her awake and there's an empty pill bottle next to her bed." Margaret's voice held a frightening urgency.

"Call 911 and tell them to take her to St. Luke's! I'll be there as soon as possible." Damn. The minute Big Joey had told her about Willowby's missed check-in, she'd been afraid that Belinda might get word of it and do something stupid.

Chantal jumped out of her chair, grabbed her purse and headed for the door.

As she drove to St. Luke's Hospital, her heart beat a frantic rhythm. This wasn't the first time Belinda had done something stupid. Twice before she'd taken an overdose of pills.

"Damn it, Belinda," she murmured. The thought of losing her created an ache inside Chantal's chest. Belinda was more sister than friend. Belinda was the keeper of secrets, Chantal's partner in joy and sorrow and she couldn't imagine not having her best friend in her life.

By the time Chantal arrived at the hospital, Belinda had already been taken into the emergency room. "I'm here for Belinda Carlyle," Chantal said to the receptionist.

"And you are?"

"Her sister, Chantal." She knew the only way to get information was to pose as an immediate family member.

"If you'll just have a seat in the waiting room I'll let them know you're here."

Chantal sank into one of the chairs and tried to still the rapid beat of her heart. Thank God she'd decided to call Belinda. She prayed they had found her in time.

"Nine-hundred-count sheets, anything by Armani, chocolate-covered strawberries." As the stress built up inside her, she began her mantra beneath her breath.

She wanted to wring Belinda's neck, kick her in her butt, and pull her against her heart and make her swear she'd never do anything like this again.

What if Chantal hadn't called her? What if Margaret hadn't gone into the bedroom? What if…what if… Those kinds of thoughts could eat you alive.

It was a little over an hour later that she was allowed into the emergency-room area where a doctor told her they had pumped Belinda's stomach and he'd summoned a mental-heath associate to speak to her.

"May I see her?" Chantal asked.

He nodded and motioned toward exam room seven. Chantal hurried into the enclosure to find Belinda with her head turned toward the wall in the semi-dark room.

"Belinda, it's me." Chantal sat in the chair beside the bed and reached for her friend's hand. Without turning her head to acknowledge Chantal in any way, Belinda released a deep, heart-wrenching sob and squeezed Chantal's hand.

For a long moment they remained that way, neither of them speaking, their hands clasped tightly together. Every woman, no matter what her age, needed a best friend in her life. Men were great for sex and opening difficult pickle jars and a few other things, but only another woman could understand the complexities, the joys and sorrows of being a woman.

It was Belinda who finally broke the silence. She turned to look at Chantal, her face pale and her eyes dark and haunted. "He's going to get away. I knew he'd never be punished. I knew somehow he'd escape."

"Belinda, you don't know for sure what's going on. Nobody does. They think it might be some sort of monitoring malfunction."

"Bullshit." The word exploded from her as tears filled her eyes. "He's going to get away with it just like he did years ago. There's no monitoring malfunction. He's running and he has the money and the means to run where nobody will ever find him, where he'll never have to face up to the lives he's destroyed."

She jerked her hand from Chantal's and half rose in the bed. "Don't you understand? It's my fault. It's all my fault. If I'd done the right thing years ago then none of those girls would have been raped. That bastard would have been in jail a long time ago."

She fell back to the bed and shook her head wearily. "At least they were drugged when it happened. They were unconscious and don't remember the smell of his breath or the feel of his hands or the things that he said."

"What things did he say?" Chantal asked. In all the times they had spoken about Willowby, Belinda had never gone into the details of the rape that night in his mansion.

She chewed on her bottom lip, her eyes feverish. "Sometimes I can't get his voice out of my head. At first he didn't say anything, he just grabbed my hand and pulled me into the bathroom. Before I even understood what was happening he was pulling up my skirt and yanking down my panties." She drew a deep breath and released a sob.

"Belinda…you don't have to…"

"No, I want to talk about it. Maybe if I talk about it I'll be able to forget it." Once again she reached for Chantal's hand and grabbed it painfully tight. "I was so shocked, I didn't even fight him. He shoved me back against the sink and it was over almost before it began. I started crying and he looked at me like I was nothing, like I was dog shit that he'd accidentally stepped in."

She shivered, as if the devil himself had grabbed her soul. "I remember as clearly as if it happened yesterday, that look in his eyes, then he said, 'You won't tell.' I told him I would, but he said nobody would believe me, that I was a fat girl with zits and he'd tell everyone I came on to him and it was nothing more than a pity fuck on his part."

A rage of indignation swelled in Chantal and for a moment speech was impossible as the anger swept over her.

"The awful part was that I knew he was right," Belinda continued as tears streamed down her cheeks. "I *was* fat and I *did* have bad skin and he was the handsome, popular Marcus who could have any girl he wanted."

"I can't take those ugly words out of your head, Belinda," Chantal said softly. "But you know you didn't deserve what he did to you."

Belinda sighed and swiped the tears from her cheeks. "I'd rather be dead than know he's out there raping more women, destroying more lives." She turned her face to the wall once again.

"Belinda, that's not going to happen," Chantal said vehemently. "He's not going to get away. If he runs, then I'll find him. Have you forgotten that that's what I do? I swear I won't let him get away."

Once again Belinda's hand gripped Chantal's and she turned her head to gaze at Chantal once again. "You promise?"

"Pinky promise," she replied, a term from their youth. "And you need to make me a pinky promise."

"I know, I know. I was stupid." She released a tremulous sigh. "When I heard that he'd missed his check-in, I just felt the deepest, blackest despair I've ever felt in my life."

"Then you should have called me," Chantal replied. "Because I can't imagine my depth of despair if I didn't have you in my life." It was true. She couldn't imagine not having her best friend in her life. "He's not worth it, Belinda. He's nothing but scum."

Dusk had fallen and night was only minutes away when Chantal finally left the hospital and headed home. She was exhausted. The afternoon had been a mental roller-coaster ride and all she wanted to do was go home and curl up in her bed.

Back at home, she headed for the master bath and changed into her favorite silk pajamas. Sam, who was curled up in the middle of her bed, glared at her balefully as she stepped into the room.

As she approached the bed he hissed and dove for the doorway, then disappeared down the hallway to an unknown destination. Just her luck, the one and only male she'd allowed in her house and he had attitude.

She slid beneath the sheets and grabbed the remote control from the nightstand. She was just in time to catch the ten o'clock news.

She sat up as an attractive reporter announced that the Willowby jury had delivered a verdict late that afternoon. "Guilty," the reporter exclaimed, as if personally pleased with the jury decision. "But the real news is that Jonathon Mathis, Willowby's lawyer, was unable to produce his client for the verdict. Tonight a warrant has been issued for Marcus Willowby. Anyone with any information as to his whereabouts is asked to call the TIPS hotline."

Chantal lowered the volume of her television and picked up the phone receiver by her bed. She quickly punched in Big Joey's number. Busy.

She got out of bed and headed for her computer, sleep the last thing on her mind. Her conversation with Belinda played and replayed in her mind and the rich anger that had filled her then consumed her now.

She hadn't realized when she'd made the promise to Belinda that Willowby had already flown the coop. Chantal didn't make promises easily and she never made promises she didn't intend to keep.

Because of her love for Belinda, because of what Willowby had done to her and to so many other helpless women, Chantal would use whatever means necessary to hunt him down and see that he faced the justice that he'd managed to escape for so many years.

"Game on," she murmured as her computer connected her to the Internet.

Chapter 3

Sleep deprivation made Chantal cranky, so did dieting, rude salespeople and non-returnable policies on anything, but lack of sleep was the worst. She was a nine-hour-a-night kind of woman and actually preferred ten to twelve whenever possible.

It used to drive her mother crazy, Chantal sleeping away half a day. "Life is passing you by while you're dreaming," Katherine would say. For a while Chantal had tried to exist on six to eight hours of sleep a night, but within weeks she was back to her normal pattern.

When she pulled into Big Joey's the next morning she was definitely feeling the effects of a night with too little sleep and she was more than a little crabby.

She'd spent most of the night printing off whatever

she could find about Marcus Willowby's life and trial. She had a feeling that somewhere in the ream of paperwork she'd printed off was a clue as to where he might run. All she had to do was find that clue.

Her foul mood instantly intensified when she pulled into Big Joey's parking lot and saw Luke Coleman standing outside the bail bonds building.

As usual, Luke was dressed in a white T-shirt that displayed muscled biceps and worn jeans that hugged his slim hips and long legs.

Despite the early-morning hour, dark whiskers covered his firm jaw, making her wonder if the man even owned a razor. The brilliant sun managed to pull highlights from his shiny, long, dark hair.

As she got out of her car she felt his gaze on her, and, as always, a small knot of tension balled in the pit of her stomach. What was it about the man's very presence on the earth that bothered her?

She wondered what he was doing standing outside the building in air that was already far too hot for mid June.

Maybe he'd been fired, she thought optimistically. Yeah, right, and maybe Paris Hilton would go to work for the Peace Corps.

"We need to talk," he said as she approached.

"I can't imagine what we'd have to talk about," she replied with just the right amount of cool disdain in her voice. "Unless of course you feel the need to apologize for your behavior on Saturday night."

One corner of his mouth curved upward and his dark

eyes lightened in obvious amusement. "Why should I apologize for saving your ass?"

"You didn't save my ass, you stole my collar." She tried to keep her tone cool and calm even though she wasn't in the mood for him, especially if he intended to gloat. "I'd staked out that bar for four nights to get Wesley Baker."

"You're handcuff-challenged and you made a lot of mistakes," he returned, "but that's not what I need to discuss with you."

"And I told you we have nothing to discuss." She walked past him and headed for the door.

"Chantal, we need to talk."

She froze at the sound of her real name and whirled back around to face him in horror. "How do you know my real name?" She'd been so careful to make sure nobody here knew her as anything but Carol Worth. How long had he known her real identity? How in the devil had he found out?

He stepped closer to her, close enough that she could smell the scent of minty soap and his spicy cologne. That's one thing she'd noticed about him, no matter how disreputable he looked, he always smelled clean and good.

"I knew who you were the day after you started working for Joey. I make it my business to know the kind of people I work with."

"I don't work with you and you need to forget anything you think you know about me." She wasn't sure why, but the idea that Crazy Luke Coleman knew her real identity made her feel vulnerable.

"Don't worry, your little secret is safe with me. I'm not worried about where you live or what's in your bank account. I'm more worried about the fact that according to my sources you now have a price on your head."

"What are you talking about?" How she wished she'd gotten more than three hours sleep the night before. How she wished she'd taken the time to put on mascara before leaving the house that morning. The utter irrationality of this thought let her know she was beyond sleep-deprived. She was positively delusional.

"Remember Perry Mundy?"

"Of course," she replied. Perry Mundy was a two-bit dope-dealing punk who had skipped bail and taken to the streets. Chantal had brought him in and she'd heard that only a week earlier he'd been sentenced to five years in prison. "What about him?"

"My street sources tell me he's put out the word that he wants you dead and he's willing to pay for the job. I'd say the best thing for you to do is to take a little vacation, get out of town until Mundy cools off and calls off his dogs."

She stared at him with a mixture of disbelief and horror. A price on her head? Was that possible? Disbelief quickly won over horror.

"What's the matter, Coleman? Can't handle a little competition?"

He frowned, eyes narrowed to mere dark slits. "What are you talking about?"

She shrugged. "I just find it interesting that yesterday Marcus Willowby jumped bail and this morning you're telling me to take a vacation because some punk has put out a hit on me. The timing is just a tad suspicious to me."

Once again she turned to go inside, but squeaked in surprise as he grabbed her by the upper arm and spun her around to face him once again.

Her heart thumped wildly as his gaze bored into hers. All trace of amusement had fled from his black eyes and his mouth was nothing more than a grim slash. "Don't be stupid," he said. "This isn't one of your little society soirees, this is a very real threat that you'd better take seriously."

She jerked away from his grip and stumbled two steps backward. "Fine. You've delivered the information. I'll take it under consideration."

She breathed a sigh of relief when he didn't stop her from going inside. It took her only ten minutes to find out that Big Joey knew nothing more about Willowby's disappearance than she'd managed to glean from the news.

However, there was an intensity vibrating in the air inside the office. Big Joey had put up the bond for Willowby and he was beside himself with rage. When Big Joey wasn't happy, nobody in the office was happy.

When she discovered he didn't have any information that she could use to find Willowby, she left, realizing she was going to have to use every resource at her disposal in an attempt to figure out where he might be.

Chantal was glad Coleman was nowhere to be seen when she left the office. She got back in her car and headed home. As she drove, she thought of what Luke had told her about the price on her head.

As dope dealers went, Perry Mundy had been small change, but he'd considered himself a bad-ass gangsta and had surrounded himself with a couple of meatheads who he called his boys.

She supposed it was possible Mundy had gotten word to his old friends on the street that he wanted her dead and was willing to pay for the pleasure. She just wasn't sure she was willing to take Luke's word on the situation.

On impulse, instead of going directly home, she headed downtown. The smart thing to do was to check out the rumor and there was only one person she knew who might have heard this latest news about a threat to her life.

Christopher Carson, Chubby Cheeks, lived on the streets near a homeless shelter in the blighted downtown district. Chantal had met him six months before when she'd been looking for a friend of his who had skipped out on bail.

She'd discovered Chubby to be an invaluable source of information about all kinds of things, in particular street crimes and people. He seemed to have his ear to the ground when it came to information.

She drove slowly down Twelfth Street and pulled to the curb in front of the Italian Pizza Place. The business had changed locations years ago, but the sign still hung in the window of the abandoned building.

Chubby sat in the alcove of the doorway and when he saw her familiar red sports car he stood, walked to the car and got in the passenger side.

He was a big man of an indeterminable age, and he brought with him the smell of the streets, the odor of unwashed clothing and sweat and filth. "Been waiting for you," he said as she pulled away from the curb.

"You got something for me?" she asked.

"You got a price on your head, baby girl."

So, Luke had told her the truth. For the first time a whisper of apprehension swept through her. "And what's the price?"

"Five thousand," he replied.

Five thousand? If she wasn't so worried she'd be offended. "I spend more than that in a year on hair products."

"You ain't careful you won't be needing any hair goop," Chubby said. "That punk-ass kid you put away seems to think he's some sort of a godfather."

Chantal slowly digested this information. Still, even though it was disturbing, she had another case to think about as well. "You know anybody in the city who provides false identification and passports?" Willowby would probably need false identification if he intended to get out of the country.

Chubby shook his head. "I know a guy works out of his car over on Grand, mostly does fake ID for kids. I don't think he's good enough to do passports or nothing like that."

Chantal rounded the block and pulled back up in front of his alcove. "You doing okay, Chubby?"

"You know me. I get by."

She pulled a twenty-dollar bill from her purse and

handed it to him. "Get yourself a decent meal." She gave him a twenty anytime she talked to him, whether he had information or not. She didn't know whether he used the money to buy food or to purchase a bottle or two of cheap wine, which he told her he had a fondness for.

He took the bill and flashed her a bright smile. "And you watch your back." He got out of the car and disappeared back into the shadows of the doorway.

Five thousand dollars was definitely insulting. But, whether the bounty was five or five hundred thousand dollars, dead was dead.

She tried to tell herself that the young men who had been friends with Mundy didn't have the intelligence to pull off a hit on her, but she knew that wasn't true. It didn't take a brain surgeon to point a gun and pull the trigger.

The only comfort she could find in the entire situation was that they would be looking for Carol Worth. This was one of the reasons Chantal had decided to use a fake name in this line of work.

Her mother was a wealthy woman all alone and Chantal's main reason for not using her real name was to protect her mother from any form of revenge that might happen because of Chantal's work.

Chantal would be a fool not to take this threat seriously. She recognized that the first thing she needed to do was stay away from Big Joey's, which wouldn't be a problem since she intended to spend the bulk of her time hunting for Marcus Willowby. He certainly wasn't going to be found at Big Joey's Bail Bonds.

A smug smile curved her lips. She had a feeling all of Luke's contacts would be of no use to him when it came to locating Willowby. The "social soirees" he'd mentioned earlier would be her ticket to the information she needed.

Willowby wasn't a common criminal and he was a creature accustomed to certain comforts. He wouldn't be found in a hole or a hovel. He wouldn't take to the streets to evade capture. She would eventually talk to somebody, one of her social peers, who would have a clue as to Willowby's whereabouts. All she had to do was identify who that peer might be.

Harrah met her at the front door of Chantal's house, notebook in hand. "Enrique called. He wants to go over the menu with you for Saturday night. Your mother called and wants you to call her. Belinda called and said they're releasing her from the hospital around noon so she's planning on being here by one or two at the latest."

Chantal had insisted that Belinda come stay with her for several days when she was released from the hospital. Chantal hadn't wanted her friend to go home and be alone while she was so emotionally vulnerable.

"Call Enrique back and tell him I trust him with the menu," Chantal said as she walked through the living room toward her office. Harrah followed behind her and stopped in the doorway as Chantal sank down at her desk. "Then call Sarah Birmington and see if it's too late for me to get a ticket to the fund-raiser tomorrow night."

Harrah raised an eyebrow. "I thought you'd decided not to go."

"I've changed my mind," Chantal replied. "It might be the perfect place for me to hear some snippet of news about Willowby. Would you check to see if my red Gaultier is back from the cleaners?" Chantal picked up the phone to call her mother while Harrah disappeared from the doorway.

Her mother's housekeeper, Edna, answered the phone and connected Chantal. "Darling," Katherine said. "I called earlier to see if maybe you were free for lunch today."

"No way. I've got tons of work to do. You heard Willowby skipped out?"

"I spoke with Rebecca this morning. The poor woman is beside herself. You know she absolutely dotes on that boy, both she and Roger do."

"Does she know where he might be? Is it possible she'd help him get away?"

Katherine paused thoughtfully. "I don't think so. She has certainly been eager for the trial to be over with and didn't believe he was guilty of the charges, but I don't think she'd encourage him to run. Rebecca isn't that kind of a woman."

Chantal frowned. She wasn't so sure. Rebecca's devotion to her only son was legendary, which Chantal suspected was part of Marcus's problem. He'd been spoiled and indulged from the moment he been born.

Rumor had it that Roger and Rebecca had suffered

infertility issues and that at the age of thirty-seven, Rebecca had finally gotten pregnant with Marcus. She and Roger had considered the boy a gift from God.

"She's distraught over the fact that reporters have camped out in front of her house," Katherine continued.

Chantal had suspected as much. The odds were minimal that Willowby had gone to his parents' house. But the moment he'd missed his check-in, cops and reporters would have descended not only on his condo, but also his parents' residence.

"I've decided to go to the Folly Theater open house tomorrow evening," Chantal said. "Are you going?"

"Yes, and I'm so pleased that you're going. It seems lately the only time I see you is at a social event."

"Do you have an escort?" Sometimes Katherine talked Jeffrey Barnes into attending functions with her.

"No, I'd planned to go alone."

"Why don't we go together? I can pick you up," Chantal offered.

"That would be lovely," Katherine exclaimed, her pleasure obvious. "It will be a girls' night out."

"Why don't I plan on picking you up at seven?"

With arrangements made for the next evening, Chantal logged on to the Internet and checked for any updates on the Willowby case.

"If I were a convicted rapist and had money and connections, where would I run? Where would I hide?" she muttered aloud.

Somehow, someway, she needed to get into Willowby's head. She needed to find out what made him tick, his thoughts, his fears, his friends and his fantasies.

She had a feeling that if she succeeded and did manage to get into his head, it would be an ugly, perverted place to be.

Chantal stood in front of her dresser mirror, giving herself one last look before leaving to pick up her mother. Chantal had never had any illusions about her physical appearance.

She was average height and average weight. Her shoulder-length hair was a medium blond, not ash or wheat, and her eyes were a simple blue, not azure or sapphire.

Her features were regular and she'd long ago accepted the fact that she would always be average. Average wasn't necessarily a bad thing, she supposed. She never had to worry about being particularly memorable.

The fire-engine-red Jean Paul Gaultier gown, with its plunging neckline and cut-out shoulders definitely made her figure look better than average. Harrah had provided her jewelry, a dazzling pair of gold earrings and a necklace to match.

She turned from the mirror to look at Belinda, who was sprawled on her bed with a drink in her hand. "Are you sure you don't want to come?"

Belinda tugged at the belt of her dressing gown and shook her head. "No, I'm not in the mood to socialize.

You go on and have fun. I'll just read some magazines and watch TV until you get home."

"Tonight isn't about fun," Chantal said. "I'm hoping I'll get some information." She sat on the edge of the bed next to her friend. "You want me to call Harrah and Lena and see if they can come over for a while?"

"I don't need a babysitter," Belinda replied irritably. "I'll be fine, I promise. Besides, I'll be waiting for you when you get home so I can hear all the gossip." She got up off the bed as Chantal checked her watch.

"I don't expect to be late," Chantal said as Belinda walked with her to the front door. "The open house runs from seven to ten and I doubt if Mom will want to stay the whole time."

"I'll be here whatever time you get home. If I happen to fall asleep wake me up."

"Sure," Chantal agreed even though they both knew that wasn't happening. Waking Belinda once she fell asleep was as easy as transforming a discount store dress into high fashion.

Twenty minutes later Chantal pulled up in front of the house where she'd been raised. The two-story home boasted over seven thousand square feet and was surrounded by five acres of lush lawn and gardens.

Chantal had been raised with the proverbial silver spoon in her mouth. She'd had the best of everything that money could buy, but she'd also been lucky enough to be raised by people who never took their wealth for granted, people who, while enjoying the fruits of their labor, never forgot their early struggles and sacrifices.

Edna answered the door and Chantal kissed the housekeeper on the cheek as she greeted her. Edna had worked for the Worthingtons since Chantal had been a baby.

"Is she ready?" Chantal asked.

"I'll go up and see."

As Edna disappeared up the wide, winding staircase, Chantal turned her attention to the photos that lined the entry. She smiled as she gazed at her parents' wedding photo. They had made a handsome couple, despite the fact that they'd both been poor as church mice.

Even though he'd only been twenty-three years old when he'd married his bride, a burning light of ambition had lit her father's eyes. He'd been a man with a dream and had lived long enough to see his dreams realized.

"Darling, you look beautiful," Katherine said as she descended the stairs.

"Thanks, Mom. You don't look too shabby yourself." Her mother wore a silver gown that complemented her blond hair and bright, not average, blue eyes. She swept down the stairs like a queen and gave her daughter a warm hug, then turned to look at the photos.

She tapped a perfectly manicured nail on the glass of a photo of Chantal's father standing next to a shiny red boat. "Who would have thought those little boats your father dreamed of building would sell so well?"

"Those little boats" had been the beginning of an empire. Worthington Bass Boats had become the indus- try standard for fast, affordable and functional fishing crafts and they had made Sam Worthington and his family millionaires several times over.

After Sam's death, Katherine, as a major stock-holder, held the position of CEO of the company, but she had little to do with the daily running of the busi-ness. Instead she relied on a loyal business manager and a staff who loved the business and had loved Sam.

It was a thirty-minute drive to the Folly Theater where the fundraiser was taking place. The two women passed the drive by chatting about upcoming events and mutual acquaintances.

By the time they arrived the fundraiser was already in full swing. The Folly Theater was located in down-town Kansas City, in an area not far from Big Joey's Bail Bonds. The Folly had begun life in the early years of the city as a house of burlesque. The building itself, both inside and out, was a masterpiece of design from years gone by.

Most recently the town leaders had been trying to decide what to do with the old lady. Tonight was only one of many fundraisers that would be necessary to raise enough money to provide the old building with some sort of future.

It was the usual champagne-and-hors d'oeuvres gathering, with the same faces that usually attended these kinds of functions.

Chantal snagged a glass of champagne from a pass-ing waiter and began to work the crowd. She talked about fashion and facials, about who was divorcing and who was getting married and managed in each conversation to bring up the topic of Willowby.

Her subtle inquiries were met with a variety of responses…blank stares, whispered expressions of shock and pointed changes of topic. What she didn't get was any information that might help her in her hunt for the convicted rapist.

By eight-thirty Chantal was bored stiff. That's when she saw him. He stood near the buffet table, looking as out of place as a palm frond on a ski slope. Although he was dressed in a respectable three-piece suit and had his hair neatly tied back at the nape of his neck, he looked only half-civilized as he perused the guests through narrow eyes.

How had Luke Coleman managed to get a ticket to this affair? She had a feeling he wasn't on anyone's list as a patron of the theater. It irked her to no end to see him here, in her world.

His gaze caught hers and he gave her that sexy half smile that twisted her stomach into a knot. She approached where he stood. "What are you doing here?" she demanded.

"And a good evening to you, Ms. Worthington." His gaze slowly slid down the length of her. "You're looking exceptionally fine this evening. Red is definitely your color."

"What are you doing here?" she repeated, refusing to be swayed by his compliment but ridiculously pleased she'd chosen the red Gaultier for the evening.

"Probably the same thing you're doing here. Fishing."

"This is a ticketed, invitation-only event. How did you get in?"

At that moment Brandy Hamilton slid up to him and smiled. "There you are," she said. "I was wondering where you'd gone. Hello, Chantal, have you met Luke?" Brandy's eyes shone with the glaze of a woman who had imbibed too much champagne and who enjoyed too little natural intelligence.

"We've met," Chantal replied. Brandy Hamilton was four years older than Chantal and although the two were social acquaintances, they had never been friends.

How on earth had Luke Coleman hooked up with the twice-divorced socialite who had the reputation for being an alcoholic man-eater?

"Luke does work for Daddy occasionally." Brandy put a hand on Luke's chest and smiled up at him. "Isn't he yummy?"

"Yummy," Chantal echoed dryly.

She murmured a goodbye and walked away. She shouldn't be surprised that Brandy was the kind of woman Luke would like. Vapid and promiscuous, of course that would be his cup of tea. Not that she cared.

Still, it irritated her that he was here. This was her territory and she didn't like the idea that he had the same access to information that she might have.

For the rest of the evening she felt his gaze on her often. She didn't like the way he looked at her. She always felt half-naked beneath his dark intense gaze.

There was some comfort in knowing that although he wore a decent suit and was accompanied by Brandy, he would still be considered an outsider and she doubted very seriously that anyone would give him any information he could use.

By nine o'clock she was ready to go home. The evening had been a bust. Either nobody knew anything about Willowby or they weren't talking about what they did know.

She rejoined her mother who indicated she was also ready to go and together the two women left the old theater. "Joan is divorcing Raymond," Katherine said as they waited for the valet to bring them Chantal's car.

"Why?"

"She found out he's been having an affair with his secretary."

"But, I thought Joan was having an affair with her yoga coach," Chantal said.

"She is, but in this case what's good for the gander is not good for the goose."

Chantal sighed. "Sometimes I think relationships are just too much trouble."

"They are a lot of trouble," Katherine agreed. "But, when they're good, they're worth every ounce of that trouble. Your father and I got it right. He wasn't just my husband, he was also my best friend." Katherine smiled at her daughter. "I hope someday you find the same kind of thing."

A wave of longing filled Chantal. She couldn't seem to get it right. Her relationships so far had been flawed in one way or another and the flaws had been too big to overlook. When she dated a man who was from her same social background and standing it didn't take long for boredom to creep in. If she dated somebody who was not of her social background she wondered if they were drawn more to her money than to her.

Although she loved her independence and loved her life there were times she wished she had somebody to share it with, somebody who would be her friend, her partner as well as her lover.

She mentally shoved away the wistful thoughts as her red sports car arrived. The two women got in and Chantal took off. She'd only driven two blocks when she first noticed the car behind them. It was a beat-up dark Chevy and it was following her way too closely.

"Doris has had a face lift since last time I saw her," Katherine said. "She says she just took a little vacation, but I'd bet the farm that she took that vacation to a plastic surgeon."

Chantal only half listened to her mother detailing the latest gossip as most of her attention was focused on the car behind them.

Back off, she thought as she stepped on the gas to gain some distance. But, before she could get any distance she came to a red light and had to stop.

The Chevy crept up so close behind her the glow of the headlights disappeared. She saw the flash in her rearview mirror just as the back windshield shattered.

"Get down," Chantal screamed at her mother. At the same time she floored the gas pedal and shot through the red light.

Chapter 4

Chantal couldn't beat up a man three times her size, nor could she figure out how to apply fake eyelashes that looked natural, but the one thing she could do was drive.

Her father used to joke that somehow Earnhardt blood had mixed with Worthington blood in her veins. From the moment she'd first gotten behind the steering wheel of a car she'd had the skills and instincts of a professional race-car driver.

She shot through the red light and took the next right corner on two wheels. The oppressively hot night air poured through the broken window as her heart pounded a frantic pace.

The Chevy squirreled around the corner behind her.

Chantal slid a quick glance at her mother, who was practically lying on the seat next to her, then returned her gaze to the rearview mirror where the Chevy was gaining on them.

There was another flash from just outside the passenger-side window and she heard the ping of bullet against metal.

She didn't waste a minute's energy trying to figure out who was driving the Chevy or why they were shooting at her. All that mattered was escape. She'd ask questions later.

"Dean Koontz novels, cell phones, Victoria's Secret," she muttered under her breath as she careened around a left turn and shot through another red light.

Several cars blared their horns to show their displeasure. She'd rather invoke a healthy dose of road rage than be dead.

"Where are the cops when you need them?" she said.

"A speeding ticket sounds delightful right now," Katherine murmured.

Chantal's hands ached as she gripped the wheel, turning down one street then another in an attempt to lose their pursuers.

Katherine peeked over the dashboard just in time to see Chantal turn down a one-way street. "Oh, my," she said as a pair of headlights careened toward them. She lowered her head to the seat as Chantal swerved a hard right to avoid the oncoming traffic.

It seemed as if it took hours, but within minutes

she'd managed to lose the Chevy and slowed to a normal breakneck pace.

Her mother didn't move from her position on the
seat, her head still covered by her hands. "Mom? I think
it's okay now," Chantal said.

Katherine slowly sat up. "Would you like to share
with me what that was all about?" She flipped down the
visor to display the mirror on the back, then pulled a
tube of lipstick from her purse, a nervous habit that
Chantal knew meant her mother was frightened.

Chantal had a feeling that if her mother was faced
with a psychopath wielding a machine gun she'd pull
out a tube of Mauve Rose and apply lavishly.

"I do believe somebody just tried to kill us," she
added. She applied a fresh coat of lipstick, flipped the
visor back up then stared at her daughter expectantly.

Chantal told her mother about Mundy and the price
on her head. Although she tried to downplay the whole
thing, there was no way to minimize a death threat.

"And you think that's who just shot at us? But, how
did they know where you'd be? How to find you?"
Katherine asked.

Chantal frowned thoughtfully. "The Folly is only a
few blocks from Big Joey's. They probably recognized
my car." She wanted to scream at her own stupidity. Of
course they'd be cruising the area, looking for her car,
and the red Mustang wasn't exactly hard to spot. She
should have thought about that before.

"So, what are you going to do?" Katherine asked.

"Get a new car." Chantal checked her rearview mirror for the hundredth time, pleased to see nobody suspicious behind them as she pulled into the development where her mother lived.

Katherine emitted a small laugh. "Silly me. I thought you were going to do something totally irrational like quit your dangerous job."

Chantal pulled to a halt in front of the house, parked the car and turned to look at her mom. "Is that what you want me to do? Quit?" Even though she'd been bounty hunting for a relatively short period of time, the thought of quitting grieved her.

Katherine's love for her daughter shone from her eyes. She sighed and patted an errant strand of hair back into place. "I want you to be safe." She placed a hand on Chantal's cheeks and Chantal felt the slight tremble in her mother's fingertips. "But you love what you're doing and I would never ask you to quit. I just want you to be careful, Chantal. You know how much I love you."

"And I love you," Chantal replied and pressed her hand against her mother's. "And I do love what I'm doing and I will be careful. I made a mistake in judgment tonight, one I won't make again."

It wasn't until her mother had gotten out of the car and Chantal was driving home that the shakes began. Her stomach bucked and kicked with queasiness and her hands trembled as she thought of how close they'd come to disaster.

She'd been foolish not to think that the only way Mundy's boys knew to identify her was by the car that carried her back and forth to work at Big Joey's. It was the same car that had carried Mundy from his girl-friend's home to the police station on the night Chantal had taken him into custody.

That single lack of attention to detail could have gotten her killed tonight, but worse than that, it could have gotten her mother killed.

The first thing she did when she got inside her house was go to the spare room to check on Belinda, who was already sound asleep, her eyes covered with a gold satin eye mask. The second thing Chantal did was call the police.

As she waited for the officials to arrive to make a report, she fixed herself a double mocha latte with an extra squirt of whipped cream. She didn't normally imbibe in the high-calorie, sinful drink but she fig-ured being shot at and surviving called for a celebra-tion of sorts.

"Hell of a night, Sam," she said to the cat who sat on top of the refrigerator staring at her with unblinking green eyes.

She sat at the kitchen table and wrapped her hands around the warm mug, fighting the chill that had taken up residency deep in her bones.

The threat that had been nothing more than words before had now become a reality. Even punk-ass kids could kill her if they got lucky. Thank God they'd been unlucky tonight.

This was the first time since she'd begun bounty hunting that she'd truly found her life in danger. Certainly she'd known on an intellectual level that it was a dangerous business, but at this moment the risks were more than just an intellectual nebulous concept.

Did she want to quit? Hell, no. She just needed to be smarter, better. She loved what she was doing. For the first time in her life she felt a true purpose of being, a commitment to something bigger than herself.

The doorbell rang and she jumped up, certain it would be the officers she'd summoned. She opened her front door and instead of uniformed officers, Luke stood on her porch.

He swept past her and into the living room before she could even protest his very presence.

"Are you all right?" he asked, his voice a low growl. He stood too close to her, invading her personal space.

"I'm fine. What are you doing here?" He looked wild, his tie had been yanked loose and his hair had escaped the confines at the nape of his neck.

"I heard the call on the scanner requesting officers at this address due to a shooting." His gaze slid down the length of her, as if checking for bullet holes. He seemed to relax slightly as he saw that she was intact. "So, what happened?"

She took a step back from him, finding his nearness nearly overwhelming. "They killed my car."

"Tell me everything." Sam appeared in the doorway of the living room and to Chantal's surprise made a beeline to Luke. He curled around Luke's feet and meowed plaintively. Luke bent down and scooped up the cat in his arms. Sam purred like a motor boat. Chantal scowled.

"The police are on their way. There's no reason for you to be here." The man seemed to fill every space in the room and her irritation only climbed as he stroked her cat…her purring cat.

"Was it Mundy's men?" He obviously intended to ignore her not-so-subtle invitation to leave.

"I can't be positive, but that would be my guess." She glared at the traitorous cat. "They were in an old Chevy and took a couple of shots at me as I was driving home from the Folly."

"What color was the Chevy?"

She frowned thoughtfully. "Black or dark blue, I couldn't tell for sure which."

Luke's jaw muscle throbbed. He set the cat on the floor and took two steps toward her. "I told you that you were in over your head. This business isn't a game, Chantal. Go back to your luncheons and charity wingdings and leave the bounty-hunting business to the big boys."

It had been a bad night and she was in no mood for him. He stood so close to her she could feel the heat emanating from his body, see the tiny flecks of silver that sparked in his dark eyes. "Of all the arrogant, chauvinistic things to say."

She fought the impulse to take off her shoe and throw it at his smug, handsome face, knowing that such a girly reaction would only feed his low opinion of her.

"I think it's time for you to go. As you can see, I'm

fine. I handled everything just fine and the police should be here anytime."

She wanted him out of her house and away from her cat, who continued to curl around his feet and meow as though he'd found his lost love.

"Chantal, the people who tried to kill you tonight aren't going to stop trying." Once again the muscle in his jaw worked overtime, making him appear more menacing than ever.

"And I'll take the necessary precautions to make certain they don't succeed," she replied. She thought she sounded competent and cool, but he eyed her with disbelief, his mouth thin with displeasure.

"I told Joey you were a mistake the day he hired you. You're going to get yourself killed. You don't know what you're doing. You don't even know how to work your handcuffs properly."

His words infuriated her. "I'm not sure why you felt the need to stop by, but it's way past time for you to leave." She walked over to the door and opened it. "I can handle myself. I've handled myself just fine for the last eight months and I'll be in this business doing well long after you're gone. Now, leave before the police arrive and I tell them you're an intruder in my home."

He hesitated, and for a moment she thought he was going to refuse to leave. She opened the door wider.

"Three numbers, Coleman. 9-1-1. I dial them and you won't just be working for Joey but you'll be in need of his services." She smiled cheerfully at the thought of him behind bars.

* * *

Luke turned on his heels and left the house. He climbed into his truck, his emotions raging from black irritation to out-and-out anger.

When the call had come over his police radio that officers had been summoned to her address because of gunshots fired, he'd half expected to find her dead.

As he pulled out of the driveway a patrol car pulled in, and the sight of the official car only fed his anger. She had no business running around like a loose cannon trying to capture criminals.

He'd seen her type before, a bored socialite looking for a little excitement in her life. She'd be better served to do something completely predictable and have an affair with her tennis coach.

And yet, as much as he wanted to dismiss her as nothing more than a dilettante in over her head, there was something about her—besides her great ass—that got to him.

He'd assumed when she started work for Joey that she'd last a month, two at the most. She'd surprised him not only by being determined to succeed, but by actually bringing in several criminals.

Still, she wasn't taking the business seriously enough. The fact that she was out driving the streets of Kansas City, attending a fundraiser while knowing there was a price on her head was a case in point.

If she didn't start taking things more seriously her shapely ass would be in the morgue and that would be a damn shame. He roared down the highway that would take him back downtown to his own apartment.

He knew what she'd been doing at that fundraiser tonight, the same thing he'd been doing. Seeking information that might lead to Marcus Willowby's whereabouts.

She'd been surprised to see him there. She probably didn't think he was capable of putting on a suit and acting respectable. She had no idea how resourceful he could be when necessary.

Chantal Worthington. She was a fashion designer's wet dream in high heels. But, if she thought she was going to be the one to bring in Willowby, she had another think coming.

Crazy Coleman never lost and he certainly wasn't about to lose to some trust-fund debutante who was playing at being a bad ass.

"Jackie? This is Chantal Worthington." Chantal spoke into the phone receiver as mid-morning sunshine danced through her office window. She watched the golf course where a well-built hunk was taking some practice swings and recognized it had been too damn long since she'd enjoyed a physical relationship with a man.

"Hi, Chantal," Jackie replied.

Chantal spun around in her chair, finding the hunk far too distracting. "I know it's short notice, but I'm having a little dinner party here at my house tomorrow evening and was wondering if you and Frank could attend. I realized this morning that it's been far too long since I've seen the two of you."

"I'll have to check Frank's schedule. Can I get back to you later this afternoon?" Jackie Shofield had the low-pitched voice of a heavy smoker, although to Chantal's knowledge the woman had never smoked a cigarette in her life. Even though she had to be surprised by the last-minute invitation, her voice didn't betray it.

"That would be fine. If I'm not here just leave a message on the machine or with my assistant, Harrah." A moment later Chantal hung up and tapped a finger on the phone as she fought a wave of frustration.

Inviting Jackie and Frank Shofield to the dinner party had been sudden inspiration. Frank and Marcus Willowby had been close friends through high school and college. Jackie was Chantal's age and while the two hadn't been the best of friends, they had been friendly.

She leaned back in her chair and rubbed the center of her forehead. The past couple of days had gone by in a blur.

She'd given a statement to the police about the shooting incident. Of course she'd been unable to give them any names or any real description of the car, but she had told them about the price Mundy had put on her head and that she was a bounty hunter. As she suspected there wasn't much the police could do without any real evidence.

Her Mustang had been picked up for repairs and she'd rented a car and had spent most of her time trying to connect with anyone who might know something about Willowby's whereabouts.

She'd stayed away from Big Joey's, using the phone

rather than personal appearances to stay in touch. She'd also seen nothing of Luke Coleman since the night he'd shown up on her front porch.

Belinda had returned to her home and there wasn't a minute of the day that Chantal didn't worry about her. The longer Willowby remained missing, the deeper into despair Belinda seemed to plunge.

She checked her watch and stood. She had an appointment with Rebecca Willowby in an hour and needed to get dressed. She had a feeling the only reason Rebecca had agreed to see her was because she'd assumed Chantal wanted to talk about some charity or another. Rebecca and Katherine were friendly acquaintances and Chantal hadn't been too ashamed to mention her mother when she'd called Rebecca.

Harrah sat in the kitchen, paperwork strewn across the table and a pair of purple reading glasses riding low on her nose.

"I'm going to get dressed for my appointment with Rebecca," she said. "How are you doing?"

Harrah pushed back from the table and stretched her long arms overhead. She'd been going through clippings of old newspaper articles that mentioned Willowby's name. She patted a stack of papers to her left. "I've already gone through these and found nothing of use." She pointed to three sheets of paper in front of her. "Those are all I've got. All three of them are from several years ago and show him with friends at various social functions."

Chantal picked up the papers and studied them one

at a time. They were newspaper clippings from the society pages, each one depicting a photo of a particular event.

The first one showed the handsome Marcus with his arm around a young woman at a Spring Fling Ball. The young woman was identified as Marcy Canon. Marcy and her family had moved to New York City several months after the photo had been taken.

The second photo showed Marcus with his parents and the third showed a group of young men, Marcus included, preparing for a charity baseball game. Chantal recognized several of the young men, including Frank Shofield.

She handed the paper back to Harrah. "You're keeping a list of any names you find in connection with Willowby?"

Harrah nodded. "You'd better go get dressed for your appointment," she advised. "I'll get through the rest of this paperwork while you're gone."

At some point over the last couple of days the reporters had abandoned their posts outside the Willowby mansion. After all, the news worth reporting in Kansas City hadn't stopped happening on the day Willowby disappeared.

She suspected that the police might be watching the house, but if they were, she saw no signs of them as she pulled into the circular driveway.

The Willowby house made the Worthington place look like a quaint summer cottage. Unlike the Worthingtons who had made their money in this century, the

Willowby fortune was old money and the mansion had been in the family for years.

Chantal had no idea how cooperative Rebecca might be, but she knew in order to get into Marcus Willowby's head, she needed to talk not only to the people who hated him, but also to the people who loved him.

It had been five days since Marcus had officially gone missing and Chantal was aware of each moment that ticked past.

As she walked to the front door, she smoothed her skirt, surprised to discover she was a bit nervous. She'd dressed carefully for the meeting with Rebecca. The powerful, dignified woman would find no fault in the beige Chanel suit and pearl accessories.

She was seeing Rebecca under false pretenses and once Rebecca knew the real reason she was here, she had no idea how she'd be received.

Her knock was answered by a uniformed housekeeper who ushered her into a living room. Chantal sat on the white sofa and declined the housekeeper's offer of something cold to drink.

As she waited for Rebecca to join her she looked around the room with interest. It had been ten years since she'd been in the Willowby house, not since the night of the party that had changed Belinda's life. The decor had changed since then, but memories of the party that night sifted through Chantal's head.

By the time Chantal and Belinda had arrived, the place had already been swarming with kids. At sixteen, Belinda and Chantal had been in the midst of teenage

crises. Belinda had been overweight and suffered from
acne, certain she was the ugliest girl on earth, and Chantal had felt invisible and far too average to survive life
on earth.

It had been typical teenage angst and drama and the
party was supposed to have been a panacea for boredom
and a lack of self-confidence.

They had been at the party for about an hour when
they got separated. Chantal had been standing by the
fireplace in this very room when Belinda had rejoined
her, urging her that they had to leave right away.

There had been a horrifying blankness in Belinda's
eyes that frightened Chantal. It was on the drive home
that Belinda had told her Marcus had raped her upstairs
in a bathroom.

A new surge of anger filled her as she thought of
what Marcus had said to Belinda, of what he'd done to
Belinda. She swallowed against the anger, knowing it
would be counterproductive to indulge it while speaking to Rebecca.

She got up from the sofa and walked over to the fireplace where the mantel was decorated with silver
frames containing photos of Marcus at various stages
of his life.

He'd been a pretty little boy who had grown up to
be a strikingly handsome man. With his blond hair and
blue eyes he looked like the all-American boy. He had
chiseled features and the strong Willowby jaw and carried himself with the confidence of a man who was
assured of his place in the world.

"Chantal. So nice to see you."

She whirled away from the fireplace to see Rebecca Willowby enter the living room. Rebecca was a tall, handsome woman with strong, almost masculine features and sharp blue eyes. She approached Chantal and held out a hand. "Your mother is doing well?"

"Yes, she's doing fine. She told me to send her regards to you."

"She's a lovely woman." Rebecca released her hand and gestured back to the sofa. "Please, have a seat. May I get you something to drink?"

"No thanks, I'm fine."

Up close, stress was obvious on Rebecca's features. Dark shadows shone beneath her eyes despite an attempt to cover them up with concealer. She looked like a woman who hadn't slept well for a month.

"I'm assuming your visit today has something to do with the fall festival dance. I understand your mother is heading up the committee. I'll be more than happy to make some sort of financial donation, but I'm afraid that's all I can commit to at the present time."

"Actually, that's not why I'm here." She drew a deep breath, then continued. "I'm here about your son." Chantal saw the sharp grief that momentarily claimed Rebecca's features. It was there only a moment, then gone beneath a mask devoid of expression.

This is a mother, she reminded herself, a mother who obviously loves her son. "I'm worried about him," she said.

"My dear, you have no idea what worry is," Rebecca

said with a trace of bitterness. She cleared her throat and straightened her shoulders.

"I'm going to be perfectly honest with you, Mrs. Willowby. I'm afraid that if Marcus doesn't turn himself in to the authorities as soon as possible he could get hurt. The moment Marcus skipped out he became a hot property among every bounty hunter in the city and some of those men aren't nice."

Chantal talked as fast as she could, afraid that at any moment Rebecca would summon security to have her removed from the house. "He'll probably go to jail if he turns himself in, but he'll have an appeal process. If a bounty hunter tries to pick him up, something bad could happen and he could wind up seriously hurt or dead."

"Don't you think I know that?" Rebecca stood abruptly and walked to a nearby window. Her back was ramrod-straight as she faced away from Chantal. For a long moment a weighty silence reigned.

"I don't understand this," she finally said, her voice filled with weariness. "I don't understand any of this. I can't imagine why those women told those awful lies about my son."

She turned back to face Chantal, her eyes burning with something akin to religious zeal. "We gave Marcus everything money could buy. He was the center of our universe, he had all of our attention, all of our love and he never wanted for anything. He's bright and handsome and wealthy. Why would he ever need to rape any woman? The whole thing is absolutely ridiculous. Money. They're obviously after money…or publicity. It's the only way to explain this…this unseemly business."

Although Chantal's initial reaction was to defend the victims, she didn't, knowing that if she did she'd lose any further opportunity to talk to Rebecca. "Do you know where he is now?"

Rebecca's shoulders slumped slightly. "How I wish I knew. We haven't talked to him since the day before he disappeared. But, if he did call me, I'd tell him to turn himself in. I'd assure him that this will all be taken care of on appeal. We'll prove those women to be liars and that the entire case against him is nothing but some sort of personal vendetta." She sat next to Chantal once again and for the next hour she told Chantal about her son.

It was as if Chantal's presence had opened up a vein in Rebecca's wrist and what poured out was a mother's love for her only son.

Rebecca spoke of her joy in finally becoming pregnant when she'd begun to think it impossible, of the rapture she'd felt when Marcus was born. She extolled his accomplishments, both as an athlete and as a scholar.

Chantal couldn't help but feel sorry for the woman, who was so obviously convinced her son was a good boy who had grown into a good man.

From Rebecca, Chantal got a list of Marcus's friends, although she told Chantal she'd contacted each of them in the last couple of days and none of them knew anything about Marcus's current location. Chantal didn't tell Rebecca that she was a bounty hunter rather she implied a deep friendship with Marcus that had her worried about his safety.

Rebecca walked Chantal to the front door and placed a hand on Chantal's arm. "You said that those bounty hunters could be dangerous to my son." She squeezed Chantal's arm, her eyes burning fervently. "You find him, Chantal. I'll do everything I can to help you search for him. But you find him and bring him back safely for me."

"I'll do my best," Chantal replied.

It wasn't until she was back in her car minutes later that she realized she had two women who wanted her to find Marcus Willowby: Belinda, who wanted to destroy him, and Rebecca, who wanted to save him.

Chapter 5

"Narcissist." Chantal rolled the word off her tongue.

"Blue-eyed bitch," Harrah retorted. "If you're going to call me names, then I'll respond in kind."

Chantal laughed and got up from her desk to stretch. "I wasn't calling you a narcissist. After everything I've read and everyone I've talked to in the last couple of days I've decided that's what Marcus Willowby is."

"He's a creep, that's for sure." Harrah capped the bottle of polish she'd been using to paint her long fingernails.

The late-afternoon sunshine slanted through the windows in the office and the scent of culinary creations drifted through the house as Enrique and his staff prepared the food for the dinner party that evening.

Harrah had spent most of the afternoon cleaning the

house and transforming the dining room from a catch-all to an atmosphere perfect for formal dining for the twelve people who had been invited to the dinner.

Chantal walked to the window and stared outside, but her thoughts were far away from the golf course and players in the late-afternoon sunshine. She turned back to face Harrah, who was in the process of blowing on her wet nails.

"It's interesting that Marcus's parents loved and indulged him just like mine did me." She found it not only interesting, but strangely disturbing. "They doted on him, gave him everything he wanted and needed, and yet he turned out to be a monster."

Harrah raised a perfectly arched black brow. "Honey, you aren't anything close to a monster." She shrugged. "Maybe his mama dressed him funny when he was a kid, or didn't breast-feed him long enough when he was a baby."

Chantal threw herself back into her chair. "Why do people always assume it's the mother who somehow screwed up a kid?"

"Okay, then maybe his daddy dressed Marcus funny or didn't breast-feed him long enough when he was a baby."

Chantal laughed again, then sobered. "I just find it interesting, you know, what makes a Marcus Willowby."

"So, what exactly is a narcissist anyway? I think I've dated some in my past."

"A narcissist is somebody who has an exaggerated sense of his own worth, somebody who can't connect to people, doesn't care about others' needs or emotions. From what Marcus's friends and acquaintances have told me, he has all the characteristics of a true narcissist."

"Is he dangerous?"

Chantal frowned thoughtfully. "I'm not sure. I think he could be. He has no moral compass except for how it relates to him and his needs. I would imagine him capable of anything if it came to his own preservation."

"Where do *you* think he is?" Harrah asked curiously. "I mean, do you think he'll ever be found?"

"I don't know," Chantal said honestly. "He could be on a mountain in Tibet or a ski slope in the Alps. He's got enough money to disappear forever, but in my gut I think he'll surface. If he's a true narcissist, then he craves attention, and deep in his heart he doesn't believe he did anything wrong."

She released a deep sigh. "He probably doesn't understand what the big deal is, so he had sex with some unconscious women and videotaped his actions, they should be happy that he chose them."

"That's so sick."

Chantal nodded. She'd spent the last couple of days trying to get into Marcus Willowby's head and once she'd felt she'd succeeded, she hadn't liked it there.

Deep inside her, in the very depths of her soul, she worried that her life and Marcus's mirrored each other's so closely. She'd been as spoiled and as indulged as he had been and the comparisons were impossible to deny.

Was there a streak of narcissism in her? Is that why at twenty-six years old she'd never had a relationship that really meant anything to her? Was she as incapable of truly loving another human being as Marcus?

"I'll tell you what would really be sick," Harrah said, interrupting Chantal's disturbing thoughts. "If your dinner guests arrive and you're still sitting here dressed in your sweats."

Chantal looked at her watch and flew up from her chair. "Why didn't you tell me it was getting so late?"

Harrah grinned. "I just did."

It was almost five and her guests would arrive at six-thirty. She still had to take a bath, dress and check the final preparations.

"I'm out of here," Harrah said, also rising. "I'll see you Monday morning."

"Thanks, Harrah." As her assistant headed for the front door, Chantal went into the kitchen where Enrique, caterer extraordinaire, had taken control.

"Don't touch anything," he commanded as she entered the room. He held a spatula in his hand like a weapon, ready to use it if necessary to keep her away from his creations.

"Don't worry, I have no intention of messing with a master at work." Chantal grinned affectionately at the large man whose reputation for temper tantrums was as big as his reputation as one of Kansas City's premier caterers. "I just wanted to check to make sure we were on schedule for dinner at seven."

"I'm on schedule, dear." He raised a bushy black

eyebrow. "But, I can't imagine that you'll look presentable by dinner time."

Enrique also had the reputation of being a catty bitch, but he was always forgiven because of his talent. "I'm headed to my room to get ready now."

"Good, go." Enrique waved his hands to get her out of the kitchen.

Minutes later in the master bathroom, Chantal sank down into a tub of hot water and scented bubbles. She leaned her head back against the cool porcelain, closed her eyes and drew a deep, long breath.

For the past week she'd felt as if Marcus Willowby was slowly consuming not only the hours of the day and her dreams at night, but also her very soul.

She'd spent the week talking to Marcus's friends and relatives and had watched as Belinda threatened to fragment into a million pieces.

Chantal's friend was drinking too much and living on tranquilizers, increasing the pressure on Chantal who had begun to think that the only way to save her friend was to find Willowby.

She'd tried to talk to the two victims, but they had refused to speak with her and had referred to their lawyers. She'd pored over the trial transcript and read the victims' accounts.

They'd met Willowby in a club. He'd been charming and pleasant and when he'd invited them back to his place neither of them had hesitated.

Once at his condo he'd offered them his specialty, a fruity drink that had gone down easily. And that's the last thing they remembered. Both of them had awakened the next morning in his spare room, embarrassed at the thought that they'd passed out.

He'd assured them that it was no problem, that perhaps he'd made the drink too strong, then he'd offered to cook them breakfast, but by that time the two had realized something bad had happened.

It was bad enough that he'd raped the women and videotaped the act while they'd been unconscious, but it added a touch of twisted perversion that the next morning he'd acted all charming and solicitous and had wanted to fix them breakfast before they left.

She thought of the dinner party tonight. Normally Chantal hated to entertain but she was looking forward to tonight for one reason, the opportunity to talk to Frank Shofield about his friend Marcus.

Frank was one of the few people she hadn't spoken with yet and she was hoping that after a few drinks and a good meal, he might be loose enough to share something that would help.

An hour later she stood in front of her bathroom mirror, checking her reflection. Tonight she looked like Chantal Worthington, heir to a fortune. Clad in a light-blue Carolina Herrera dress and bedecked with jewelry by Harrah, there was no hint of Carol Worth, bounty hunter, in the mirror.

She turned away from the mirror and as she left her bedroom the doorbell rang. The first of her guests had arrived.

Two and a half hours later, dinner and dessert had

been consumed and everyone lingered at the table over coffee. Frank Shofield pulled a pack of cigarettes from his pocket and looked at Chantal questioningly. "Do you mind if I step outside?" he asked.

His wife, Jackie, rolled her eyes. "I've managed to break him of most of his vices, but that's a habit stronger than me."

"It's not a problem," Chantal replied, secretly pleased as she got up and led Frank to her patio door. She stepped outside with him and gestured to the ashtray she kept for her smoking friends.

Frank lit a cigarette and gestured toward the golf course. "You play?"

"No, but I like the view. What about you? Do you play?" She knew he did, knew that one of his golf partners was Marcus.

"As often as I can."

Chantal tried to figure out a way to smoothly work the topic of Willowby into the conversation. "Terrible about Marcus Willowby, isn't it?" she finally said, smoothness be damned. "You and he were good friends, weren't you?"

Frank drew on his cigarette, his forehead wrinkled in a frown. "I guess as much as anyone was friends with him." He leaned with his back against the patio table. "Even though we basically grew up together and hung out, I never felt like I really knew him."

He shook his head and drew another drag on his cigarette. "But I would have never suspected him of doing the kind of crap he was arrested for."

"You never saw anything that would make you think he was capable of raping a woman?"

"God, no." He shook his head vehemently, then frowned again. "But, in a lot of ways Marcus was a private person. Oh, he could be fun and he could charm a snake out of his skin, but he didn't talk much about important stuff."

"You have any idea where he might be now?"

Frank took another long drag on his cigarette. "No, I haven't talked to him since before his arrest. Why are you interested?" he asked.

"Just curious. I was just wondering where I'd run if I were a fugitive from justice."

"He could be any of a dozen places, but my money would be on Tamillo."

"Mexico?" Excitement surged through Chantal's veins. This was the first hint she'd gotten of any location where Willowby might be found. "Tamillo…why would he be there?"

Frank shrugged and stubbed out his cigarette. "That was his place to go and escape. He'd fly down there for a week or two about four or five times a year. He loved it there, said it was his haven away from the madding crowds. Me, I'd head for Switzerland." He flashed Chantal a smile. "I like to ski almost as much as I like to play golf. We'd better get back in there or Jackie will give me hell tonight."

An hour later Chantal told her guests goodbye. She couldn't kick them out the door fast enough. She wanted to get to her computer and do a little research on the Mexican town.

She had spent time in Mexico visiting Puerto Vallarta and Cancun on several occasions, but she'd never been to the smaller town of Tamillo.

By midnight she had all the information available on the booming resort town. Up until five years ago, Tamillo had been a quiet little coastal town mostly populated by fishermen.

Beautiful beaches and a depressed economy made the area ripe for development and in recent years five-star hotels and restaurants had sprung up and the town promoted itself as the new playground south of the border.

She clicked off her computer and reared back in her chair, her mind working as effectively as an experienced shopper figuring out a thirty-three-percent discount without a calculator.

In the relatively short time she had been bounty hunting, she'd learned several truths about criminals. One, they were never as bright as they thought they were, and two, they were creatures of habit.

It wasn't out of the realm of reality that Willowby would go someplace he'd been before, a place where he'd felt safe. Any place in Mexico made sense. There were no laws of extradition and the country had long been a refuge of fugitives fleeing the long arm of American law.

She rubbed her eyes and slid her chair back from the desk. She needed some action. She'd spent far too much time in the past week sitting at her desk and talking on the phone.

While she'd been chasing down leads on Willowby other criminals were running the streets or being brought in by Coleman.

It pissed her off that some scum-sucking punk-ass dope dealer had put a price on her head. It pissed her off even more that she had to take the threat seriously and in doing so, she'd had to change her routine and stay away from Big Joey's.

It pissed her off that Luke Coleman was probably cleaning up the streets of Kansas City without any real competition. She could just imagine his monumental ego getting bigger with each day his crown as king of the bounty hunters wasn't challenged.

As she walked from the office to her bedroom she unzipped the back of her dress and smiled. Let Coleman run around the streets of the city picking up penny-ante bail jumpers.

She had visions of a bikini, a bottle of sunscreen and the beautiful beaches of a quaint Mexican town called Tamillo.

"You're on an eleven o'clock flight tomorrow morning," Harrah said the next morning as she entered the office where Chantal sat at her desk. Even though it was Sunday, Harrah had agreed to come in to help with the clean-up after the party. "The ticket is going to be faxed here in the next few minutes."

"Great. What about a hotel reservation?"

Harrah sat in the chair opposite the desk. "You're booked into the Hacienda Hotel, one of the newest upscale hotels in the area. I told them you needed an open-ended reservation and that wasn't a problem."

Chantal nodded. "Perfect. That gives me today to take care of last-minute details."

A deep frown cut across Harrah's broad forehead. "Are you sure you want to do this? I mean, do you have a plan?"

"Sure. Find Willowby and bring him back."

Harrah's frown deepened. "You make it sound so simple but Willowby isn't going to just let you waltz right up to him and handcuff him. Honey, you don't know how dangerous he could be."

Chantal leaned back in her chair. "I'd like to tell you that he's not dangerous at all, that a man who rapes unconscious women is nothing but a coward and therefore not a threat. But I'd be a fool to believe that."

"A man who rapes women is capable of anything," Harrah exclaimed.

"A man who has been convicted of rape and sentenced to years behind bars definitely is capable of anything when it comes to maintaining his freedom," Chantal agreed.

"That's what I'm talking about. I wish you weren't going to try to do this all alone."

She smiled at her assistant. "Harrah, I'm not a stupid person and I don't intend to put myself at risk. I'm just going down there to check things out. Right now I don't even know if Willowby is there. It's very possible I'll have a couple of days in Tamillo and will only discover Willowby is nowhere in the area."

"Maybe you should just let this one go," Harrah said softly.

She stared at Harrah in surprise. "What are you talking about?" She'd never seen Harrah so serious. "You know I can't let this one go." Her stomach knotted at the very thought. "You've seen Belinda, you've talked to her. She's falling apart and the only thing that's going to put her back together again is if I get Willowby in custody."

Harrah raised a hand to her neck and worried her beaded necklace between two long fingers. "I've just got a bad feeling about all this."

"Maybe it's heartburn," Chantal replied dryly.

Harrah gave her a dirty look. "I'm serious, Chantal. The last time I had a feeling like this my mother died."

A wave of apprehension swept through Chantal, but she offered Harrah a reassuring smile. "I'll be fine. I promise. I don't intend to take any unnecessary chances. The worst that will happen is I'll get a sunburn while I'm there."

"That's not the worst that can happen and you know it," Harrah replied with a scowl. She sighed and dropped her hand back to her lap. "How long do you think you'll be gone?"

"Three or four days…a week at the most. You'll see to Sam and water the plants?"

At that moment the fax machine began to work, spewing out the e-ticket for the flight the next day. Harrah got up to retrieve the ticket. "I'll put this on the kitchen counter for now."

Chantal nodded absently, then stood as well. "I've got some errands to run. Why don't you meet me back here about nine in the morning to take me to the airport."

Harrah nodded, although Chantal could tell her friend didn't want her to go. "It will be fine, Harrah. I promise."

"Yeah, that's just what my mama said when the doctor told her it was just a shadow on her X-ray. Three months later she was dead."

"Believe me, I have no intention of being dead anytime soon." She offered Harrah a reassuring smile. "And now, I'm going to start packing, then meet my mother for a late lunch."

It took her over an hour to get packed. Not only did she pack beach and casual wear but also clothing for clubbing and upscale restaurants.

When she'd finished with the packing she left to meet her mother for lunch. Katherine had survived the wild car ride no worse for the experience and their lunch together was pleasant. After lunch Chantal shopped for a few last-minute items for her trip.

She hadn't talked to Joey all week and felt cut off from everything and everyone there. Unless she disguised herself she didn't think it would be a great idea to go to the office. She hadn't forgotten the taste of fear that had filled her mouth the night in the car with her mother.

"If the mountain won't come…" she murmured and punched in the number to the office. "Hi, Monica. It's Carol," she said when the phone was answered.

"Hey, girl, you've been scarce the last few days."

"I think I've got some punks hunting me down so I've stayed away. But, I'm having withdrawal and wondered if maybe you'd be interested in meeting me for dinner and filling me in on any news."

"I'm on duty here most of the night. About all I could do is meet you at Danny's for a quick bite around six."

"That would be great and if you could bring me copies of anything new that's hit the boards or new information on any pending cases, I'd appreciate it."

"Will do. See you at Danny's at six."

Chantal disconnected the call and headed back home. She had several hours to kill before meeting Monica and she intended to use those hours making phone calls to Tamillo.

Using the Internet she got a listing of hotels in the city, then called each one and asked to be connected with Marcus Willowby's room.

Although most criminals would not be foolish enough to use their own names, Chantal knew that Willowby was no ordinary criminal. He might just be arrogant enough to register under his own name.

None of her calls hit pay dirt. Each establishment told her there was nobody registered by that name. Of course, that didn't mean he wasn't there, it just meant that he might be smarter than she'd given him credit for or he was staying someplace other than one of the hotels listed.

At five-thirty she was back in her car driving toward Danny's, a diner three blocks away from Big Joey's. She felt relatively secure in the fact that she was driving a rental car nobody would recognize and the young men who were working for Mundy would probably be watching the bail bonds business for signs of her.

If you were into low-carb, healthy food, Danny's was not the place to eat. The moment you walked into the small diner your very skin seemed to absorb cholesterol and carbs.

Monica hadn't arrived yet when Chantal walked through the door. She chose a booth toward the back of the restaurant and sat facing the door so she could see when her friend approached. She flipped open the menu even though she knew she'd probably order what she often did when eating here.

As she read the fare offered, her thoughts were still consumed with Willowby. It was possible he hadn't used his real name but some variation thereof.

It was a common occurrence among criminals. Jeffrey Davidson became David Jeffries or Jeff David. She knew Willowby's full name was Marcus Maxim Willowby. He could be registered as Max Willow, Will Marcus or any number of variations. There was no question that the easiest way to know if he was in Tamillo was to go there and look for him.

She knew from the Web sites that Tamillo wasn't a huge place. She couldn't imagine that Willowby would hole up in a hotel and never step outside. He'd like his creature comforts and that would include good food and nightlife.

Harrah was right about one thing. She needed a plan. She figured once she saw that he was there, where he was staying and the circumstances, a plan would eventually unfold. Seat-of-the-pants planning, it was the only way she knew how to work.

She closed the menu and looked up to see Monica fly through the door. Chantal guessed that Monica was somewhere between the ages of thirty-five and forty-five, but when it came to her energy level she was like a two-year-old on speed.

She slid into the seat across from Chantal, tossed a folder on the table, picked up a menu and signaled the waitress all at the same time. "How you doing, girlfriend?"

"Good. What about you?"

"I'm thinking about killing Joey." She smiled brightly at the waitress who appeared at their booth. "I'll have a grilled chicken salad, dressing on the side and a diet cola."

"I'll take the chicken-fried steak, mashed potatoes and gravy and corn. Oh, and throw an extra one of those buttered rolls on," Chantal said.

Monica shook her head as the waitress departed. "I don't know how you can eat like that and stay so slender."

"I only eat like that occasionally," Chantal replied. "Trust me, I suffered through plenty of fat days when I was younger. When my best friend and I were in high school our weight was a constant battle. I think we tried every diet on the market."

Chantal tried not to think about the hateful, vile things Marcus had said to Belinda. Maybe that was the moment in time that Belinda had begun her anorexic eating habits.

"Well, something worked. You look great."

"Thanks, now tell me why you're ready to kill Joey."

Monica rolled her green eyes and shoved a strand of

her bright red hair off her forehead. "Joey has been an ill-tempered monster ever since Willowby skipped out. I've never seen him like this. It's not just about the money, although that's bad enough. But, for some reason he's taking this one personally."

"Why?

Monica frowned thoughtfully. "You know, Joey has been in the business for a lot of years. He's posted bonds for thousands of people, some of them wealthy, important people. He's used to being stiffed by the common riffraff, but until Willowby he'd never been stiffed by one of his wealthy, influential clients."

She picked up her fork and twirled it on the table as if to vent some of her manic energy. "I think Joey's pissed because he believed that people who had money and influence also had honor and this has proven how wrong he was."

"There's certainly no honor in what Willowby did to those women," Chantal replied.

The two women fell silent for a moment as the waitress reappeared with their meals. "I met him, you know," Monica said when the waitress had left once again. "I went with Joey to get the paperwork signed." Monica stabbed at a carrot in her salad. "I've got to tell you, that man is one of the most handsome I've ever seen, but he gave me the creeps."

"Was it something he said? Something he did that made you feel like that?" Chantal asked with interest.

"I'm not sure. Maybe it was because I knew what he'd been charged with, but there was something in his eyes, a cold, calculating shine that totally creeped me out." Monica shivered.

"He raped one of my best friends years ago." Chantal's heart squeezed at thoughts of Belinda. "He didn't drug her. He raped her in the bathroom at a party."

"She didn't report it?"

Chantal shook her head. "I tried to talk her into reporting it, but she was too scared." Again anger edged through her as she thought of everything Belinda had told her.

Monica sighed. "Most people don't understand the trauma of rape, the aftermath is often just as terrible as the act itself."

Chantal thought of Belinda popping pills and guzzling booze, taking chances by being promiscuous and playing roulette with her health with her eating habits. Monica was right. Belinda had lived through the rape, but without an angel or two watching over her she wouldn't survive the aftermath.

As the two women ate, their conversation flowed easily. Monica talked about her twenty-three-year-old son who had just joined the police force and they talked about the bail bonds business in general.

"Enough about business, tell me about your love life because I'm sure not having any fun with mine," Monica said. "The last time I had sex a Democrat was in the White House."

Chantal laughed. "Love life? What's that?"

"Damn, I thought maybe I could live vicariously through you."

"Not when it comes to men." Chantal raked her fork

through the mound of mashed potatoes on her plate. "I can't even remember the last time I had a warm, hard body next to me. I've been so focused on work."

"Speaking of work." Monica checked her watch and grimaced. "I'd love to sit around and chew the fat, but I've got to get back."

She forked the last bite of salad into her mouth and motioned the waitress to bring her check. She motioned to the folder on the table. "That's copies of anything I thought might be of interest to you that's come in during the last week."

"Thanks, Monica. I appreciate it."

Monica grabbed a twenty from her purse, wiggled her fingers in a goodbye, then walked toward the cash register right inside the restaurant entrance.

There was no way Chantal was leaving until she'd eaten every bite of the fattening food on her plate. She rarely indulged herself so, but when she did she enjoyed it.

As she ate she opened the folder Monica had brought and flipped through the pages inside. Several mug shots with accompanying information about the latest bail jumpers. A robbery suspect, a flasher, but nothing concerning the Willowby case.

She'd just finished eating and had signaled the waitress for her check when the door to the diner burst open. Two men wearing ski masks stepped inside. Chantal didn't have to be a rocket scientist to realize she was in deep shit.

She grabbed her purse and dove to the floor.

Chapter 6

There was a moment of silence, then all hell broke loose. Several people screamed, dishes crashed to the floor and in the melee Chantal grabbed her gun from her purse and slithered on the floor across the aisle to the booth on the opposite side of the restaurant. It was an act of pure survival based on nothing more than instinct.

"Maple syrup on pancakes…*Sex and the City* reruns…books that make me cry…" she muttered under her breath as she flipped the safety off her gun.

A shot rang out followed by more screams and the meal she'd just consumed threatened to come up. She'd never had a reason to pull her gun before this moment, had never really contemplated whether she could aim and fire at another human being.

She didn't need to contemplate it now. As another shot rang out she knew if she could, she'd have no problem taking down the gunmen. Were they here to rob the place? If so, she hoped they grabbed the cash from the register and ran before somebody got hurt.

With her gun gripped firmly in her hand and adrenaline pumping wildly, she peeked her head around the base of the booth.

Two more shots rang out, the bullets slamming into the booth where she had just been sitting enjoying her meal. The acrid scent of gunsmoke filled the air.

Her blood iced as she recognized that these men weren't interested in robbing the establishment. If they had only been interested in robbery they'd have already reached for the cash register and been gone.

The red leather of the booth where she had been sitting now sported bullet holes with foam stuffing showing through. No, these men weren't here for money— They were here for her.

As they fired several more times at the booth across the aisle, she also realized they didn't know she'd changed positions.

She pressed herself against the floor, considering her options. She knew the minute she returned fire they'd realize she was no longer where they thought she was. But, if she didn't do something fast, somebody was going to get seriously hurt.

"Get down! Stay down!" A male voice shouted.

"Help us, Jesus," a woman cried.

Chantal couldn't wait for the cops to arrive or for

divine intervention. Once again she peeked around the corner, this time with her gun leading the way.

One of the masked men stood in the aisle between the booths. Beneath the ski mask his eyes looked wild as he waved his gun first in one direction, then another. He was a perfect target.

She drew a breath, aimed and fired. He screamed and dropped his gun, grabbing his bloody thigh as he fell to the floor.

She flattened herself on the floor as bullets ripped through the booth. Above the gunshots and screams she heard the faint sound of an approaching siren.

But the cops couldn't get here fast enough to stop the second gunman. He screamed obscenities and fired again, one of the bullets ripping into the wood base less than an inch from her head.

"Put down your weapon," a deep, familiar voice yelled from the back of the restaurant.

"Screw you!" the gunman screamed and fired again.

Luke returned fire from his position behind Chantal. Chantal looked around the corner of the booth once again and saw several police cars squeal to a halt out on the street. Right behind them was a news van.

"Throw your gun down, because if the cops don't kill you, she will," Luke said.

With a sob of outrage, the gunman looked around frantically, then threw down his gun. Chantal stood and Luke was instantly by her side.

"If you don't want the entire city to know what Ms.

Worthington does in her spare time, I suggest you go out the back door and get the hell out of here," he said quietly.

She didn't wait to be told twice. As police stormed through the front door, Chantal raced through the back. The kitchen help were huddled together in a corner, their faces frozen in various expressions of terror.

"It's all right now. The police are here," she said to them as she flew out the back door. Her car was parked out front and there was no way she was going back for it. Instead she ran as fast as her legs would carry her to the next block.

She ran until she could run no further, then stopped to catch her breath, pulled her cell phone from her purse and called for a taxi.

It wasn't until she was in the back of the taxi taking her home that she allowed herself to think and to process what had just occurred.

That had been close…too close. Once again she recognized that she'd made a mistake, underestimated the men who wanted her dead.

Damn it, it was bad enough she'd put herself at risk, but it was unforgivable that she'd put innocent people in danger. She hoped, prayed that nobody had gotten hurt. It had been impossible to know in the chaos.

She would have never guessed there would be a time when she'd be glad to hear Luke Coleman's voice, be grateful for his presence. While she'd been confident she could have handled the situation, without his help she would right now be talking to police and reporters.

Her life would get considerably more complicated if

reporters had gotten hold of the information that socialite Chantal Worthington moonlighted as Carol Worth,
bounty hunter. It would make a wonderful human-in-
terest story and would destroy not only her credibility
but her ability to sneak up on bail jumpers.

She leaned her head back against the seat and closed
her eyes as the adrenaline that had pumped through her
slowly began to ebb away.

Maybe it was a good thing she was leaving tomorrow
on the trip to Mexico. Some time and distance from the
problem might give her a reasonable solution where
Mundy and his death threat was concerned.

She prayed nobody had gotten hurt or killed at
Danny's, and until the price on her head was resolved
she'd take care to make sure she didn't do anything or
go anywhere that might put others at risk.

The moment she entered her house, she went directly
to the television and turned it on, seeking news of the
gun battle that had taken place at the diner.

She channel-surfed, finally seeing a breaking news
flash. "This just in," a male reporter said. "A shooting at
a local diner. Details are sketchy at this time, but at ap-
proximately six-thirty this evening two gunmen entered
Danny's Diner on Grand Avenue and began shooting. It's
unclear at this time if it was an attempted robbery or
something else. Both suspects are in custody. One is being
treated at an area hospital for a gunshot wound to the leg."

As regular programming resumed, she shut off the
television and went into the kitchen. She needed a drink
and she wasn't even considering coffee or tea.

She fixed herself a gin and tonic with a double lime twist, then carried the drink out on her back porch and sipped it as she watched a group of golfers scrambling to finish their round before night crept in.

The sight of normal life going on reassured her after the scene she'd just left. The scent of gunsmoke left her senses, being replaced by the smell of green grass and summer flowers.

Definitely time to get out of Dodge for a while, she thought. Maybe by the time she returned from Mexico Mundy's thugs either would have killed each other or all been arrested. And if that didn't happen she was going to have to figure something out, because she was not going to be ruled by a little creep and his power play.

She didn't realize she'd been expecting him until she heard the doorbell. She carried her drink with her to the front door.

"You okay?" Luke asked as he strode past her and into the entry. He turned to face her, his eyes as dark, as fathomless as she'd ever seen them.

"Fine. Was anyone hurt?" Although the news report hadn't indicated injuries to anyone other than the gunman, she held her breath as she waited for his reply.

He smiled then, that slow lazy grin that caused a slight burn to begin in the very pit of her stomach. "You mean other than the one you got with a perfectly well-executed shot?"

His backhanded compliment sent a ridiculous wave of pleasure through her. She nodded. "Nobody else was shot?"

"No. You got another one of those?" He gestured to the drink in her hand.

"Yeah, come on in." Under normal circumstances she never would have invited him in or offered him a drink, but these weren't normal circumstances and she figured she owed him a drink, at the very least.

He followed her through the living room and into the kitchen where he sat on one of the stools at the counter while she got out the gin and tonic to fix his drink.

As always, he seemed to command the space around him and brought with him a frenetic energy that pulsed in the air. He was dressed as usual in a pair of worn jeans and a T-shirt. Although his facial expression appeared relaxed, his eyes held a dark intensity that unsettled her.

"You know you could have been killed in there," he said.

By nature Chantal was not a woman who blushed easily, but she felt the warmth that colored her cheeks. It wasn't a blush of embarrassment but rather one of guilt.

"I know, but more importantly, innocent people could have been killed." She set the drink in front of him and pulled up a stool across from him.

He raised a dark eyebrow. "I figured you'd tell me you had it all under control and that I just got in your way."

"You didn't get in my way. If you hadn't been there I'd still be there probably fighting off reporters. Besides, I'm not stupid enough to think that in a situation like that anyone is in complete control."

She raised her glass to take a drink and tried to ignore the tension that coiled in her stomach, tension that was always present when he was near.

The bite of the gin tingled in her mouth and warmed her stomach, relaxing some of the taut tension. "I'm guessing it was some of Mundy's boys?"

Luke nodded. "Two of his lieutenants in his little army of lowlifes."

"The one I shot? He's going to be all right?"

"He'll survive."

"I wonder how they knew I'd be in the diner? I'm not driving my own car."

"You made a mistake," he said, his smile gone. "You reverted to habit by going to Danny's. It's possible they followed Monica and saw you there. You only get so many mistakes in this business, and then you get dead."

She frowned at his words, wishing she had the ammunition to protest, but she didn't. She knew he was right. "How did you know I was there?"

She wanted to think that she could have handled the situation on her own, but there was no doubt Luke's presence there had kept her cover from being blown and had probably helped contain the situation.

"I was at Joey's when Monica came back from supper. She told me she'd met you and I decided to get some dinner and see if you were still there." He paused a moment to take a drink. He tilted his head back and she noticed not only the whiskers on the underside of his jaw, but also the smooth, tanned skin of his throat.

Why was she so acutely aware of everything about him? She'd never before noticed the faint scar on the left side of his forehead or the length of his dark lashes. She frowned and tried to focus on the conversation, not the man.

He set the glass back down then continued. "When I drove by I saw those two punks just outside. My gut instinct told me they were up to no good and I never ignore my gut instinct. I parked in the back and went in through the kitchen entrance and waited to see what might happen."

Chantal rubbed two fingers in the center of her forehead, where a headache threatened to appear. "Do I need to call the police? It's my bullet the doctors are going to dig out of that leg."

"No. I took care of everything. If the authorities have any questions they'll call me."

"Thanks."

"Don't thank me." Again the corner of his mouth curved upward in a half smile "I've got to admit, you surprised me in there."

"Surprised you how?"

"You stayed calm, stayed low and stayed in control."

She flashed him her best smile despite the fact that his words irritated her. What had he expected from her? Hysterics and tears? "I told you I was good."

"It's going to be interesting to see just how good you are," he replied. There was something in his smooth deep tone, something in his eyes that made her wonder if he wasn't talking about something other than bounty hunting…something more delicious, something more dangerous.

He lifted his glass and took another drink. "You need to figure out what you're going to do about this threat of Mundy's."

"I intend to take your advice," she said.

Once again, one of his dark eyebrows rose. "What advice?"

"You told me to take a vacation, to get out of town until things cooled down. That's exactly what I'm doing tomorrow morning."

"You're taking a vacation?" There was the faintest hint of suspicion in his gaze. "Where are you headed?"

"Paris," she lied. Even though he'd helped her out tonight that didn't mean she owed him anything. "I figured I'd do a little shopping, maybe visit the Louvre and just relax for a couple of weeks."

She held his gaze, hoping he wouldn't see the lie there. The last thing she wanted was for him to know she had a possible lead on Willowby.

At that moment Sam made an appearance. The cat entered the kitchen with a plaintive meow and ran to Luke's feet. Luke leaned down and scooped up the cat, who purred with audible pleasure. "What's his name?"

"Sam. I can't believe he's so friendly with you. He hates me."

Amusement lightened Luke's eyes. "Maybe he's just playing hard to get."

"I'm not into playing those kinds of games," she replied.

Heat flashed through her as his gaze left her face and settled momentarily on her breasts, then returned to her face. It wasn't an overt leer, but rather appeared to be a natural male assessment of a female. Her nipples tightened in response and the tension in her stomach renewed itself.

"Interesting, I thought all women played games." He set the cat on the floor.

"Well, I don't," she replied, wondering how the conversation had gone from Sam's name to something more personal.

She felt the need to escape him before things got any more personal. She looked at her watch, then back at him. "And now, I hate to be rude, but I need to finish packing for my trip tomorrow."

He tipped his glass and drained it, then stood. "I've got to admit, things won't be as much fun around here with you gone," he said as he followed her back to the front door.

"I'm sure you'll manage just fine without me," she said dryly.

He paused at the front door, that infuriatingly sexy smile on his lips again. He took a step closer to her, so close she could smell the tangy lime and biting gin on his breath. For just a brief, insane moment she wanted to lean forward and taste his mouth. Instead she took a step backward.

"Between now and the time you get on your plane in the morning you watch your ass, because personally I think it's a damned fine ass."

She watched speechlessly as he walked toward his

truck in her driveway and wondered why in the hell her heart pounded as frantically now as it had when she'd had two masked men firing guns at her?

There was nothing better than a seat in first class on a plane carrying you to a sandy beach south of the border, Chantal thought as she eased down in aisle three, seat A.

She intended to sleep through the entire flight, especially since what little sleep she'd gotten the night before had been haunted by dreams…terrible dreams.

In the first nightmare of the night she'd dreamed that Marcus Willowby was fixing her breakfast. As he stood at the stove stirring a skillet filled with scrambled eggs, a video camera had whirred in the background. She'd sat at the kitchen table totally naked and unable to move as the camera captured every moment of the event.

"If you tell," he said in the dream, "nobody will believe you. This is nothing more than a pity breakfast. You're nothing but average and nobody will ever believe I made you bacon and eggs."

That dream had faded only to be replaced by another, equally disturbing one. This time Belinda cried Chantal's name over and over again as Willowby chased her through a bathroom as big as a house.

Each time Marcus managed to touch Belinda, she seemed to fade, like a photograph left out in the sun for years. Chantal knew if she didn't stop him, Belinda would be gone.

She'd awakened with a gasp, damp with sweat and

her heart beating a million miles a minute. She'd been unable to go back to sleep in spite of the early-morning hour.

Now, all she wanted was this seat, a pair of head-phones with some light easy-listening music and a person sitting next to her who wanted privacy and quiet as much as she did.

She grabbed the in-flight magazine and flipped through the pages as the plane continued to fill with passengers. She stifled a yawn and checked her watch.

Fifteen minutes and the plane would be taking off, carrying her to the small resort town of Tamillo. It wasn't a direct flight. They'd land in Mexico City, then she'd board a smaller plane bound for Tamillo.

She closed the magazine in her lap and leaned her head back and shut her eyes. She tried not to think about the shooting the day before, the worry that had darkened Harrah's eyes as she'd told Chantal goodbye and that damnable Luke who had kept her tossing and turning in her bed before the nightmares had begun.

Okay, so he'd said she had a nice ass. She didn't have a problem with him thinking she had a nice ass, she had a problem with the fact that she was oddly pleased he thought she had a nice ass.

She was willing to admit that even though she thought he was arrogant and needed a complete make-over, he intrigued her on some base level.

She checked her watch once again. Five minutes to takeoff. Maybe first class wasn't full and the seat next to her would remain empty. That was fine with her. That meant she could sprawl and not worry about bumping elbows or thighs with a stranger.

Although the trip was prompted by her desire to find Willowby, she intended to work in some beach time as well. Chantal loved the beach and Kansas City certainly offered none of the beach life to its residents.

Again she opened the magazine in her lap and thumbed through the pages, at the same time imagining the sound of the pounding surf, the heat of the sun on her skin.

She looked up to see him step through the doorway and into the plane. Shock stabbed through her along with disbelief. What was *he* doing here?

Luke offered her a full smile of amusement as he made his way down the aisle. He was dressed in a pair of worn jeans and a blue-flowered Hawaiian shirt, and he carried a small leather attaché with him.

No! A voice in her head screamed in protest as she stared at him in open-mouthed shock. It had to be a hallucination. Please, let him be a figment of my imagination.

To her utter horror he sank down in the seat next to her, shoved the attaché beneath the seat, then looked at her with a chiding amusement.

"Paris, my ass," he said.

Chapter 7

"How…how did you…what did you…" Chantal sputtered like one of her father's motor boats just hitting the water without enough gasoline in the tank.

"How did I know you were going to Mexico?" He held her astonished gaze with a look of lazy amusement. "I'd like to tell you that I have the same contacts you do, but that wouldn't be the truth."

"Then how…"

"I saw your plane ticket last night on the kitchen counter and figured if you were going to Tamillo, Mexico, there must be something…or someone interesting down there."

"That's despicable," Chantal finally managed to get out a sentence, even if it was only a two-word one.

"On the contrary, it's how I work." He grabbed his seat belt and buckled it over his slim hips. "You know, in this business you use whatever means necessary to get the information you need."

"You aren't stealing this one from me," she exclaimed. "You might be in the same city as me, but if Willowby is there, I'm going to be the one bringing him in."

She turned her gaze toward the window. He might be going to Tamillo, but the minute the plane touched down she intended to lose him.

She wasn't about to lead him to another capture he could steal from her. *And when I get home I'm going to fire Harrah for leaving that ticket on the counter where Luke could see it,* she thought even though she knew she'd do no such thing.

She couldn't believe he was here, couldn't believe that she'd have to suffer his nearness for the duration of the flight.

The plane engines began to wind up, the humming noise filling the cabin. She glanced at Luke and saw him curl his fingers over the ends of the armrests as the plane began to back away from the airport building.

She stared at his hand. He had long fingers and his nails were clean and neatly clipped. But what surprised her was that he gripped the armrest so tightly his knuckles were white.

Fear.

With surprise she shot a glance at his face. A muscle ticked in his jaw and his mouth was a grim, taut slash.

He was afraid. Big, bad bounty hunter Crazy Luke Coleman was afraid of flying.

A wicked delight swept through her as she digested this bit of information. "There's nothing better than being on a plane a hundred miles above the earth," she mused aloud. "Soaring with the eagles in a steel cylinder that by all rights shouldn't be able to lift off the ground."

He said nothing, but the muscle in his jaw ticked faster as the engines whined in pre-takeoff fervor.

Chantal settled back in her seat and smiled. "Up, up, up in the big, blue sky," she continued. "No strings attached and…"

"Shut up, Chantal," he said and flashed her a dark look that held not only a dangerous warning, but also a subtle plea.

She shut up. That single moment of vulnerability shining from his eyes made it impossible for her to tease him anymore. It would be like kicking a little puppy dog. This thought made her shake her head in amazement. Who would have ever thought she'd consider Luke as innocent as a puppy?

They didn't speak again until the plane had left the ground and had stopped climbing. His fingers relaxed their hold on the end of the armrest and he released a deep, audible sigh.

"I've never liked to fly," he said.

"It's safer than driving a car."

"Yeah, well, in a car I'm in control. Up here I'm not."

She should have known it was a control issue. She

had a feeling Luke Coleman was a man who prided himself on always being in control.

The irritation that had momentarily died beneath the knowledge of his fear reappeared. "How do you know I'm not headed to Tamillo just to spend some time on the beach and relax and wait for Mundy to cool down?"

"Because if that was the case you wouldn't have lied to me about where you were going. Because I get the feeling you're taking this Willowby thing way too personally and that's definitely dangerous in this line of work."

"Why on earth would you think that?" She eyed him coolly, not about to share with him just how personal Willowby's capture had become to her. "I'm a bounty hunter, hunting skips is what I do. Willowby is no different than any other criminal I'd go after."

"But that's where you're wrong." Whatever else he was about to say was pre-empted by the captain speaking over the intercom system.

Chantal turned her head and stared out the window as the captain droned on with his welcome speech. She couldn't believe Luke was not only on his way to Mexico but seated next to her for the ride. How in the hell had he managed that?

Damn, if only that airplane ticket hadn't been out on her kitchen counter the night before. If only the shooting in Danny's hadn't occurred and he hadn't come to her place. If only he hadn't been able to get a seat on this plane.

Even with her gaze out the window she was acutely conscious of him next to her, far too close to her for comfort. She could smell him, that clean male scent of minty soap, spicy cologne and fresh-scented shampoo.

She supposed she should be grateful he'd obviously bathed before boarding the plane. She'd once spent a long plane ride seated next to a man who'd smelled like a sweaty armpit. It had been horrendous.

What was it about him that twisted her insides into knots? She wanted to believe it was intense dislike, but she knew that wasn't it at all. She didn't know him well enough to dislike him completely.

Whenever he was near she felt as if she couldn't draw quite enough air. Her heart beat just a little faster and she felt slightly flustered, slightly breathless.

The captain finally finished his spiel and she looked at Luke once again. "What do you mean I'm wrong about Willowby being like any other criminal?" she said, picking up their conversation where it had stopped before the interruption.

"The men you've been chasing for the past eight months have been small change." He bent down and reached for the attaché beneath the seat and placed it on his lap. "They've not been especially bright, without any real resources and fairly predictable. Willowby is none of those things."

"I know that," she replied tersely. "I've done my homework."

He unzipped the case to reveal a laptop computer. It surprised her. She'd never have guessed him as a computer kind of guy. "What do you do with that? Visit porn sites?" she asked dryly.

"Yeah, and I've got to say, that last picture of yourself that you posted didn't do you justice."

"Ha ha," she replied.

He quirked a dark eyebrow. "You want to ask stupid questions, I'll give you stupid answers."

Her cheeks warmed and she decided it was definitely intense dislike that she felt for him. She watched as he turned on the computer and pulled up a file.

She was stunned, stunned that he not only had a computer but that the file he pulled up appeared to contain background material on Marcus Willowby. In spite of her reluctance to have anything to do with him, she leaned closer to him to peek at the file.

"This guy is definitely not your garden-variety creep," Luke said. "He spent all of his college years on the dean's list and considered going to medical school. He toyed with the idea of becoming a psychiatrist."

"Where did you hear that?" she asked with interest.

"You have your sources, I have mine."

"Can you imagine," she mused. "Dr. Marcus Willowby with the power to prescribe medication to women seeking help. If he'd become a psychiatrist he could have drugged them into unconsciousness and done them in his office." The thought sickened her.

Luke's expression showed her that he felt the same way. "I can't imagine why a guy would want an unconscious partner for sex."

"If you had sex with Brandy Hamilton then surely you came as close to that experience as a man can."

He laughed, a low smooth sound that twisted the

knot in her stomach even tighter. "Careful, Chantal, I'll think you're jealous."

"Don't be ridiculous," she scoffed and straightened up in her seat once again. "I couldn't care less who you sleep with."

"Or don't sleep with," he replied. "I've had my share of conquests, but Brandy Hamilton isn't one of them. Actually, I'm a friend of her father and Brandy definitely isn't my type. But she was useful as a companion at that fundraiser. Anyway, back to Willowby. My original point is that he's brighter and more calculating than most criminals."

"And this is supposed to worry me?"

He frowned and shut down the computer. "If you find him, what's your plan?"

"Plan?" she repeated evasively.

His frown deepened. "You don't have a plan?"

"Of course I do," she snapped. "My plan is to sleep for the rest of this airplane ride." She lowered her seat, turned her face toward the window and shut her eyes.

She didn't need Luke Coleman trying to freak her out where Willowby was concerned. She knew Willowby might be dangerous. Luke thought he knew everything, but he wouldn't be on this plane if he hadn't seen her ticket on the counter.

She might have fallen asleep if they hadn't begun serving lunch, although lunch was a relative term. There was only one thing that would make her put up with Luke and that was the promise of food.

She straightened her seat as she was served a chicken

sandwich, a bag of chips and a soda. Luke got the same meal, but he ordered a Scotch and soda to drink.

"I've got a proposition for you, Chantal," he said once they had been served.

"I'm not interested in any of your propositions and don't call me Chantal. Once I get to Tamillo I won't be using my real name."

"What name are you going to use?"

"I haven't decided yet what my cover is going to be." And she certainly didn't intend to tell him when she did make up her mind.

"Aren't you afraid Willowby will recognize you? I mean, you and he ran in the same crowd for a lot of years." Luke ignored his sandwich and took a deep swallow of his drink.

"I've thought about that. We never really hung out together. He's a couple of years older than me and I never had a conversation with him." She frowned thoughtfully. "I'm not that memorable."

He looked at her, his gaze sweeping over her face, then taking a fast trip down the length of her. "Don't underestimate yourself."

"I'm not. I'm being realistic. I used to mourn the fact that I'm average, but in this business that's a plus." She took a bite of her sandwich and thought about what he'd said.

It was true. She and Marcus had never been friendly or even casual acquaintances. They'd both attended various functions when they'd been teenagers, but she couldn't remember ever speaking to him or his gaze ever meeting hers for any length of time.

Surely he wouldn't recognize her. It was important that he not. If she wanted to get close to him, close enough to clap handcuffs on him, she needed him to believe she was somebody who would have no idea of the trouble he was in.

She hadn't decided the best way to play it yet, but she knew for a fact he probably wouldn't trust Chantal Worthington. He had to know that her mother was friends with his mother.

"Sure you don't want to hear my proposition?" Luke asked, pulling her from her inner thoughts. "I think it would benefit both of us."

She eyed him suspiciously. "Okay, what?"

He finished his drink in one swallow. "Like I said before, Willowby is smart. He'll know that bounty hunters are after him. He'll be suspicious of anyone getting close to him, anyone asking questions. I think we should work as a team on this one."

She nearly spat out her bite of sandwich. "You've *got* to be kidding." It was as ludicrous an idea as Brandy Hamilton becoming a brain surgeon.

"I'm not kidding. I think we need to work together to bring him in. Think about it, Chantal. We're going into a country where we have no jurisdiction. We aren't going to get any help from the authorities and Willowby isn't going to just waltz up and allow himself to be taken. It's a two-man job."

"I work alone."

His eyes flashed with a hint of impatience. "And you can continue to work alone on other cases, but this one is too big, too complex to work alone. We can split the fee."

"It isn't about the money," she replied. "And I'm not interested. Now, if you'll excuse me. I'm going to take that nap." Once again she lowered her seat, turned her head toward the window and closed her eyes.

The very idea of them working together was ludicrous, she thought. You couldn't partner with somebody you didn't trust, and she definitely didn't trust Luke Coleman. She hadn't forgotten that he'd walked away with the prisoner that by all rights should have been hers.

He probably just wanted to use her to find Willowby, then he'd waltz off with him and be the big hero. No way, no how would she be stupid enough to trust him.

Not in this lifetime.

Luke leaned his seat back and tried to relax, but tension rippled through him, making any real relaxation impossible. It wasn't just the fact that he hated to fly that had him on edge.

It was Chantal.

She'd had him on edge since the moment she'd waltzed into Big Joey's wearing a scandalously short skirt and a pair of red high heels that had made her legs look sexy as hell.

Hell on heels, that's what he'd thought when he'd first seen her. There had been a challenge in her eyes, a determined thrust to her chin and a stubborn set to her full lips that had only intensified her attractiveness.

Sexy or not, she was in way over her head on this particular case and didn't seem aware of that fact. He had to admit she obviously had sources he didn't. If he hadn't seen her airplane ticket he wouldn't have thought about Tamillo as a potential place where Willowby might hide.

Mexico had been in his sights as a potential place to hunt, but he hadn't pinpointed a specific town and in fact had been leaning toward one of the more popular resort areas. He'd figured Willowby would want to get lost in the crowd of a bigger resort.

Luke was willing to concede that Chantal was bright and resourceful, and she seemed to possess a single-minded determination that was admirable.

He slanted his gaze in her direction. Although her eyes were closed, he knew she wasn't sleeping by the way she breathed. He took the opportunity to study her.

The coral blouse she wore complemented her blond coloring and flawless complexion and accented the thrust of her breasts and slender waist.

She might consider herself average-looking with her medium-blond hair and even features, but there was a spark in her eyes, a touch of the devil in her smile and a sexy sway to her hips that elevated her beyond average.

And that's what had him worried. He'd studied the profile of Willowby's victims and Chantal fit that profile. And if she proved herself as bright as he thought she was, she'd play on that aspect to get close to the rapist.

He tore his gaze from her and instead focused unseeingly on the seat in front of him. The day she'd started working for Big Joey, Luke had made it his business to learn everything he could about her.

He knew that she was worth a fortune, that she was close to her mother and liked shopping at the Plaza. He knew she worked out at least three times a week at a gym and had a personal assistant named Harrah and a best friend named Belinda Carlyle.

He'd learned the charities she preferred, the fact that she was well liked within her circle of friends and that she could handle herself well in a stressful situation.

What he didn't know was what drove her? What made her tick? Why would a woman with her background, her money, want to be a bounty hunter?

He'd initially thought she was nothing but a bored socialite looking for a little fun, but over the months of watching her work, seeing her results, he'd slowly begun to change his mind about her.

What they did was hard, often tedious work and if she'd been just looking for fun she would have gotten bored and moved on months ago. But she hadn't. Rather she'd continued to learn, to focus more and more on the bounty hunting and less on her social obligations and fun.

He glanced at her once again and caught the sight of blue sky out the window. A wave of disquiet filled him. There had been a time when flying had been a big part of his life.

His father had been a commercial airline pilot and had also enjoyed flying his small private plane on occasion. Luke's childhood had revolved around weekend trips with his parents and younger brother to locations around the country.

He'd been twenty-two when his parents had decided to fly from their home in Chicago to Denver for a weekend of skiing. They'd asked Luke to go with them, but he'd declined. He'd preferred to hang out with his friends and party. They'd also asked Luke's brother, Seth, but he'd also turned them down, preferring to spend the weekend with his fraternity buddies.

In a freak ice storm his parents' plane had gone down and they'd been killed, leaving Luke with enough grief, enough guilt to last a lifetime. After that, he'd also developed a fear of flying.

Five months after his parents' death, his brother had been killed in a convenience-store robbery. Seth had been in the store to buy a soda when a gunman had burst in to rob the place.

Nobody knew exactly what had taken place that night in the convenience store. The first thing the gunman had done was shoot out the camera. When all was said and done, Seth and the store clerk had been shot and the gunman had escaped with all of $32.50.

Seth had lingered for two days in the hospital although he'd never regained consciousness. They had been two of the most difficult days of Luke's life.

It had been a year of tragedy for Luke and the result had been he'd closed off, shut down and been in a dark place for a very long time. He'd crawled out of the darkness when the man who'd killed his brother had been arrested. The shooter had been wanted in another state and had skipped out on his bail. It was at that time that Luke knew what he wanted to do with his life.

Once again he directed his gaze to the back of the seat in front of him as his thoughts returned to the problem at hand.

Luke had been bounty hunting, or bail-bond enforcing, as it was now called, since he was twenty-seven years old. He'd had five years of experience and in those five years he'd faced a hell of a lot of criminals, some more dangerous than others.

Something about Willowby's crime and his character made Luke think that Willowby might just be one of the more dangerous skips he'd gone after.

He thought the man a sociopath, without conscience, without empathy for any other human being. Those were the worst kind of criminals and the most unpredictable.

Damn it, there was no way Chantal was ready for a job like this one. Granted she had handled herself admirably the night before in Danny's Diner, but she couldn't even use her handcuffs properly. He had a bad feeling about this one, a very bad feeling.

Somehow, someway, he had to convince Chantal that she couldn't do this alone. He had to make her agree to partner up with him.

He checked his watch. He had two hours of the flight left to make her see things his way.

Chapter 8

Luke Coleman was nothing if not persistent. By the time they boarded the smaller plane in Mexico City bound for Tamillo, Chantal had a raging headache that had his name written all over it.

The worst part was that the more he talked, the more he made a crazy kind of sense. "I'm telling you, Chantal, this isn't a one-man job. Even if you do manage to get him handcuffed and into your custody, you still have the job of keeping him contained and getting him back to the States," Luke said. "How do you intend to do that all by yourself?"

She rubbed her forehead and frowned thoughtfully. Her ultimate goal in being here was to get Willowby back into custody to serve his sentence for his crimes.

She had to decide what was more important, her pride and independence or getting the job done right. "All right, let's just say I'm considering your proposition of working as partners on this one," she finally said. "Do you have a plan as to how this would all work?"

He grinned at her, that smile that made her think she probably didn't want to have anything to do with whatever plan he might have.

"I've given it a lot of thought," he replied. "You need a cover and I need a cover. Willowby has got to know that he's on the A-list of most wanted for bounty hunters so he's going to be suspicious of anyone who tries to get near him. So, I think a reasonable cover is for us to pose as newlyweds."

Surely she'd misheard him. He couldn't have said newlyweds. A flush of heat swept through her at the thought, a heat she didn't understand. She stared at him in disbelief. "Excuse me?" she finally said.

"You heard me. Think about it, it makes perfect sense. Tamillo is a haven for honeymooners. We could hang out at all the local nightclubs, spend time eating together at the restaurants, jump from hotel to hotel and keep an eye out for our man."

"Did you used to do drugs?"

"No, why?"

"Because only an addled brain could come up with such an idea," she exclaimed.

"What's addled about it? I'm telling you it makes perfect sense. Nobody will be suspicious of a couple of honeymooners."

"I'm better off sticking to my own plan," she replied.

He raised an eyebrow. "And what plan would that be?"

Damn. At the moment there were two things she would love to possess, a seat on another plane and a plan. "I'll check into my hotel, pretend to be a sexy single woman on vacation and find Willowby," she said.

"Okay, my first question is how are you going to check into a hotel under an assumed name? I would bet you used a credit card to reserve your room and that credit card will have your name on it."

Double damn, she thought. "I never said my plan was completely flawless. What about you? Your name is far more recognizable than mine when it comes to the bounty-hunting business."

"I've got a set of identification and a credit card under the name of Luke Kelly. I use it in situations like this when I don't want to use my real name."

She wasn't surprised. She'd always believed he didn't always walk on the right side of the law. The fact that he had fake ID just reinforced the point.

"I can check us in as Luke and Carol Kelly. That way if Willowby tries to check us out he won't find anything to make him suspicious."

"It's still a ridiculous idea," she said.

"What's so ridiculous about it?"

She looked at him and deliberately slid her gaze from the top of his head to the bottom of his feet. "No offense, but there's no way anyone would ever believe that a woman like me would be married to a man like you."

He opened his mouth to protest, but she hurried on. "Look, Luke, we both know that Willowby is not the type to forego the finer things in life just because he's a fugitive from United States' justice. He's going to be staying in one of the best hotels, dining in one of the best restaurants and clubbing at one of the most exclusive clubs. He's going to be in my world and frankly, you just don't look like you belong in that world."

His expression didn't change and she wasn't sure if she'd angered him or not. She knew her words made her sound like a first-class snob, but the truth was there was a class system and clothing and manners and haircuts defined not only her class but Willowby's as well. As Luke was now, he would stick out like a Volkswagen parked in a row of Ferraris.

Rather than holding anger, his eyes now held a glittering challenge. "You think I can't fit into your world? Chantal, you vastly underestimate my talent."

"I don't think so," she replied warily. She didn't trust that gleam in his eyes.

"I'll tell you what, when we get to Tamillo I'll check us into a hotel as Mr. and Mrs. Kelly. While you unpack and relax I'll transform myself into the kind of man who will fit into your world, the kind of man you would marry."

She grinned, certain that he couldn't make a Gucci bag out of the proverbial sow's ear. "All right, but if you don't meet my standards, then the deal is off. You get me a separate room with your credit card and we forget the husband-and-wife cover and figure out something else."

"Any other cover will be second-rate."

"I'd rather settle for a second-rate cover than a second-rate husband."

He laughed. "Is that why you aren't married? Because you're a snob and have impossible standards?"

"I'm not a snob," she protested as he looked at her in disbelief. "Okay, maybe I'm a little bit of a snob, but I'm not married because I haven't found a man I could tolerate longer than six months at a time. And what about you? Why aren't you married?"

"I've never found a woman who could tolerate me for longer than six months," he answered easily.

At that moment the plane began its descent, banking sharply to the left as it approached the runway. Once again Luke's hands gripped the ends of the armrests and his face paled slightly.

Chantal almost felt sorry for him. She knew what it was like to be afraid, how fear could twist your gut and send a chill through your heart. She felt that way sometimes at night in the dark when she was alone with just Sam's presence for company.

At those times she thought about what it would be like if she didn't have Belinda as a friend or her mother or Harrah in her life and she recognized that what she feared most was loneliness.

Other than Belinda, most of her acquaintances her age were either already married or in a committed relationship. Maybe she was too picky.

The problem she had now was that the men in her social group expected her to be nothing more than eye candy. They wanted a wife who would create wonderful dinner parties and do charitable work and not much more. They certainly wouldn't understand or accept her desire to bounty hunt.

If she dated men who weren't in her social group the concern was that they saw her money instead of her. Both of her parents had instilled in her a healthy respect for how money could bring out the best in people and the worst. They'd also warned her about men who would love to help her spend her inheritance.

She liked to believe she was a woman who could spend her life alone if it came to that, but deep in her heart she knew it wasn't true. For one thing she liked sex too much. It wasn't as though she was a slut or anything like that, but she did enjoy a lusty bout of sex occasionally.

And it had been a long time, too long since she'd indulged herself, she thought as the plane touched down on the runway.

She glanced over at Luke. At least she didn't have to worry about anything sexual happening with him even if they did play house for a couple of days. He wasn't her type at all.

"We'll get checked into the hotel, then I'll take care of the little business of making myself into the man of your dreams while you get settled in the room," he said as the plane came to a halt.

"If you aren't coming back to the room until you've transformed into my dream man, then I guess we'd better say goodbye now," she replied.

"There you go again, underestimating me." He

reached out and ran his fingers across the back of her hand. "You'd be surprised by what I can pull off. I'm a man of many talents."

She felt his touch even after he pulled his hand away and leaned down to retrieve his attaché case. She couldn't remember Luke ever touching her before, although she knew he had at one time or another. There was no explaining the electric currents his touch had shot through her.

Crazy, she thought as they prepared to leave the plane. She dismissed the moment from her mind as they entered the small Tamillo airport and headed for the baggage area.

"I thought I'd go ahead and rent a car from here," she said as they waited for the bags to appear on the conveyor belt.

He shook his head. "They won't have what we need here. We'll find a place to rent once we get settled into the hotel. I want something with both speed and off-road capabilities."

"Okay," she agreed easily. "Then we'll take a taxi from here to the hotel." She grabbed one of her large suitcases from the conveyor belt.

"Is that it?" he asked and grabbed a small black duffel bag.

"There's one more," she said.

He frowned and looked at the size of her suitcase. "How long were you planning on staying?"

"A week or so."

"Don't believe in traveling light?" he asked dryly.

She didn't reply as her second large suitcase appeared. She pulled it from the conveyor belt then looked around to find a Skycap to help her with the luggage.

Luke handed her his duffel, then grimaced and picked up her two suitcases and headed for the airport exit.

Chantal hurried after him, deciding that even though she found him arrogant and underhanded in his dealings, he was at least handy when it came to grunt work.

Within minutes they were in a taxi and headed for the hotel. Chantal rolled down her window and looked out with interest.

The streets of Tamillo were narrow and cobblestoned and lined with white adobe homes, each sporting a red tile roof and flower-laden wrought-iron balconies.

Hot, humid air, scented with the fragrance of the Gulf and the flowers that seemed to be everywhere, drifted into the cab through her open window.

"Nice. You ever been here before?" Luke asked from beside her.

"Never. I've been to Acapulco and Puerto Vallerta, but never here. It's much smaller than I'd expected."

"That definitely works to our advantage," he said. "According to my research there are only four five-star hotels and maybe half a dozen clubs where somebody like Willowby would hang out. We should be able to check everything out within a week easily."

She nodded her agreement. If Willowby was here in Tamillo, surely within a week they could sniff out his scent. As much as she didn't particularly want to work with Luke and definitely wasn't thrilled about their cover as newlyweds, she reluctantly admitted that he was right about this being a two-man job.

She glanced over at him once again. At least she didn't have to worry about becoming intimately involved with him. With his long hair, worn jeans and floral shirt he looked like a nightmare tourist from the seventies. Definitely not her type.

It was just after four when the taxi pulled up in front of the Hacienda Hotel, a luxury high-rise structure on the shore of a sandy beach.

A middle-aged man clad in a crisp red uniform greeted them as he loaded their luggage on a brass carrier. Together Chantal and Luke headed inside for the check-in desk.

The lobby whispered of elegance and Chantal immediately felt at home. If she couldn't be in her own house then a five-star hotel was the next best thing.

Although the reservation Harrah had made was in Chantal's name, Luke paid for the room with his credit card and registered them as Mr. and Mrs. Luke Kelly.

He took one of the two keys provided, then grinned at her. "I'll be back in a little while. Prepare to be amazed."

"Whatever," she replied. She watched him head back toward the front door, noting the confident set of his shoulders.

She immediately dismissed Luke Coleman from her mind as she took an elevator to her room on the fifteenth floor. The bellman followed just behind her with the luggage.

Within minutes she was in her room alone, having

tipped the bellman and sent him on his way. She looked around, pleased that the tense knots that had formed in her stomach at Luke's appearance had relaxed when he'd disappeared.

The room was sumptuous, large and airy and furnished with oversized furniture in dark wood with black wrought-iron trim. The bed was a king-size with a massive wrought-iron headboard. A table and four chairs graced one corner of the room.

Chantal placed one of her suitcases on the bed, but before she began the task of unpacking, she went to the French doors, opened them and stepped out on the balcony.

The scene before her nearly stole her breath away. White sandy beach and sparkling blue water stretched seemingly endlessly before her.

People sprawled beneath colorful umbrellas, frolicked in the waves and lounged on oversized towels. She moved closer to the edge of the balcony and stared at the people below.

Right at this very moment it was possible Marcus Willowby was tucked into a swim suit and chatting up his next potential victim. She hoped they could find him before he added another rape to his list.

She walked back into the room and thought about calling Belinda, but rejected the idea. She'd called her friend that morning to tell her that the next time she spoke to her it would be to tell her that Willowby was in custody. There was no point in calling her again right now.

Instead she focused on the task of unpacking. The

first suitcase yielded her handcuffs, which she set on the nightstand while she finished removing and hanging her clothing.

Because of the rigid security standards she hadn't packed her gun and hoped they could get Willowby in hand without the need for a weapon.

Although she'd agreed to Luke's plan where their cover was concerned, she had no intention of allowing him to run the show fully.

That was the problem with men, she thought as she began to unpack her second suitcase. They all had major control issues. That had been what had ended each and every relationship she'd had: the man's need to control her.

That wasn't going to happen with Luke. She'd make sure he understood that just because she'd agreed to work with him didn't mean he got to be boss. They were partners, and that meant fifty-fifty. She'd play nice as long as he played nice as well.

She finished her unpacking, then went into the bathroom and stared at the Jacuzzi tub with longing. She'd love a long, hot soak, but didn't want to take time for such a luxury.

She caught her reflection in the mirror and frowned. Was it even remotely possible that Willowby would recognize her?

She supposed it was conceivable. Maybe she should change her hair color, go darker. She could pick up a temporary color and do it herself. Surely she could find a nearby drug store or market and buy a box of transformation.

She left the bathroom and once again wandered back to the balcony and stared out at the beach below. It was possible this trip was a waste of time, that Willowby was not even in Mexico. There were a million places a man like Marcus could run to to escape facing the sentence the jury had handed down.

But her gut instinct told her he was here, that he would have escaped to a place he knew, a place where he'd been before, a place where he felt safe.

Tamillo held all the ingredients that would make it a haven for the escaped criminal. First and foremost because he'd traveled here in the past there would be a familiarity for him here. The exciting nightlife would draw him, the upscale living would please him and the scantily clad women on the beach would tempt him.

This place made sense more than any other place on earth and she knew in her gut he was here, it was just a matter of finding him.

Luke had said on the plane that he had the feeling that she was taking this case too personally. She'd protested his assessment at the time, but the truth was she took it very personally.

Whenever she thought about what Marcus had done to Belinda, it made her sick. It would have been better had Belinda been one of his drugged victims, if she'd awakened the next morning with no memory of the violation that had taken place. Of course, it would have been better if the crime had never taken place in any shape or form.

But it had, and Chantal wanted to be the one to bring the bastard in. She needed to do this for Belinda. It might prove to be the one thing that would save Belinda's life. It might be the one thing that would get Belinda off the pills, off the booze and back to living a happy, productive life.

Her thoughts turned back to Luke. It was strange. She didn't trust him as far as she could throw him when it came to their work, but she trusted him enough to share a room, share the intimate spaces of a bed with him.

She wasn't at all convinced that he wouldn't use her to get close to Willowby, make the collar himself then leave her high and dry. But, she instinctively knew she could trust him with her personal safety.

She didn't know how long she stood on the balcony, thinking about Luke, about Willowby and about how to catch a narcissistic rapist when she heard the hotel-room door open then close.

She left the balcony and took only two steps into the room before stopping, frozen in stunned surprise. Luke stood just inside the door, but it wasn't the Luke Coleman who had left over an hour before.

His long hair was gone, replaced by a short, stylish cut that emphasized his starkly handsome features. He was clad in beige linen slacks and a beige-and-pale-green shirt that fitted across his broad shoulders as if it had been tailor-made. He looked ruggedly elegant and unbelievably hot.

"Hi, honey, I'm home," he said and smiled that grin

that instantly retied the knots of tension in the pit of her stomach. He dropped a large shopping bag on the floor.

It was at that moment that Chantal recognized what exactly it was that always caused her tension whenever he was around. Lust. It roared through her with a force that threatened to knock her right off her feet.

"Bagels from Benny's, Times Square, scented candles." Her mantra sprang to her lips unbidden.

"Excuse me?" He sauntered toward her, a confident smile on lips she'd never noticed were quite so full, quite so...so...hot-looking.

"Nothing," she exclaimed.

"So, what do you think?" He stopped just in front of her, close enough that she could feel the heat radiating from his body, see the flecks of silver in his dark eyes. "Do I meet your standards?"

Her stomach fluttered and her heartbeat revved up as the full extent of her desire filled her. "You'll do," she managed to reply, then swallowed hard once...twice in an attempt to gain control.

"You know, I've been thinking." He took one last step toward her, his chest mere inches from hers. He reached up and stroked a hand through her hair, down her cheek, then his fingers lingered on the curve of her jaw. "I was thinking if we really want to pull off this newlywed stuff, maybe we should practice a little."

Even as she recognized that she wanted him, she wasn't mindless enough to follow through on it, and, in truth, she was suspicious of his motives.

"Practice? Just what do you have in mind, Mr. Kelly?"

She tried to keep her voice light, even though her blood thundered in her veins and her suspicion of him grew.

What was his game? Other than telling her she had a nice ass, he'd never shown any kind of a personal interest in her before.

Was this some sort of control thing? Maybe he figured that if he could get her into bed then she would be more malleable as a partner.

He wrapped an arm around her back and pulled her close against him. "I was thinking that if I'm going to play your groom then I should know what you taste like right here." He dipped his head and pressed his lips against the hollow of her throat.

His mouth was hot and under any other circumstance Chantal would have followed where he led, but the truth was she didn't trust Luke Coleman and she sure as hell wasn't going to tumble into his bed.

And that might just be a damn shame, she thought, because he definitely knew how to use his lips on her neck and she could easily imagine how those lips would feel on other areas of her body.

Despite the fact that he knew how to kiss a neck and Chantal's neck had always been particularly sensitive to a man's lips, she fought against the sensations his lips evoked.

She pushed away from him and moved toward the side of the bed. "If you really want to practice playing newlyweds, maybe we should get into bed." She gave him a come-hither look, all the while wondering how far he'd push this particular game.

She had her answer when he kicked off his loafers and quickly stretched out on the bed. He lay down on his back, then opened his arms as if to welcome her.

Apparently if she allowed it he'd take it all the way. But she had no intention of allowing it.

She moved to the side of the bed and with one hand unbuttoned the first button on her blouse. He stared at her, a hint of hunger darkening his eyes.

For just a brief moment she wondered what it would be like to have sex with Luke? She had a feeling he'd be good at sex, that he'd be the kind of man who knew not only how to take pleasure, but to give it as well.

As she unfastened the second button of her blouse, with her other hand she reached behind her and grabbed her handcuffs off the nightstand.

With one smooth movement she leaned over him, cuffed his wrist, then yanked his arm up to snap the other cuff over the wrought-iron headboard. She wanted to crow with success as she realized that for the first time her cuffs had locked tight.

As he bolted upright, she jumped back from the side of the bed. "Does this mean you're into kinky stuff?" he asked, his eyes now glittering with just a touch of danger.

"No, it means I'm not into playing newlywed with you. Oh, and in case you haven't noticed, I'm no longer handcuff-challenged."

"Point taken, now unlock the cuffs." Although his voice remained deceptively smooth and calm, she noticed that muscle ticking in his jaw.

"I'm heading down to the bar for a drink and I'm

going to scout out the hotel a bit. I shouldn't be too long." She grabbed her purse from the dresser and headed toward the door.

"Chantal." She paused at the door and turned to look at him. He grinned. "Just keep in mind that payback is a bitch."

Chapter 9

Chantal supposed she should be worried about Luke's threat, but she was too busy celebrating her success with the cuffs to worry too much.

She figured she'd go to the bar, have a quick drink then go back to the room and release him. No harm. No foul. She knew she should also feel guilty about what she'd done, but she didn't.

He'd deserved it. There was no way she'd believe that he hadn't had some sort of ulterior motive in trying to get her into bed. Maybe he thought he'd blow her away with his lovemaking and she'd become a mewling, passive partner he could take advantage of.

No way. No how.

She'd probably pay for her little bit of fun, but the

shocked expression on his face when she'd snapped the cuff onto the headboard had been worth whatever the consequence.

As she headed toward the hotel bar she recognized that it was going to be difficult sharing her space with Luke. When she'd initially agreed to his plan she hadn't really thought it all through, hadn't really considered that the plan meant they'd share the same room, share the same bathroom...the same bed.

At the time she'd agreed she hadn't recognized that there was some perverse part of her that was drawn to him on a physical level. Jeez, when he'd walked through that door, every hormone in her body had jumped to life.

If he thought his little act of seduction would make sharing a room with her easier, he'd definitely miscalculated. As hot as she thought he looked with his new haircut and clothes, she wasn't about to muddle up this tenuous partnership by having sex with him.

The lounge in the Hacienda Hotel was called the Sombrero. A long polished wooden bar ran the width of the room and behind that bar the wall was decorated with a variety of fancy, glittering, sequin-spotted Mexican hats.

Several couples were seated at the tables but Chantal headed for one of the empty barstools. She hoped the bartender, an attractive Hispanic young man, spoke some English, for her Spanish was rusty at best.

"Good evening, *señorita*," he greeted her with a diamond-bright smile. "What can I get for such a pretty lady?"

Belinda would slather this dark-eyed, dark-haired man on a cracker and eat him right up, she thought as she remembered the fundraiser at the Kansas City Club. "How about a margarita and a little information?" she replied.

"What kind of information?" he asked a moment later as he placed the drink on a napkin in front of her.

Chantal opened her purse and took out a small picture of Marcus Willowby. She'd gotten the photo from Rebecca Willowby and it showed the young man standing on a porch, the sun sparking off his blond hair.

"I'm looking for an old college friend of my husband's," she said. "We heard he was down here in Tamillo and thought we would look him up while we were here." She slid the photo toward the bartender. "Have you seen him around here?"

The bartender, who wore a nametag that identified him as Carlos, picked up the photo and looked at it. "I'm not so good with names, but I never forget a face," he said, then shook his head. "Nah, I've never seen him before." He handed her back the photo.

She hadn't expected it to be easy. She tucked the photo back into her purse then asked Carlos about the location of the nearest drug or discount store.

She'd decided to color her hair. She didn't want to take any chances that Willowby might recognize her if they ran into him.

He'd just answered her when two hands fell on her shoulders. She stiffened, then turned to see Luke and jumped out of her seat to face him.

"Ah, here you are, darling," he said, his eyes glittering darkly. "I'm sorry I'm late. I was all tied up."

Before she could guess his intention, he grabbed her to him and took her mouth with his in a hard, punishing kiss that quickly transformed to something softer and far more dangerous.

She wanted to shove him away, punch him in the stomach, but she was conscious of Carlos watching the interchange with amusement.

It was only when the tip of his tongue touched hers that she broke the kiss and staggered a step back from him on legs that threatened to buckle. Damn, but the man definitely knew how to kiss.

"Darling, now is not the time or the place," she said and shot him a look that should have dropped him dead in his tracks.

Luke winked at Carlos. "When you're newlyweds the time and place are always right for a little romance. Right?"

Carlos laughed. "Ah, *amor*. It makes fools of both men and women."

"Why don't you give me what she's having." Luke gestured toward Chantal's drink. "And why don't we get a table, darling?"

Chantal grabbed her drink from the bar and walked to a nearby table while Luke waited for his drink. Her mouth still burned with the imprint of his and she took a deep drink of her margarita to banish the taste of him.

"How did you get loose?" she asked him as he joined her at the table.

"There's not a pair of handcuffs made that I can't pick open." He took a sip of his drink. "That wasn't a nice thing to do, Carol. If I was a different kind of man that little incident might have started our married life off on the wrong foot."

"Get bent," Chantal exclaimed. "I agreed to work with you, not sleep with you."

"Then I guess you don't believe in combining business with pleasure?" He raised a dark eyebrow.

"What makes you think sleeping with you would be a pleasure for me?" she countered.

He leaned back in his chair and smiled. "Because I know what I'm good at. I've never had any complaints."

"Enough of this nonsense, we need to get down to business." She did not want to think about or talk about Luke's skill at sex. It made her uncomfortable. It made her feel as if she suffered a fever. "We need to see about a rental car and I've decided maybe it would be a good idea if I dye my hair before we really go on the hunt for Willowby."

"I already got us a car," he replied. "It's parked in the hotel garage right now. And later tonight I'm meeting a man about a gun." He kept his voice low so their conversation wouldn't be overheard by anyone else nearby.

Chantal frowned. "You really think that's necessary?"

He shrugged. "I believe in erring on the side of caution. I don't like being here without a weapon. As far as Willowby is concerned, I'm still not sure what he might be capable of."

"Who is this man you're supposed to see?"

"A friend of a friend of a friend."

Chantal took another sip of her drink, then said, "Is that wise?"

"Wise or not, it's necessary. Mexico might be beautiful, but there is a high crime rate here and we aren't exactly here for a luxury vacation." He eyed her curiously. "What color?"

"Excuse me?"

"What color are you going to dye your hair? I think you'd make a good redhead."

"Dark brown," she replied, although she had been leaning toward red. She leaned back in her chair and realized it was difficult for her to look at him. Without the long hair there was nothing to detract from his strong, handsome features, chiseled features she'd never noticed before.

"So, what exactly is our plan for this evening?" she asked. "I've already shown a picture of Willowby to Carlos and he said he's never seen Willowby in here."

"Why don't we get your hair stuff and go back to the room. We can order room service for supper while you're doing your hair. After we eat and your hair is done we can take a look around the area until it's time for me to meet my man."

Chantal finished her drink and stood to leave. "Carlos told me there's a drug store in the next block. I'll go get what I need then meet you upstairs in the room."

He stood as well. "I'll go with you. Even though this is a resort, it's not safe for a woman, especially not a woman who looks like you, to be walking the streets alone."

"I can take care of myself," she said. "I'm not exactly your typical helpless female."

"Far be it for me even to suggest such a thing. I just figured if I took the walk with you, I could get a feel for the neighborhood."

"Whatever." Chantal waved to Carlos as she and Luke left the bar and headed toward the front door of the hotel.

The evening air was still quite warm and humid as they walked outside. "Carlos said the store is this way," she said and pointed to the left.

Darkness had begun to fall. Shadows clung to the sides of the buildings, deeper in the alley they passed. In the shadows of the alley a gang of young men milled about and they didn't look as though they were exchanging business cards.

Luke stepped closer to her side and despite the fact that she knew she could handle herself against a single attacker, she was grateful for his presence as they passed the alleyway and the group of men.

The shop where Carlos had told her to go was small, but carried a vast array of items, including a box of cocoa-brown hair dye, which Chantal purchased while Luke picked up a couple guide books and visitor information brochures, then they left to make the return walk to their hotel.

In the few minutes they had been in the store darkness had fallen completely and the streets had begun to come alive with the exciting nightlife the travel brochures promised.

Lively music poured from several open doorways and well-dressed groups of people walked the streets, apparently seeking entertainment.

Chantal felt the thrum of energy deep in her veins and despite the fact that she was tired from the flight she felt a second wind coming on.

Perhaps Willowby was right now arriving at one of the clubs. He'd be dressed to kill, flashing his charming smile and picking a victim for the night.

Why had he chosen Belinda that night? Had he sensed some kind of weakness in her that would make her a perfect victim? She'd read someplace that criminals, rapists in particular, seemed to have a sort of radar for likely victims. They honed in on the vulnerable.

That night of the party so long ago, the house had been filled with pretty girls, more than a few of whom would have willingly fallen into bed with Marcus.

Why hadn't he picked on Chantal? She would have fought back. Even at the age of sixteen she hadn't been as vulnerable as Belinda had been.

When they returned to the room, Luke stretched out on the bed with the brochures and Chantal disappeared into the bathroom to transform her looks.

Less than an hour later she stood in front of the bathroom mirror and stared at her reflection. Amazing what a bottle of goop and forty minutes could do, she thought as she studied herself.

The dark brown hair definitely changed the way she

looked. Her eyes appeared bluer and her round face looked thinner. If Willowby had any memory of her at all, she felt confident he wouldn't recognize her now.

She heard a knock on the door and knew it was probably room service delivering their dinner order. A moment later, Luke knocked on the bathroom door.

"Carol, dinner is here."

She opened the bathroom door and stepped out. "Perfect timing," she said. She touched her hair self-consciously as Luke stared at her. "What do you think?"

He gazed at her hair thoughtfully. "It looks good. It definitely makes you look different."

"That was the idea." She walked over to the table and chairs where their meals had been laid out, complete with a fresh-cut floral centerpiece.

They both sat at the table. "Now that our makeovers are complete, we can really get down to business," she said.

"We're not going to really get down to business until I get a gun," he replied. "We can really start our hunt for Willowby first thing in the morning."

For a few minutes they ate in silence and Chantal found herself wondering about Luke's personal life, his history. "I know you've worked for Big Joey for about five years. What did you do before that?"

"Little bit of this, little bit of that. Drifted mostly, worked as a bouncer in a couple of bars, roped some cattle on a ranch in Texas."

"Really? Where are you from originally? Where's your family?"

"I grew up in St. Louis and I've got no family. My parents died when I was twenty-two."

"I'm sorry."

He shrugged. "It was a long time ago."

"But, it must be tough...being all alone."

"I don't mind being alone. When you depend only on yourself you never have to worry about people disappointing you or leaving you behind." There was a darkness in his eyes that subtly warned her this particular conversation had reached an end.

She wondered who had disappointed him? Who had left him behind? But, she knew better than to pry by the expression on his face. "How did you meet Big Joey?" This seemed a better choice for conversation.

"I was bouncing in a bar on the south side of Kansas City. He came in one night and we got to talking and before I knew it he'd offered me a job. He'd heard I wasn't just brainless muscle, that I had a degree in criminology and he thought bounty hunting would be a good fit for me. He was right."

Chantal stopped eating and stared at him wordlessly for a moment. "You have a degree in criminology?" The idea was as foreign as Versace designing clothes for gas-station attendants.

"Don't look so surprised," he said dryly. "I told you I'm a man of many talents."

So, she wanted to ask but didn't, why would a man with a degree in criminology be working as a bouncer in a bar? The last thing she wanted was to get personal with Luke Coleman. The less she knew about him the better.

It was already distracting enough to realize that beneath all that hair and bad clothes lurked a drop-dead gorgeous man who stirred her hormones into a near frenzy.

But no matter how fine he looked, no matter how his nearness stirred her up inside, she couldn't get distracted from her job and that job was to find Willowby and bring him to justice for Belinda's sake.

The heart of Tamillo was a five-mile stretch of luxury hotels, fancy restaurants and nightclubs, tiny shops and food bazaars. Bright lights and crowds of people filled the street despite the fact that it was nearly midnight. The sound of laughter and raucous music rode the humid salted air, proclaiming to visitors that Tamillo was open for fun.

But, as with all resort towns, there was a seedy underbelly away from the bright lights and laughing tourists. Chantal maneuvered the Jeep down the narrow street lined with shanties and trash, grateful that she didn't have to make this trip alone, that Luke sat in the passenger seat beside her.

She'd been pleased with his choice of vehicle and even more pleased when he hadn't argued when she'd said she'd drive. She was also glad that he wasn't a backseat-driver kind of man. Other than giving her directions to their destination, he said nothing.

They both understood the danger of what they were going to do. They were in a foreign country and about to buy an illegal gun from a man they didn't know. It was possible they could wind up in jail, ripped off or dead.

It was the dead part that had Chantal more than a little nervous as they passed sullen-faced teenagers and men with angry expressions standing on the street corners.

In this part of the town the developers' money hadn't changed life, poverty was rampant and where there was poverty, there was rage.

"Up ahead, on the right," Luke said tersely. "La Cantina. Pull up in front and keep the Jeep running, and whatever you do, don't get out of the Jeep for any reason."

"You might think I'm stupid, but I'm not," she said as she tightened her fingers around the steering wheel. She pulled up in front of the cantina where a handful of men stood looking pumped and primed for trouble.

"I'm looking for a man named Ramos," Luke yelled out in perfect Spanish.

One of the men broke away from the group and stepped closer to the Jeep. "There are many men named Ramos. Why are you looking for one?"

"We have a mutual friend," Luke replied.

"And who might that friend be?"

The man leaned down and his glittering dark eyes connected with Chantal. She averted her gaze from his, not wanting him to perceive any kind of personal challenge coming from her.

"Escobar Diaz sent me." Luke opened the Jeep door and Chantal fought the impulse to grab his arm and keep him inside the vehicle.

The gang of men seemed to be holding their collective breaths as Luke climbed out of the Jeep. Several of them wore grins, not smiles of welcome or glee but rather of anticipation.

Hands had disappeared into pockets and Chantal had a feeling that if a frisk was conducted of the gang, enough weapons would be found to stock a small army. She tightened her grip on the steering wheel.

"So, is Ramos here or should I go back to my friend Diaz and tell him Ramos couldn't be found?" Luke asked.

A tall man broke away from the group and approached Luke. "I am Ramos. My friend Diaz mentioned I might have an American visitor, but I didn't realize it would be so soon."

The man called Ramos motioned for Luke to step away from the Jeep. The other men gave the two a wide berth, but their dark gazes remained fixed on Luke.

Chantal's heart banged unsteadily against her ribs. The air was electric with tension, with the portent of unexpected danger. She kept the gas pumped and her foot firmly on the clutch, ready to pop it and go in a heartbeat.

She could no longer make out the words Luke and Ramos exchanged in rapid-fire Spanish, but as their voices raised her heart crashed faster.

What was happening? The two men were out of her direct line of vision and all she could see was the group of men who looked meaner by the moment.

Voices raised, Spanish coming in short staccato bursts and suddenly Luke flew into the passenger seat and slammed the door. "Go!" he yelled.

Chantal popped the clutch and stepped on the gas. The Jeep flew out of the parking space at the same time as she looked in the rearview mirror and saw several men piling into an old battered car.

"What happened?" she asked as they flew down the narrow street, the car behind them gaining ground.

"I got the gun," he said.

"They're chasing us. What did you do, stiff them?"

"No, I paid the money Ramos wanted, but he decided he wanted a fringe benefit."

"Fringe benefit? What?"

"You. I suggest you lose them unless you want to be a night's entertainment for a bunch of horny men."

It was one thing to participate in a car chase in the city where you'd been born, where you knew the streets, the alleys and the dead ends.

It was far more frightening to participate in a car chase in a city you'd never visited before, where one false turn could lead to a blind alley with no escape.

She stayed on the main street as the car behind them crept closer and closer. She came to an intersection and at the last minute turned left, nearly running down an old man.

The turn was so sharp she felt two wheels leave the ground. Luke cursed beneath his breath and grabbed the roll bar overhead. She didn't ease up off the gas.

"Sushi, SPF15 lip balm, tinted sunglasses," she muttered under her breath. Adrenaline spiked through her as she passed a slow-moving car and shot back into her lane seconds before a head-on meeting with a pickup truck. She heard Luke's swift intake of breath.

"Take it easy," he muttered.

"Easy for you to say, none of those boys look the type to be interested in your ass," she exclaimed between clenched teeth. She made a fast right turn and at the same time flipped off her lights.

The road was dark and without streetlights or headlights she had to focus all her concentration on the road ahead. She prayed that nobody darted out into the street in front of her, that no animal ventured into her path.

By the time she'd made two more unexpected, last-minute turns she realized there was no sign of the car that had been chasing them.

She slowed and headed toward the main road that would take them back to their hotel.

Luke released his hold on the roll bar. "Where in the hell did you learn to drive like that?" There was an edge of admiration in his voice.

"You're a man of many talents? I'm a woman of many talents," she replied as the adrenaline kick slowly began to ebb from her veins.

"Obviously."

They didn't speak again until they had parked the Jeep in the hotel garage and were in the elevator going up to their hotel room. Luke held a brown paper sack that she assumed contained the weapon and ammunition.

"I've got Mundy's lot in the United States chasing me and now I've got a bunch of drunken men in Mexico after my ass."

Luke grinned. "I told you it's a great ass."

She scowled at him. "I'll tell you right now, we may be working together on this case and sharing the space of a hotel room, but that's all we're going to be sharing so get my great ass right out of your mind."

"I'll try," he said, "but there are some things beyond a man's capacity."

The elevator door whooshed open and Chantal got off, her mind scattered in a million different directions. She still tasted the danger of the chase, felt the electric energy of fear and what she needed more than anything at the moment was some time to decompress and a good night's sleep.

Luke had thrown her off-kilter from the moment he'd shown up on the plane, and he had completely discombobulated her by his startling transformation and the damned kisses he'd planted on her.

She definitely needed some down time to process everything. When she got into the room she grabbed her nightgown and makeup case and disappeared into the bathroom without saying a word to him.

She removed her makeup and washed her face, still vaguely surprised by the brown hair that now covered her head. She undressed and pulled her nightgown over her head, grateful that she'd packed a plain cotton gown instead of one of her silky, flimsy ones.

The one thing she had no intention of doing was getting all breathless and prissy about sharing the bed with Luke. They were both rational adults.

The bed was a king-size, there was plenty of room for both of them and despite the fact that his kisses had been pretty awesome, she had no intention of sharing anything else more intimate with him.

She knew Luke Coleman was a man accustomed to being in control, that in both his professional and his personal life he didn't abdicate control for anything or anyone. From what little he'd told her about himself, it was also obvious he was a man who didn't get close to people, gave nothing of himself.

She left the bathroom to find Luke stretched out on the bed clad only in his slacks. He'd taken off his shirt and the sight of his broad bare chest kicked her hormones into overdrive and her stomach clenched with what she now recognized as sexual tension.

This would be much easier if he'd had a concave chest and love handles. It would also be easier if she had a man in her life, if it hadn't been months since she'd had sex and if she'd decided to become a nun once Willowby was behind bars.

She had a definite feeling that no matter how strongly she lusted for him, getting personally involved with Luke Coleman would only be a study in pain.

If she was interested in that she'd get a Brazilian wax. It would probably be as painful, but a lot less complicated.

Chapter 10

She awakened only once during the night to find that she was no longer on her own side of the bed but rather on Luke's. His arm was slung around her waist and his warm body was pressed against her back.

Somewhere in the back of her sleep-fogged brain she knew she should pull away, crawl back to her own space, but it was obvious Luke was sound asleep.

She was warm and comfortable and instead of moving she closed her eyes and went back to sleep.

When she awakened the second time she was alone in the bed. In fact, she heard no sounds coming from the bathroom and suspected she was alone in the room.

She rolled over on her back and stared up at the ceiling. Today was the day they got serious about finding

Marcus. What if he wasn't here in Tamillo? What if all of this was wasted effort on their part?

She refused to entertain her doubts for more than a minute. She wondered where Luke had gone. Maybe he'd already begun the hunt. She wouldn't put it past him to find Willowby, take him into custody then send her a note bragging about his success.

A vision of Belinda filled her head. Not a picture of the woman she'd said goodbye to yesterday, but rather an image of Belinda on that night so long ago.

Her face had been so deathly pale and her eyes…the emptiness in her dark eyes would haunt Chantal for the rest of her life.

"We have to leave now," Belinda had said, her voice a faint almost sing-song whisper. Her blank eyes had stared at Chantal.

Chantal jerked herself up and out of the bed. She grabbed what she intended to wear that day then padded into the bathroom.

A few minutes later she stood beneath the spray of a hot shower. She had to tell Luke he was right. She was taking this particular case very personally. She had to make him see how important it was, how much she wanted to be the one to clap the handcuffs on Marcus Willowby's wrists.

She needed to look Willowby in the eyes and let him know that Belinda sent her regards and hoped he endured his own brand of hell in prison. At the moment it was the most important thing in her life.

A half hour later, showered and dressed, with make-

up and hair done the way she liked them, she left the
bathroom to see Luke sitting at the table with his laptop
computer powered up in front of him.

He looked up as she entered. "I was beginning to
wonder if you intended to sleep the day away."

"I'm not much of a morning person," she replied.
Once again he looked casually elegant in a pair of blue
slacks and a blue-and-silver short-sleeved shirt.

"And you're definitely a bed hog." He grinned.
"Every time I woke up in the night you were wrapped
around me like duct tape."

She wanted to protest, but recognized he might be
right. She shrugged. "You can't hold it against me, I was
unconscious."

"Are you conscious enough now to get some breakfast? I'm starving." He shut down the computer and
closed the lid.

"Sounds good," she agreed.

Minutes later they entered the Hacienda Café just off
the hotel lobby. Luke indicated he wanted a table near
the back, then took the chair that faced the entrance.
"This way I can see who comes in," he said as Chantal
took the chair across from him.

A waitress appeared immediately to take their orders,
then poured them each a cup of coffee and left. "I figured we'd spend the day sightseeing," Luke said.

"There's only one sight I want to see," she replied.
She took a drink of her coffee, then unfolded her napkin
in her lap. "Luke, you told me yesterday you thought I

was making this case too personal. You were right. It is very personal."

He took a sip of his coffee and said nothing, as if waiting for her to explain.

"Ten years ago my best friend and I went to a party at Marcus's parents' house. We weren't really friends with him, but a ton of kids were going and we thought it would be fun. We arrived at the party and it was a bit wilder than we had expected. A lot of drinking, a lot of drugs and kids in every room."

She paused a moment to take another sip of her coffee, a chill sweeping over her as it always did when she revisited that night. "We'd agreed we'd stick together, but I saw some girls I knew and before I knew it my friend and I had gotten separated. She found me about thirty or forty minutes later and I could tell by her expression that something bad had happened. She said we needed to leave and it wasn't until we were in the car and driving away that she told me Willowby had pulled her into the bathroom and raped her."

Luke leaned back in his chair and frowned. "She didn't report it?" he asked.

"No. She was young and afraid and he'd said terrible things to her. I couldn't talk her into going to the authorities. But Marcus Willowby destroyed her life. She's never been the same."

Her hand clenched around her coffee cup. "Willowby took her virginity, now she's promiscuous and incapable of forming any real commitment to a man."

"Has she had therapy?"

Chantal sighed. "Not really. She sees a couple of psychiatrists who prescribe pills that she pops like candy. She drinks too much, she medicates herself into a stupor."

Luke leaned forward, his gaze softer than she'd ever seen it. "Sounds like she doesn't need just a good friend, she needs a rehab center as well."

"She needs Marcus Willowby to be behind bars and I need to be the one to accomplish that." She was interrupted by the arrival of the waitress with their orders.

Once the waitress had departed, Chantal held Luke's gaze intently. "I need you to promise me something, Luke. Promise me that you won't steal this one from me. I don't care about the fee. You can have it all, but I want to be the one to handcuff Willowby, I need to see the look in his eyes when he realizes he's busted."

Luke's frown deepened. "I can't promise you that. You know there are no guarantees in this business. I can't control the conditions. What I can tell you is that I have no intention of stealing this one from you. If it's at all possible then you can be the one to get him into custody, but that's the best I can do."

She nodded, not happy but satisfied. A promise was easy to make, lip service to keep her pacified. She respected the fact that he hadn't taken the easy way out and made a promise he had no intention of keeping.

"You know, this case reminds me of another one," he said as they began to eat.

"Andrew Luster," she replied. He looked at her in surprise. "One of the first news stories that broke the day that Marcus disappeared mentioned the Luster case and I remembered vaguely that there were some similarities and looked up the old case."

"Both men are wealthy, both used GHB to render their victims unconscious," Luke said.

"And both of them made videotapes. But Luster was charged with something like eighty-six counts of kidnapping and rape. Willowby was only charged with two counts of rape. Although I have a feeling there are a lot more victims out there who don't even know what happened to them."

"But, if we're right and he's fled to Mexico, then he's following Luster's lead. Luster fled jurisdiction and wound up being captured in Puerto Vallarta."

Chantal smiled. "He was captured by a bounty hunter who got his own reality show. Just think, if we're successful, when this is all over maybe you can be a television star."

He laughed and somewhere on another level she recognized that she liked the sound of his deep laughter. "I'm not interested in being a television star," he said.

"I just don't understand why men would want to drug a woman into unconciousness to have sex with them," she added.

"I suppose it could be considered the ultimate sex without commitment."

She shot him a dirty look. "That's awful."

"I didn't say I understood it," he protested. "I'll tell you this, GHB has become a lot of college-aged kids' wet dream. It can be mixed up in a dorm room and in most cases the victim doesn't even know it's been consumed."

"Sex without commitment, is that what you're into?" she asked.

His gaze slid down the front of her in a lazy, heated trail. "Why? You offering?"

"In your dreams," she replied, appalled to recognize that with just the power of his gaze he'd managed to make her sexually aware of him. "But it's a new century, there's nothing wrong with women enjoying sex without commitment the way men have done for years."

"Amen to that." He drained his coffee cup and motioned the waitress for a refill.

"I'll bet we're the only couple in here talking about drugs, rape and sex," she said when the waitress had filled their cups once again and left.

Luke looked around, amusement crinkling the corners of his eyes. There were several couples at tables in the café. "Oh, I don't know. Maybe all of them are talking about the amazing sex they shared last night. I'm probably the only schmuck in here who didn't get lucky last night."

He leaned forward, his eyes glittering. "You better hope I never get the opportunity to handcuff you to a bed because if that happens I'm not leaving the room to have a drink in the bar."

For just a brief moment her mind filled with a vision of herself handcuffed to the bed while a naked Luke slid his lips all over her body. She was way too young to suffer hot flashes, but at that moment she felt as if she was in a menopausal moment. She felt light-headed and far too warm and she grabbed her coffee cup hoping another jolt of caffeine would banish the image.

"I think we need to finish breakfast and get to work," she finally managed to say. "I didn't come all the way to Mexico to indulge in foreplay with you."

"You're absolutely right. I think we should skip the foreplay altogether."

Chantal sat up straighter in her chair. "What are you doing, Luke?"

He looked at her innocently. "I'm sitting here having breakfast."

"You know what I'm talking about," she replied.

He opened his mouth as if to give another flip answer, then closed it and hesitated before finally replying. "I think what I'm doing is attempting to seduce you. Since you had to ask, I must not be doing a very good job of it."

Oh, you're doing just fine, she thought. Although his seduction might not be as smooth, as subtle as other men, it was all the more effective because it was up front and in her face. She was almost relieved that it was now on the table between them instead of simmering under the surface. "Why?"

"Why?" One of his eyebrows raised slightly. He leaned back in his chair and frowned thoughtfully. "Because from the moment you walked into Big Joey's with that short red skirt and those spike high heels, I wanted you. I can't explain it. Hell, I'm not even sure I like it. But, it's there."

Chantal folded and refolded her napkin in her lap,

for a moment lost for words. It amazed her that he remembered what she'd worn the first time she'd gone into Big Joey's. But, what amazed her even more was that she remembered what he'd been wearing the first time she'd seen him.

He'd had on a pair of worn jeans that had hugged his hips and legs as if they'd been sewn specifically for him. He'd also worn a black turtleneck that had molded to his muscled shoulders and broad chest.

"I just think it would be better if we kept things strictly business between us," she said. Even though she was flattered and very, very tempted, she still didn't trust him.

More than that, she realized she didn't trust herself where he was concerned. It was one thing to talk about sex without commitment and certainly there had been a few times in her life when she'd enjoyed having sex with a man without any kind of emotional tie. But for some reason Luke scared her just a little. She had a feeling he would be harder to forget than the other men who had drifted in and out of her life.

"All right," he agreed, then smiled. "But, that doesn't mean I'm not going to try to change your mind."

"I hope you like a challenge."

His grin widened. "Honey, there's nothing I love better."

She balled up her napkin and placed it on the table. "I think we need to focus on the real challenge here, and that's finding Willowby."

"Then let's get to it."

Minutes later they hit the streets of Tamillo. Even

though Chantal tried to put their conversation in the back of her mind, as they wandered through an open-air marketplace, she couldn't stop wondering about what sex would be like with Luke.

Damn the man anyway. She didn't need the distraction. All she wanted to do was get Willowby, save Belinda and get back home to her life.

The open-air marketplace was huge and clogged with tourists and natives. Exotic scents rode the breeze. Vendors called to them to buy a silk scarf, admire the beauty of a beaded serape or pick a plump chicken, but neither of them paid any attention. They weren't shopping for anything other than a certain man and they kept their gazes on the crowd.

Bright-eyed children begged for coins from passersby, often chased away by screaming vendors. The entire scene was one of controlled chaos.

They wandered the area for about an hour and a half and finally stopped at a booth to buy a bottle of water and sit on a nearby bench.

"It looks like everyone in town is here except for who we're looking for." She unscrewed the top of her water bottle.

"Nobody said it was going to be easy," Luke replied, still observing the people passing by.

She took a long swallow of the lukewarm water, then lowered the bottle from her lips. "You know, this all might be a wild-goose chase. For all we know, Willowby could be in China or Switzerland or any other place on earth."

He directed his gaze to her. "It was a good lead that brought you here?"

She nodded. "One of his closest friends told me that Willowby came to Tamillo four or five times a year for a week or two each time, that he considered it his own little haven away from everyone."

"That's a good lead," Luke said. "Most fugitives flee to somewhere familiar."

"What lead did you get that brought you here?" she asked curiously. He had to have developed some leads on where Willowby might be hiding.

"The only lead I had was the sight of your plane ticket on your kitchen counter," he confessed with a grin. "I'd never even heard of Tamillo before that night."

She laughed and shook her head. "You are some piece of work, Luke Coleman. If it wasn't for me you would have no idea where to start hunting for Willowby."

He took a deep drink of his water and she watched his throat work as he swallowed. Wow, even his throat looked sexy to her. "Why are you doing this, Chantal?" he asked when he'd finished with the water.

"What? Hunting Willowby? I told you why, because of my friend."

He shook his head. "No, I'm talking about bounty hunting in general. Why are you in this business?"

"I'd bought all the baubles I wanted, dated all the men who were acceptable and was just bored out of my silly little socialite head."

"Knock it off," he said roughly.

"Well, isn't that what you thought about me?"

He took another swallow from the water bottle, then gazed out among the crowd. "Yeah, initially that's what I thought. I thought you were a bubble-headed heiress slumming for some excitement."

She'd always believed that's what he'd thought of her and it was why she'd disliked him so much. She'd sensed his lack of respect, a vague contempt that had simmered just beneath the surface whenever he spoke to her, whenever he looked at her. That was one of the reasons why it had been important to her that none of the bounty hunters knew her real identity.

"And now?" she asked, unsure why she cared so much what he thought of her.

He studied her for a long moment and she felt his intense gaze someplace deep inside her. "Now I know you're intelligent, mentally stronger than I'd imagined and, I suspect, hard-headed to a fault. And I still don't know why you're bounty hunting."

She stared toward the booth across from them where the vendor was selling shell jewelry. "To be perfectly honest, I'm not sure why I'm doing this. I kind of fell into it accidentally, but at least for right now it feels right. In fact, it's the first thing that's felt right for a very long time."

She turned and looked at him. "Why do you bounty hunt? With a degree in criminology you could be doing all kinds of things."

It was his turn to look away but just before he did she saw a whisper of something dark, something painful in his eyes. She held her breath, sensing that she was about to learn something about the forces that drove him, the kind of man he was.

"I thought I had my life all mapped out when I was twenty-two years old. I was going to graduate, then join the police academy. Eventually I'd marry and have a couple of kids, live the American Dream as an officer of the law. Then my parents died in a plane crash."

He paused a moment, swallowed once…twice, then continued. "Their deaths hit me hard. We'd been a close-knit family. My younger brother, Seth, and I took care of all the details, I finished school and life went on…until five months later when my brother was killed in a convenience-store robbery."

Chantal sucked in her breath, her heart aching with the weight of his tragedy. She wanted to touch him, to take his hand or stroke his face, to offer some sort of human touch to ease the pain she felt emanating from him. But before she could, he stood abruptly and threw his empty water bottle into a trash can nearby.

When he returned to the bench his brow was smooth and there was no hint of turmoil in his eyes. "Anyway, I didn't handle things well. I started drinking too much and drifted from place to place. If I felt myself getting too close to anyone or too comfortable in any one place, I moved on."

He stood once again. "And speaking of moving on, maybe we should check out the beach and see if Willowby is a sand-and-surf kind of guy."

As they walked toward the beachfront, although

Chantal kept her gaze on the people around them, her thoughts were on the man beside her.

That little glimpse into Luke's past, into his pain, had been dangerous, because the last thing she wanted was to care about Crazy Luke Coleman.

Chapter 11

The Mi Casa nightclub was already hopping when
Chantal and Luke arrived at ten o'clock that evening.
They'd spent the rest of the afternoon on the most populated area of the beach, checking out the people, flashing Willowby's picture and coming up empty.

They'd returned to the hotel, showered and changed,
then eaten in one of the restaurants nearby that had a
reputation for fine dining.

After dinner they'd gone to several lounges, ordering
a single drink, checking out the people inside, then
moving on to the next one until it was time for the
nightclubs to come alive.

If the waiters and waitresses hadn't been clad in tight
black toreador pants, white shirts and little matador

hats, the Mi Casa club would have looked like any other in the United States.

Luke led her to a small empty table near the dance floor. They sat down across from each other and a waitress immediately appeared to take their drink orders.

The large dance floor made it impossible for them to see who might be gyrating on the other side, and before the waitress reappeared with their drinks, Luke got up, pulled Chantal to her feet and gestured toward the dance area.

Chantal loved to dance, but was often dismayed at her partners' lack of rhythm or lack of grace on the dance floor. It was amazing how many good-looking, physically fit men couldn't dance.

She half hoped Luke had two left feet, that he was one of those fools who got on the dance floor and seemed to lose all control of their limbs. She figured that if he were pathetically bad at dancing it would dissipate some of the underlying desire that thrummed in her veins for him.

Unfortunately, he danced as well as he seemed to do everything else. He moved with perfect rhythm, perfect control—and a fire ignited deep in the pit of her stomach.

She averted her gaze from her dance partner and instead searched the dance floor for their quarry. She had to keep her mind focused on Belinda and on Willowby.

When the music slowed, she found herself in Luke's arms, his body tight against hers and the fire inside her flamed hotter.

"I don't think he's here," she said, hoping it was

the last fast dance that had made her breathless and nothing more.

"Maybe it's too early. We need to hang around for a while. This is supposed to be the hottest night spot in Tamillo."

It was hot all right. His smell was hot, the solidness of his chest against hers was hot and the gleam in his dark eyes as he pulled her more tightly against him was hotter than anything she could ever remember experiencing.

She wished he hadn't told her he wanted her, for the knowledge now whispered in her mind with tantalizing seduction.

The minute the dance was over she excused herself to go to the restroom. She needed some distance from Luke, a moment to regroup.

She stood at the sink and dampened a paper towel, then ran it across her forehead and down her neck. When she'd agreed to work with Luke she hadn't known that their partnership would suddenly become complicated by desire.

She ran a brush through her brown hair, reapplied a layer of lipstick, then left the restroom. This wasn't the case of what happens in Vegas stays in Vegas. If she had sex with Luke here in Mexico, she would have to face him once again when she returned to her life in the States.

When she returned to the table she'd made up her mind that no matter how good he was at his game of seduction, she had to be better at rejecting his advances.

The night seemed interminably long. Even though they stayed until just after midnight, she refused to dance any more with him. Instead they sat at the table and stared at the people who came and went until finally agreeing to give up and go back to the hotel.

"Maybe he's not here," Chantal said dispiritedly when they were in the back of a cab headed back to the hotel. "Maybe while we're spinning our wheels here in Tamillo some other bounty hunter is closing in on him in another Mexican town."

Luke shifted positions, his thigh pressed warmly against hers. "We've only been at it a day. I'd say a little patience is in order."

She sighed. "I know. I'm just eager to get this over with and get back to the States."

He leaned closer to her and took her hand. "What's wrong, darling? Not enjoying our honeymoon?"

She snatched her hand from his, amazed that merely his touch had quickened her heart. She was tired and she knew she was getting cranky. "You've got to stop it, Luke. You're distracting me from the real reason I'm here."

His eyes held a dark hunger. "You find me a distraction? Good. Because I've been distracted all night long by how that little black dress hugs your body, by how you smell and by how you felt in my arms when we slow-danced."

His words momentarily stopped her breathing. For a brief moment she wanted to just say screw it, pull up her dress and climb onto his lap. She wanted to end the wanting and just have mindless hot sex with Luke Coleman.

He must have seen something in her eyes, for he groaned as if in anticipation but at that moment the cab pulled up in front of the hotel.

She released a shuddering sigh as Luke cursed softly beneath his breath. He paid the cab driver and together they walked toward the lobby without speaking. The insanity of that single moment was lost and wouldn't be reclaimed.

When they reached the room he went directly to the mini bar. "Want a nightcap?" he asked.

"No, thanks. I'm exhausted. I just want to go to sleep." She disappeared into the bathroom to change out of her clothes and wash her face.

She didn't know what was stopping her from simply indulging in a lusty bout of lovemaking with Luke. Certainly she'd had uncomplicated, uncommitted sex before, although not often.

Why was he different? She didn't have the answer. She only knew deep in her heart, deep in her soul, that having sex with Luke would somehow complicate her life.

When she came out of the bathroom Luke wasn't in the room but the door to the balcony was open, the warm night air flowing in on a faint breeze.

She thought about stepping out there and joining him, but with the memory of his hunger still filling her head and the tiny flicker of desire still burning in the pit of her stomach, she crawled into bed and turned out the light. It was safer that way.

She was still awake nearly an hour later when he came in from the balcony, undressed in the dark and slid into the bed next to her.

If he touched her in any way, she knew she'd be lost. She wouldn't have the resources to deny him, to deny herself. But he didn't touch her. Her last thought before she fell asleep was that she wasn't sure if she was relieved or disappointed.

"I checked in with Big Joey this morning while you were still sleeping," Luke said the next afternoon as he and Chantal walked a different area of the beach than they'd walked the day before.

"Don't tell me, some other bounty hunter found Willowby and brought him in and Big Joey is happy once again."

Luke laughed. "Nope. Joey is pissed as hell. Nobody has seen hide nor hair of Willowby. The news outlets are reporting he vanished into thin air."

"Unless he was taken aboard an alien space ship, he hasn't vanished." She gazed out at the throng of people enjoying the afternoon sun. "He's here," she said more to herself than to Luke. "I don't know why, but I just feel it. He's here somewhere and it's just a matter of time before we spot him."

"Woman's intuition?"

"I guess. Silly, huh?"

He shook his head. "I never discount a woman's intuition."

They walked for a few minutes in silence, the sand

hot beneath Chantal's thin sandals. "The morning that
my mom and dad left on their last plane ride, my mom
called me from her cell phone," he said. "She just
wanted to tell me that she loved me and my brother. I've
always wondered if somehow she had a sense of what
was about to happen? If some woman's intuition was
at work that morning."

Chantal touched his hand lightly. "I'm sorry, Luke. It
must have been horrible for you to lose your whole family
in the space of five months." She sighed. "Sometimes I
feel guilty because my life has been so wonderful."

"But you lost your father."

"Yes, and it was horrible, but I had my mother. We
supported each other through it all. It sounds like you
had nobody."

"I had myself. That's all I needed." There was a remoteness to him that let her know he was finished talking about his personal past.

Luke was a man of many layers, and in the brief time
she'd spent with him she felt as if she'd only peeled
away one or two of the transparent outer ones. One
thing was clear. He was a man comfortable with being
alone.

She leaned down and picked up a pretty shell. "I
should collect some of these for my assistant, Harrah.
She makes jewelry."

"And she has a brother serving five years on drug
charges." Chantal looked at him in surprise. "I told you
I checked you out when you started working with
Joey," he said.

"That doesn't quite seem fair. You seem to know everything there is to know about me, but I hardly know anything about you."

"What do you want to know?"

She leaned down and picked up another shell and added it to the first one in her pocket. "How old are you?"

"I'll be thirty-five on my next birthday."

"And you've never been married?"

"Never. Never stayed in one place long enough to develop that kind of relationship with any woman."

They walked around a group of people sunbathing. "But you've been in Kansas City working for Joey for five years or so. That's a long time," she said.

He nodded. "Longer than I've ever stayed in one place. Like you, this feels right for the moment. I like Kansas City, I like Joey and I like what I'm doing. I don't know what tomorrow might bring, but for right now, I'm doing what I want to do."

If Chantal needed another reason not to get involved with Luke, this was it. She had the feeling that at any moment he could disappear in a puff of smoke, vanish like a platter of petits fours at a baby shower.

"You ready to head back to the room?" he asked.

"Why don't you go ahead? I think I'm going to walk to the marketplace and buy a couple of pieces of jewelry for Harrah."

He frowned. "I'll go with you."

"Nonsense," she scoffed. "Just because we're working as partners doesn't mean we have to be joined at the hip twenty-four seven. I'm perfectly capable of going alone to the market and getting back to the hotel safe and sound."

He hesitated another moment, his frown deepening. "All right, then I'll see you back at the hotel within an hour or so."

She nodded, then watched as he turned and walked away from her. For the first time in three days she felt as if she could breathe more easily. She'd needed some time alone, some time separate from him.

She'd felt more comfortable around him when she'd thought she disliked him, when his hair had been ridiculously long and they weren't sharing little pieces of each other.

Things had been easier when she'd thought he was an arrogant loner she couldn't trust, a man she'd never want to get involved with.

But in the days and nights she'd spent with him she'd recognized that he was far more than an arrogant loner and there was no denying her attraction to him.

For the next few minutes she continued to pick up shells from the beach, then decided to head toward the marketplace. She needed to buy the items she wanted, then get back to the room to shower and dress. Tonight they planned to go to another nightclub, one of the last upscale clubs the resort town had to offer.

With each minute that passed she was trying not to get discouraged over the fact that not only had there been no sign of Willowby, but also the people who had seen his picture might be denying ever seeing him before.

As she walked toward the market place she remained aware of the people around her, not only seeking out the face in the crowd she'd most love to see, but watching for threats as a solitary female tourist.

It was impossible to be in the marketplace for any length of time and not feel a lightening of spirits as you breathed in the festive air. Even though it was a Wednesday afternoon, the place was once again packed. Everywhere she looked smiling faces greeted her, music wafted through the air and her momentary depression about not finding Willowby disappeared.

After all, they'd only been looking for two days. Maybe tonight he'd show up at the club. Maybe tomorrow they'd spy him on the beach. One thing was certain. She believed Marcus Willowby was like any other rapist. He was driven by compulsion.

There was no way he'd be able to hole up someplace and not seek to scratch his itch, no way he'd be able to isolate himself for any long period of time. Eventually the compulsion would be too strong to ignore, too agonizing to disregard. He'd leave his hiding hole and go hunting for a victim.

She bought a necklace and matching bracelet for Harrah, a beautiful rose scarf for her mother and a pale blue one for Belinda. She had a feeling the vendors had gotten far more for their wares than they should have. Chantal had never been good at dickering, but she was happy, they were happy and it was time to head back to the hotel.

She was on the outskirts of the marketplace when she saw him. A tall blond man clad in a pair of dark blue shorts and an unbuttoned light blue shirt. His back was to her and a pair of burly Hispanic men flanked him on either side. They stood in front of a booth that was offering a variety of items for sale.

Her heart crashed into her ribs and she almost dropped her packages in shock. Was it him? Certainly the build was right, as was the blond, neatly styled hair. She couldn't tell from this angle. She needed to see him from the front. She needed to get close enough to be certain.

If it was him she had no intention of trying to take him down alone, here in the middle of the crowd. Even though what she'd like to do was whip out her handcuffs, contain him and get him to the States as soon as possible, she was too smart even to attempt such a thing.

Besides, the two men with him didn't look like lightweights. They wore expressions of menace and their body language told her these were men who knew how to take care of themselves. Friends of Willowby? She somehow didn't think so.

Hired help? Possibly. Willowby knew he was a wanted man. Maybe he'd hired some of the local talent to work as bodyguards. She frowned. The presence of bodyguards definitely made things more complicated.

She needed to follow him, find out where he went. He might lead her to the place where he was staying.

First things first, she thought. She needed to make certain it really was him.

She moved quickly, her heart still beating rapidly. What if it *was* him? What if he recognized her? A million doubts, a million concerns shifted through her head.

As the trio stepped away from the booth, the tall blond man turned and flashed his familiar grin. Willowby.

She felt momentarily light-headed. It was him. He was here in Tamillo. She'd been right. A swell of pride filled her, but it didn't last long. She wouldn't celebrate until he was in her custody.

Now all she needed to do was follow him and his buddies and see where they led.

She kept as far behind them as she could while still keeping them in her sights, impatiently watching as they stopped at various booths, sat on benches and enjoyed a shaved ice drink, then flirted with a couple of young women.

Chantal's blood boiled as she watched him flash his charming smile and saw the obvious pleasure and preening of the young women. She wanted to run up and scream at the women to run, to get away before they were raped by the handsome American with the charming smile.

Instead she could do nothing but watch and hope that she wasn't looking at two more of Willowby's victims. She was aware of time ticking by.

She'd told Luke she'd be back to the hotel room within the hour and she'd already missed that deadline. But, there was no way in hell she was going to lose sight of Willowby until she knew exactly where he was staying.

As she followed and observed, she realized her first impression was probably correct. The two big men with Willowby were hired help. They walked just behind him, their eyes sharp on the crowd surrounding them. They were making sure nobody threatening got close to Willowby and Willowby was definitely hunting.

She felt sick as she watched the handsome man eye the women who passed his way, saw him stop first one, then another for a friendly chat. Never once did he look in her direction, which was fine by her. She considered this a bit of a reconnoitering detail and the last thing she wanted to do was draw attention to herself.

It was nearing dusk when Willowby and his cohorts left the marketplace and headed down the beach. Chantal trailed far behind, realizing they weren't headed in the direction of any of the local hotels, but rather toward a strip of bungalows that lined the beachfront.

So, that's why they hadn't seen him in any of the hotels. He wasn't staying in a hotel. He had a bungalow. Afraid of following any further, she sat down on the sand where a few other people were enjoying the last rays of the day and watched as the trio disappeared into the third bungalow in a row of six.

"Busted, Mr. Willowby," she murmured aloud.

She stood and dusted the sand off as best she could, then turned to go back to the hotel, eager to share with Luke what she had learned and the new plan that was formulating in her head.

* * *

"Where in the hell have you been?" Luke was on her almost before she got through the hotel-room door. His features were taut with tension, his eyes dark as the chocolate in her favorite Godiva box.

She dropped her bags as he grabbed her by the shoulders. "You told me an hour. You said you'd be back here within an hour. It's been almost two. Good God, Chantal, how could you be so damned thoughtless?"

She pushed his hands off her shoulders and stepped back from him. "You aren't my father and you aren't my husband. Just because I've agreed to partner up with you for the moment doesn't mean I owe you an accounting for every moment of my time."

He drew a deep breath as if to steady himself. "That's true," he said, his voice deadly quiet. "But I would think a woman with your upbringing would at least understand the concept of common courtesy." He raked a hand through his hair. "I was worried." The words seeped out of him as if with great regret.

With those three simple words he managed to banish the anger that the confrontation had created. "I'm sorry. I didn't mean to worry you. I found him." She sank down on the edge of the bed.

"Willowby? Where?" A new tension rippled from Luke.

"He was in the marketplace. It looks like he's traveling with bodyguards...two big Hispanic men. I followed him, that's why I'm late. I followed him to see where he's staying."

"Did he make you?"

"No. I don't think he noticed me at all."

Luke sat on the bed next to her. "And you found out where he's staying?"

"A bungalow on the other side of the public beach. There are six and he went into the third one. I'm assuming that's where he's calling home these days."

"Then I guess we don't need to hit the clubs tonight," Luke said. "Want to order some dinner from room service? We can talk about a plan while we eat."

"That sounds perfect," she said, a plan already in mind. If they went with her plan, then this would be the last meal she'd eat with Luke.

Luke ordered their meal and while they waited for it to be delivered, Chantal went to shower. She not only felt as if she needed to get rid of the sand from the beach, but also the dirty cloying feel of watching Willowby hunting for new victims.

It won't be long now, Belinda, she thought as she stood beneath a steaming spray of water. That animal would go to jail and Belinda could reclaim her life.

She got out of the shower and pulled on a sundress, wondering how Luke would respond to her idea for getting Willowby.

She left the bathroom and found a lamp on in the corner of the room, but no sign of Luke. The door to the balcony was open and she peeked out to see him standing there.

He had his back to her as he stared out on the water. For a moment she remained behind him, wondering what thoughts were going through his head. Funny, she couldn't remember the last time she cared much what a man was thinking.

He turned, as if he sensed her presence. "Beautiful, isn't it?" He returned his attention to the watery night-scape.

She stepped out on the balcony and moved to stand next to him. "Yes, it's beautiful, although the beauty is somehow tainted to me now, knowing that Willowby walks on that beach."

"We need to find out what we can about the men who were with him," he said. "And we need to find out if they're with him all the time or only when he leaves the bungalow."

"Everyone I spoke to about Willowby mentioned that he was a fairly private person. I can't imagine that he'd have anyone staying with him all the time. It would definitely cramp his style if he did have other people in the bungalow."

"Still, we can't move in until we have more an-swers."

A knock on their door announced the arrival of their dinner. They left the balcony and within minutes were seated at the table discussing the case as they ate their meal.

"You know, I was thinking this afternoon that it would be much easier to get Willowby back to the States if we didn't have to try to take a commercial flight and we didn't have to drive him," she said. "A handcuffed passenger makes people on a plane nervous and driving will take too long."

He looked at her with interest. "You have another idea?"

"The Worthington Boat Industries private jet," she replied. "I could arrange with my mother to have it flown here. I'm sure there's some sort of a small airstrip near here that would accommodate us for the right amount of money. The jet could be ready to take off whenever we had Willowby in custody."

"Ah, the perks of wealth," he said dryly.

She sat back in her chair and eyed him curiously. "Most of the men I know either resent my money or want to help me spend it. Which kind are you?"

"Neither. I don't give a damn how much money you have in your bank account." His tone of voice held no rancor. "I haven't done too badly myself when it comes to putting money in the bank."

"Money certainly doesn't solve every problem," Chantal replied. "My friend Belinda is worth ten times what I'm worth and yet she's the most miserable person on the face of the earth." She shook her head to dispel her concerns about her best friend. "My parents taught me that being wealthy comes with responsibilities and some moral obligations."

"It's nice when people who have money do good things with it, which I know you do. It's not great when the people who have money abuse the power that often comes with it."

He cut into his steak, then continued. "I'll be the first to admit that knowing the kind of fortune you have, when you first started working for Big Joey, I wrote you off as a bored rich girl looking for some excitement. I figured you'd play at working for a while, then go back to your ivory tower. And I'm the first to admit that I was wrong about you."

His words pleased her more than anything else she'd experienced for a very long time. "So, what do you think about the jet?"

He grinned. "I think it's one time when it would be nice to take advantage of your wealth and connections."

"Good, then I'll call my mother after dinner and arrange it."

For the remainder of the meal, they didn't talk about Willowby's imminent capture, but Luke entertained her with stories of his life before Big Joey's and bounty hunting.

It was as if they'd mutually agreed that while they ate they would not discuss Willowby. She was almost grateful for the respite. Willowby could take center stage after the meal. For now she just wanted to focus on the food and the interesting conversation.

As he spoke about the relationship he'd shared with his parents and his brother, she felt the pain of his loss. She had the definite impression that the losses he had suffered had defined the man he'd become, a loner unwilling to allow closeness with anyone else to avoid suffering any meaningful loss again.

It was after they'd eaten and had returned the dishes to the serving cart and pushed it out of the room that they sat at the table to discuss their plans for getting their man.

"Tomorrow we'll check out those bungalows and the area surrounding them to get a general idea of what we're up against," Luke said. "We need to figure out his patterns and I want to get a look at those two men you saw with him, see what I can find out about them."

"I can tell you one thing, they were big and they looked mean."

"Big and mean doesn't scare me," he replied, his eyes glittering with challenge. "I'm fairly big and I can get pretty mean myself. What we don't want is a scene of any kind."

"I have an idea of how to bring him in without a public scene," she replied. She got up from her chair and began to pace in the small confines next to the bed.

"He's hunting, Luke. When I saw him today he was hunting for a victim. I could see it in the way he interacted with the women he talked to, I could see it in the way his gaze followed women that he passed." A wave of nausea swelled up inside her as she remembered the way Willowby's gaze had slid over each woman.

"So what's your point?" Luke asked.

She stopped pacing and faced him. "I think we need to drop the honeymooning-couple cover."

"And do what?" His eyes narrowed and that telltale muscle in his jaw began to tick.

Chantal swallowed hard, fighting against a surge of dread as she thought of what she intended to do. "I think I need to be a single woman traveling all alone. I think with just a little bit of work I could be Willowby's next victim."

Chapter 12

Luke stood so abruptly his chair teetered on two legs before settling back to the floor. "Are you insane?" He left the table and moved to within inches in front of her and glared.

Warmth swept into her cheeks as she held his gaze defiantly. "Of course I'm not insane and I don't really intend to let him rape me." She took a step back from him.

"Well, there's a relief," he said sarcastically.

"Think about it, Luke. We know Willowby's weakness is vulnerable women. Why not use that weakness against him?"

In the faint glow from the lamp in the corner she could see his jaw muscle tick faster and his mouth compress into a taut line, but she continued, talking as fast as she could before he could speak.

"From everything I know, Willowby isn't an exhibitionist, he indulges in his crimes alone in his bedroom. If he's going to dismiss his bodyguards it will be for a night with a woman. If I can get him interested in me, then he'll invite me to his bungalow. He won't feel threatened by a female so he'll probably dismiss his guards for the night. I can take him down in his own living room."

"We're not using you as bait." There was a finality in his voice that infuriated her.

"Then this partnership is ended and I'll do things my own way. You need to just walk away and let me do what I came here to do." She gasped as he grabbed her forearm and pulled her closer to him.

"What are you going to do if he fixes you a drink? What are you going to do if he insists you drink it and it's spiked? You may think you're something of a wonder woman, Chantal, but even you can't fight the effects of GHB. You'd be unconscious within ten minutes and he'd be raping you within fifteen. If you really think I can just walk away and let that happen to you then you don't know me."

Before she could formulate any kind of reply, his mouth slammed down to hers. It was a hard kiss of punishment and possession. If any other man had kissed her like that she would have slapped him.

Instead, she welcomed the raw emotion that his kiss ignited in the depths of her. She wrapped her arms around his neck and kissed him back just as hard, just as demanding.

His hands grabbed her buttocks and pulled her closer, so close she could feel his hard arousal and in that instant all thought of Willowby disappeared from her mind. The temptation she'd been fighting for days, perhaps for months for Luke exploded inside her.

He moved his hips against hers, rubbing against her with a rhythm that intensified her desire for him. He pulled his mouth from hers and stared at her with a hot, hungry gaze. "Now is the time to stop this if you're going to." His voice was deep and husky and held a tremble that let her know just how badly he wanted her.

Now was the time to say no, she thought in some distant place in her mind. Now was the time to halt this, but for the life of her, she couldn't think of a single reason to stop.

She stepped back from him and saw the dark disappointment that flashed in his eyes, a disappointment that vanished as she began to unbutton the tiny buttons that ran up the front of her sundress.

"Why would I deny myself what I want?" she asked, unsurprised to realize her voice held the same slight tremble that his had.

He stood as if frozen for the longest minute of Chantal's life. He reached into his slacks pocket and withdrew his wallet. He opened it, pulled out a foil package and placed it on the nightstand, then he moved her trembling fingers aside and used his own to unfasten the buttons on her dress.

As each button was unfastened she felt the heat of his fingers on her bare skin, a heat that flashed through her like wildfire.

When he had the buttons unfastened to her waist, she shrugged out of the dress and it fell to the floor at her feet, leaving her clad in a pair of whisper-thin panties and a matching bra.

He started to reach for her once again, but she stopped him. "My turn," she murmured and reached for the buttons of his shirt.

He didn't move a muscle as her fingers worked the buttons, exposing inch by inch his lightly haired, solid chest. When she got to the last two buttons, he yanked the shirt off, popping away the final buttons.

He wasted no time with his slacks. He kicked off his shoes and yanked off his pants with an alacrity that might have been amusing under different circumstances. Clad only in a pair of briefs, he stole her breath away.

He was absolutely magnificent with his desire straining against the white cotton, his rippling abs taut with tension and eyes dark with a hunger more intense than she could ever remember seeing in a man's eyes.

Her knees felt like rubber and she sank to the bed, afraid that her legs wouldn't hold her another moment. That familiar smile curved his lips. "I've wanted you naked and in my bed for months," he said.

"I'm not naked yet," she replied, then licked her lips which suddenly felt too dry.

"Let me be of assistance in rectifying that little detail." He joined her on the bed and drew her against the length of him as he kissed her once again.

This time the kiss held no hint of punishment, only the promise of unrelenting desire. His tongue teased hers, his teeth nibbling first on her upper lip, then on her lower, driving her frenzy of need higher.

As he teased her mouth with his, his fingers worked the hooks of her bra and unfastened it. She shrugged out of it and he threw it aside, replacing the wispy material with the warmth of his chest against hers.

His hands continued to move up and down the length of her back, his palms warm and slightly rough. Their kiss ended, but he moved his mouth to the hollow of her throat, the sensitive skin behind her ear.

Shivers of pleasure shot through her and she undulated beneath him, arching her hips upward to make contact with his erection. He pulled his head back and stared down at her, his breathing short and uneven.

Her own breaths were just as quick, just as irregular and when he dipped his head to take the tip of one of her breasts in his mouth, a deep, low moan escaped her.

He sucked on one nipple, then turned his attention to the other, licking with his tongue, teasing with his teeth. She clutched her fingers in his hair, then grabbed at his shoulders, his muscles steely hard beneath her fingers.

Almost mindless with the intensity of the sensations he evoked, she reached down between their bodies and rubbed the length of him through his briefs.

It was as if something inside of him snapped; whatever control he'd been maintaining was gone. He tore at his briefs and when he'd removed them he took the waist of her panties and shimmied them down the length of her. He reached for the condom package on the nightstand and with an efficiency of movement had the protection out of the package and on himself within seconds.

He moved into place on top of her and with a deep, low groan of his own, entered her. When he was deep inside, he froze, as if any movement at all would push him completely over the edge.

In the faint light of the room his features were taut. He drew a deep, shuddering breath and only then did he begin to move his hips against hers.

Her need clawed at her and she arched beneath him and met him thrust for thrust. She'd never felt such crashing need for a man before, never felt so completely out of control. Higher, higher she felt herself climb and the intensity of their joining was greater than any she'd ever experienced.

"*People* magazine, fashion shows, pink nail polish." Her mantra sprang to her lips as their movements became more frenzied.

She wrapped her legs around his hips, pulling him closer, deeper into her as her release became imminent. The tension inside her coiled so tightly she felt as if she couldn't breathe. She cried out as the tension snapped. It was like shattering into a million pieces as wave upon wave of pleasure nearly drowned her in sensation.

She was vaguely aware of his deep, primitive groan,

of his body shuddering against hers and knew that he, too, had found ecstasy.

He rolled to her side and gathered her into his arms, neither of them speaking as they waited for their heartbeats to slow.

"That was intense," he finally said.

Intense. Yes, that was the perfect description for what they'd just shared. It hadn't been sweet or romantic, but rather it had been intense…and hot.

"That's an understatement," she replied.

She wondered if it would have been as fierce if they hadn't been arguing right before falling into bed. She also wondered if this had somehow been a ploy on his part to soften her up and get her to see things his way. If that was the case, he was going to be disappointed.

She'd had the feeling that he was somehow dangerous to her, that having sex with him would be a mistake. If it had been a mistake it had been a wonderful one, and if he was dangerous to her mental well-being, then she'd accept the danger, for, even now, sated by what they'd just shared, she wondered when they'd do it again.

He raised up on one elbow and gazed down at her. "What's that thing you do?"

"That thing? What thing?" Oh God, what had she done while in the throes of passion? Had she done something totally embarrassing? Had she drooled or made strange, funny noises?

"You list things. You murmured something about nail polish and magazines."

"Oh, that." She relaxed. "It's just something I do when I'm feeling nervous or frightened."

"Did I scare you?" he asked in surprise.

"No, it was just…just…intense. Anyway, when I feel that way I list my favorite things. I know it probably sounds crazy, but it calms me."

"It doesn't sound crazy," he replied with a small smile. "Everyone has little tricks they use to calm themselves down."

"What do you do?" she asked curiously. She loved the way he felt lying so close to her, his body radiating warmth and strength. She was in no hurry to jump out of bed and continue the fight they'd been having before.

"I think of my brother. Seth was the calmest, sanest person I ever knew. Even though he was two years younger than me, he was the one who could calm me down when I was angry, make me feel better if I was upset."

Chantal grabbed his hand and held it tight.

He stroked his other hand through her hair and gazed at her soberly. "You can't save her, you know," he said softly. "Getting Willowby into custody isn't going to save your friend. From what you've told me about her she needs intensive therapy and probably a stint in rehab."

A tightness banded around her chest as she thought of Belinda and that night so long ago. "You're right, but getting Willowby into custody will make her feel better."

"And will it make you feel better? Will it ease the guilt you feel about that night?"

She sat up, the band compressing tighter, hurting her heart. "I don't know what you're talking about," she replied.

He sat up as well. "I think you do. It wasn't your fault, Chantal. You aren't responsible for what happened to your friend." His gentle voice should have soothed her, but it didn't, rather his words sent a fresh shaft of pain through her.

To her relief he got out of bed and disappeared into the bathroom. She lay back down and stared up at the ceiling, tears blurring her vision.

He didn't understand. He couldn't understand. It was her fault. If she hadn't left Belinda alone, then Willowby wouldn't have preyed on her. If she'd remained at Belinda's side throughout the evening, then Belinda wouldn't have been raped and her life wouldn't have been destroyed.

They had agreed to stick together, but Chantal had wandered off, leaving her friend alone. Belinda wouldn't need therapy or rehab if Chantal had done what she should have done. She swiped at her tears, angry with herself for the momentary meltdown.

She got out of the bed and found her clothes and pulled them on, wanting, needing to be dressed when Luke came back into the room.

When she was dressed she stepped back out on the balcony, the humid night air wrapping around her the way Luke's arms had been around her moments before.

Right or wrong, good or bad, she knew what she had

to do and she could either do it with his help or not, but she intended to follow through on her plan to get Willowby.

She owed it to Belinda. It was the only way she could live with herself. It was the only way she could forgive herself.

She was still on the balcony when Luke joined her there. He'd taken the time to pull on his slacks and he came up behind her and turned her around to face him.

"All right," he said. "I don't like it. I don't like it one damned bit, but we'll do it your way. We'll work it together so there's as little risk to you as possible and with the understanding that if I feel it becomes too dangerous for you, then we go to an alternative plan."

"Okay, that sounds reasonable," she agreed, relieved that he wasn't going to fight with her on this but rather intended to support her.

"I also want you to promise me that you won't do anything until we have more information about the two bodyguards and Willowby's current living situation."

"All right. I've told you before I'm not suicidal." She placed a hand on his chest. "Thank you, Luke."

He flashed her a dark look. "I've just agreed to let you be bait for a convicted rapist. Don't thank me yet. I just hope to hell I haven't just allowed you to become Willowby's latest victim."

The sun beat down with the dazzling rays of a twenty-karat perfectly faceted diamond. From behind her sunglasses Chantal surveyed the beach as she stretched out on a hot-pink striped beach towel that perfectly matched the bikini she wore.

This was her second day on the beach. She'd spent most of the afternoon the day before hoping Willowby would show up, but all she'd had to show for it at the end of the day was a healthy dose of frustration and a gorgeous tan.

Luke had spent the day two days before finding out what he could about Willowby's living arrangements. By asking a few discreet questions and pretending to be interested in renting one of the bungalows he'd learned that Willowby lived in bungalow three alone.

The estate agent had said that Marcus often spent his afternoons on this end of the beach and was never seen outside without the hired muscle—brothers who lived on the other side of Tamillo.

"Do you have any idea what those places rent for?" he'd told Chantal when he'd returned from his fact-finding mission. "Twenty-five hundred bucks a week! Jesus, that's more than most people pay for their monthly mortgage."

Chantal now glanced over her left shoulder to where Luke sat on a bench with a newspaper opened in front of him. She knew he wouldn't be reading. She could feel his gaze on her, knew that he had her back.

She pulled a tube of sunscreen from her beach bag and began to rub it on her legs. While he had been checking out the bungalows, Chantal had contacted her mother and arranged for the Willowby business jet to fly into Tamillo. The hotel had a private airstrip about ten miles from the town and she'd arranged for the jet to land there and be ready at a moment's notice to return to the States.

It was impossible to formulate any real plan for the capture of Willowby. There were too many variables to consider. But she and Luke had done what they could to be ready should the opportunity present itself.

Luke. It was difficult for her to believe that just a week ago she'd thought him a hateful, arrogant bastard with no redeeming qualities.

In the past couple of days he'd proven himself to be an extraordinary man. The fact that he'd had the insight to understand the forces that drove her, the need to redeem herself by capturing Willowby, stunned her. She hadn't recognized how much she was driven by guilt until he'd astutely pointed it out to her.

Logically she knew she wasn't responsible for what had happened to Belinda at that party a decade ago. Only one person was responsible for the crime against Belinda and that was Marcus Willowby. But just as Chantal was depending on Luke to cover her back now, Belinda had counted on Chantal to cover her back years ago, and Chantal had failed her.

She knew Luke was right about something else as well. Belinda needed more help than her friends could give her. She was popping too many pills, drinking too much alcohol and when Chantal got back to the States she intended to encourage Belinda to seek help for her substance abuse and to get therapy.

Chantal had been on the blanket only about twenty

minutes when a tall, dark-haired man approached her. She could tell by his affected swagger as he came toward her that he was on the make and thought he was all that and a bag of chips.

Just before he made eye contact with her she saw him suck in the slight pouch of a stomach that threatened to spill over the top of his shorts.

He stopped at the edge of her towel and flashed her a big grin. "Are my eyes deceiving me or is it the girl of my fantasies come to life?"

"Thanks for stopping by, but I'm not interested," Chantal replied. He looked much older up close.

"Honey, how can you possibly know you aren't interested unless you have a drink with me and we do a little personal exploration into our souls?"

Was this guy for real? She had a feeling there was only one rejection he'd truly understand. "I appreciate the offer, but I'm not into men's souls."

"Ah, a woman who functions strictly on the physical plane, that's fine with me, babe."

"No, you don't understand," she said and pulled off her sunglasses. "I'm not into men's souls. I'm into women's souls. In fact, I've got my eye on that hot blonde over there in the blue bathing suit." She gestured toward a busty blonde lying on her back, silicone breasts standing up like twin soldiers beneath a skimpy suit.

The man stepped back, obviously disappointed. "So, you're one of those lesbos?"

"'Fraid so. As far as I'm concerned you're packing

extra parts that don't interest me. So, see ya." She returned her glasses to the bridge of her nose and waggled her fingers in a goodbye.

She breathed a sigh of relief as he walked away. At least he hadn't insisted that all she needed was a good man to change her sexual orientation.

She glanced back at Luke who had risen from the bench and stared in her direction, poised to provide help if she needed it. She gave a faint shake of her head and lay back down on her towel.

There was only one man she wanted to try picking her up, and that was Willowby. The beach was littered with beautiful women, but few of them were completely alone. She was hoping that by appearing to be a lonely, vulnerable woman she'd catch Willowby's attention if and when he hit the beach.

By the time an hour and a half had passed she was sweaty and bored. She alternated her gaze between the crowd around her and the bungalow in the distance, willing Willowby to appear.

She got up from the towel and walked to the edge of the water, dipping her feet into the refreshing waves, then bending over to splash her shoulders and cool off her face.

She was still standing there when from the corner of her eye she saw Willowby and his two grunts leave the bungalow and make their way toward the beach.

Nerves jangled inside her as her heart rate quickened. She glanced toward Luke and saw him sit up straighter on the bench.

Willowby was here. She was here. Now all she had

to do was catch his attention and make him interested in her. She hoped the bright pink bikini she wore worked like a red flag in front of an angry bull's face. She wanted Willowby to charge her so she could deliver a death blow with the sword of justice.

She bent over once again and splashed her shoulders one last time, watching the trek of the three men. Willowby was dressed in a pair of white shorts and a white-and-tangerine shirt opened to expose a tanned, muscled chest. His blond hair glistened in the sunlight, and if she didn't know what he was capable of, what he had done, she might have found him attractive.

If they continued in the direction they were going they would cross between the water's edge and Chantal's towel. If she timed it just right she could reach her towel just about the same time they walked right in front of it.

She held her breath, waited for the perfect moment, then turned and sauntered back toward her towel, almost colliding with Willowby.

"Whoa," he said as they nearly made contact.

"Oh, gosh. Sorry, the sun had me blinded for a moment," she replied. She flashed him a smile that she hoped looked a little shy, a little interested and a little apologetic.

He offered her a bright smile, his eyes hidden behind designer sunglasses. "American?"

"That's right." She noticed that the two big men hung back slightly, as if they were accustomed to Willowby stopping often to talk to pretty women.

"What brings you to Tamillo? Don't tell me, you're on your honeymoon."

She forced a light laugh. "I wish. Honeymooners seem to be everywhere, but I'm not one of them. This is my last stop on a prolonged vacation. I heard it was a beautiful place where the hotel rates hadn't caught up with those in Puerto Vallarta or Cancun. What about you? On vacation or on your honeymoon?"

"No honeymoon for me," he replied.

"I'm Carol Kelly." Although she didn't want him touching her in any way, she held out a hand toward him.

"Hi, Carol. I'm Mark Wills." He took her hand in his and shook it. He cocked his head to one side, his gaze intent on her face. "Have we met before?"

Chantal's heart plunged to her feet. She frowned thoughtfully, hoping her features betrayed nothing of her concern. "No, I don't think so. I've only been here a day and I'm sure I would have remembered you."

He nodded as if satisfied. "Yeah, I'm sure I would have remembered you, too. You just look a little familiar."

She laughed lightly. "Lots of people tell me that. I guess I just have one of those faces."

"Are you here all alone or traveling with friends?"

"No friends, just little old me," she replied.

"Maybe as the only two non-honeymooners in Tamillo we should have dinner together."

"That might be nice," she replied and pulled her hand from his. She fought against a shudder of revulsion.

"I could cook for you at my place."

"Oh, I don't know about that," she said hesitantly. She wasn't sure exactly how to play it, but suspected if she appeared too eager, too easy, he'd lose interest. Besides, did women really go to a stranger's house for a first date?

"If you aren't comfortable with that, why don't we meet for dinner in one of the hotel restaurants?"

She hesitated a moment, then smiled at him. "I'd like that."

"Tonight? Around seven? How about the Seaside Room in the Tamillo Grand Hotel?"

"All right. Seven o'clock it is," she replied. "And it was nice meeting you, Mark."

He took her hand once again in his. "I look forward to this evening, Carol." He raised her hand to his lips and kissed the back of it lightly, then released it. "I'll see you later."

She watched as he turned and walked away, his cohorts following close behind. Her stomach quivered with nerves and the back of her hand burned with the disgusting imprint of his mouth.

She returned to her towel and picked it up from the sand. There was no reason to remain on the beach. She'd accomplished what she'd set out to do. She'd made a date with a rapist.

Chapter 13

"**D**on't you have something else you can wear?" Luke's dark gaze swept over her as she stood in front of the dresser mirror and put on her jewelry.

"What's wrong with what I'm wearing?" She turned to look at him. He was seated on the edge of the bed, dressed in a pair of charcoal slacks and a gray-and-white striped shirt. He looked unbelievably handsome except for the tension that tightened his features and the eyebrows tugged together to create a deep frown.

"I don't know. I just don't think it's right," he replied.

She turned back to face her reflection. She'd bought the dress that afternoon in a boutique in the hotel. It wasn't a designer label, had not been too expensive and she'd thought it was the perfect attire for Carol Kelly.

The scoop neck of the light blue dress was low enough to be interesting but not low enough to be obvious. It was fitted through the bodice and the waist, then flared into a flirty skirt. High-heeled silver sandals adorned her feet.

"What's not right about it?" she asked as she fastened a tiny silver hoop to her ear. She liked the way the pale blue complemented the tan she'd acquired during her two days at the beach.

He got up from his seated position and came to stand just behind her. He placed his hands on her shoulders and moved them in a caress as he held her gaze in the mirror.

"You look way too sexy, way too hot. You make me want to put my hands all over you and the thought of Willowby thinking the same kind of thoughts I'm thinking right now makes me sick."

His words sent a wave of heat through her...not because of the way her appearance might affect Willowby, but rather because of how her appearance affected Luke.

It had been less than twenty-four hours since they'd had sex for the third time and it thrilled her that what she saw in his eyes was fevered want.

She turned to face him once again. "Stop looking at me like that."

"Like what?" He stepped closer to her, his breath warm on her face.

"You know what I'm talking about," she replied. She pushed against his chest to back him up, afraid that if she didn't they'd tumble to the bed and screw up her date with Willowby.

He sighed and shoved his hands into his pockets. "I

don't know why in the hell I let you talk me into this crazy plan."

"Because you know it's the best crazy plan for getting him. Tonight is just about dinner, Luke. Nothing is going to happen as long as we're in a public place. Besides, you'll be in the restaurant, too. It isn't like I'm going into this all alone." She checked her watch. "And I need to get going, otherwise I'll be late."

Nerves jangled inside her as she and Luke rode the elevator to the lobby together. Once in the lobby she would get a cab and Luke would drive to the restaurant located in a hotel three miles away.

They had both agreed not to try to take Willowby tonight. What she hoped was that dinner tonight would be a prelude to something more intimate later. The absolute best possible place to get Willowby into custody was in the privacy of his bungalow. They wanted no spectators, no third-party involvement…just a nice, uncomplicated take-down.

Minutes later she was in the back of a cab carrying her to the Tamillo Grand Hotel and her date with Marcus. But she found her thoughts drifting from the task ahead to the man she'd just left behind.

There was no question that she and Luke shared a nearly overwhelming physical attraction to each other, but what frightened her just a little bit was that other feelings, deeper feelings, were beginning to build inside her for him.

He was nothing like what she'd imagined him to be. Just as he'd stereotyped her as a bored socialite, she'd stereotyped him as a crass, insensitive lowlife. He was none of those things.

Falling in love with Luke Coleman would be as stupid as hitting a sale without a charge card in hand. Investing emotionally in Luke Coleman would be as stupid as buying a dozen pairs of size-five shoes in the hope that her feet would eventually shrink.

Luke himself had indicated that when people tried to get too close to him, when he got uncomfortable with a situation, it was nothing for him to pick up and move on to a new job, a new location.

No matter how much her heart got involved with the man, she knew the worst thing she could do would be to let him see that he meant anything to her. If he had any indication that she might be getting involved, she had a feeling he'd run for the hills.

They were partners on this particular case and at the moment enjoying each other sexually, but she knew better than to expect anything more from him.

She shoved aside thoughts of Luke, needing to clear her mind and prepare herself for what was to come with Marcus Willowby.

By the time the cab pulled up in front of the hotel a cold calm had descended over her, a calm that was comforting in that it was familiar. It meant she was centered and knew what she had to accomplish with this dinner. She felt as if this was a role she'd prepared to play her entire life.

As she walked through the hotel lobby she noticed the two bodyguards seated in the bar area. So, Marcus hadn't come alone this evening.

A maître d' greeted her at the entrance of the Seaside Room and ushered her to a table next to a window where "Mark Wills" awaited her.

He was clad in a pair of navy dress slacks and a light blue shirt that intensified the blue of his eyes. He rose as she approached, his signature charming smile curving his lips.

"Carol," he said in greeting. "You look lovely."

"Thank you. It looks as if we color-coordinated, with both of us in blue." She slipped into the chair opposite his and offered him a shy smile. "I wasn't sure you'd really be here this evening."

He crooked a blond eyebrow upward. "Why? Did I strike you this afternoon as the kind of man who would stand up a lovely lady?"

"The only impression I walked away with this afternoon was that you were a handsome man and had asked me to dinner," she replied.

The appearance of a waiter at their table interrupted the conversation. He ordered a good bottle of wine then they placed their orders for the meal.

"So, where in the States are you from?" he asked once he'd poured them each a glass of the wine.

"A little town in South Dakota," she replied. "What about you?" She intended to keep the topic of conversation on him whenever possible.

"I'm from the Midwest, but I'm thinking of making this my permanent home," he replied.

"I'm jealous. It's a beautiful place to live."

"You mentioned you were on a prolonged vacation. You don't work?"

She stroked her fingers up the stem of the wineglass. "Up until six months ago I worked as an executive secretary for a businessman. For the last five years I've done nothing but work and sock away what money I could for my dream vacation. Six months ago I decided to go for it."

"So you've been traveling for the past six months?"

She nodded. "I've been to France, Germany and England and have visited all the wonderful sights I ever wanted to see." She pursed her lips in a moue of disappointment. "Unfortunately, I'm on the last of my money, so probably next week I'll be back in North Dakota looking for my next job."

"At least you have another week here in paradise," he said.

"That's true, and I intend to enjoy every moment of it." She leaned back in her chair and took a sip of her wine, at the same time glancing around the dim restaurant.

She spied Luke seated alone at a table on the other side of the room. She quickly averted her gaze from him although she was glad he was near in case something went terribly wrong.

"I'll bet your family misses you," Marcus said. "Six months is a long time to be away from family."

"I don't have any family," she replied. "My parents died three years ago in a car accident and I've been on my own since then."

She knew this was probably just what Marcus

wanted to hear. A perfect victim would be somebody without family support, in a foreign place and without friends nearby.

For the next two hours she and Marcus ate and talked about myriad subjects. Chantal wished she could get a handle on what drove him, what dark forces dictated his perversion, but he displayed no hint of being anything other than a well-adjusted, handsome man.

He was one of those men who had the enviable talent of making a woman feel as though she was the most important person on the face of the earth. He was charming and bright, with a good sense of humor, but there was something just beneath the surface that simmered occasionally in his eyes, something that made her skin crawl.

He conducted himself like a perfect gentleman, flirtatious enough to let her know he might be interested, but not so overt that she would be turned off.

As he talked, he touched her often, the back of her hand, her forearm and her shoulder. Each and every touch made her skin want to crawl right off her muscles.

This was the man who had brutally raped her friend. This was the man who had laughed about it afterward, said horrid things to Belinda in an effort to keep her silent.

This was the man who drugged women then raped them while they were unconscious, the ultimate violator working on his next potential victim.

"I've enjoyed this," he said as they lingered over coffee after the meal.

"Me, too," she replied. Yeah, she always enjoyed dining with a pervert, she thought.

He gestured to the waiter, then smiled at her. "It's still early. Can I talk you into a nightcap at my place?"

"Oh…I don't think so." She gave him her best imitation of a teasing smile. "I make it a habit never to go to a man's place on the first date."

She held her breath, hoping…praying she wasn't blowing it all by playing it too safe. But she and Luke weren't prepared for the whole enchilada to play out tonight and there was also the little glitch of the two behemoths she'd spotted outside the restaurant.

"Look, I'm not trying to get you into bed," he said. "I just make a mean special fruity drink and thought it would be fun if we spent some more time together and had a few drinks."

He looked so earnest, so absolutely innocent. God, he was good.

"I just don't think it would be a good idea tonight." She gestured toward the empty bottle of wine. "I've already drunk more than my limit. But perhaps another time?"

"What about tomorrow night? You have any plans?" Although he asked nonchalantly, she felt his energy in the air, a sick energy that made her want to puke.

"I think I'm going to have special fruity drinks at a new friend's place," she replied with a smile.

His eyes glittered almost feverishly. "Good. Great. You know the beach where we met this afternoon? I'm in one of the bungalows there. Bungalow three, the third from the left as you're facing them. The actual address is 3 Gulf Drive. Why don't we say around eight tomorrow night?"

"All right."

He paid the bill and they left the restaurant together. When they reached the lobby the two bodyguards stood and moved closer to where she and Marcus stood.

"Aren't those the two men who were with you at the beach today?" she asked.

"Yeah, they were with me this afternoon."

"Are they waiting for you?" She frowned in pretend confusion. "Do they go everywhere with you?" she asked. "Are they friends, or what?"

"It's a long story," he said smoothly.

She raised an eyebrow. "Will they be having drinks with us tomorrow evening?" She let him know by her tone that she found the presence of the two pretty weird.

"Not a chance," he assured her with a dry laugh. "I promise you won't see hide nor hair of them to-morrow night."

"Good, because the odds would definitely be un-comfortable," she replied. She much preferred the odds be in her and Luke's favor. "Thank you for a lovely din-ner, Mark."

He smiled and took her hands in his. His hands were slightly damp, as if just the idea of having her in his home the next night made him excited...sweaty. "I should be thanking you. I really enjoyed it and I'm looking forward to continuing tomorrow evening. Are you staying here in this hotel or do you need a lift somewhere?"

"Thank you, but I'll be fine under my own steam." She didn't want him to know exactly where she was staying.

He nodded, pulled her forward and kissed her cheek. His lips left behind a wetness on her skin and she fought the impulse to wipe it away. He released her hands and stepped back from her. "Good night, Carol. I'll see you tomorrow evening."

She watched as the trio disappeared out of the hotel. At that moment Luke approached from the restaurant. They didn't speak to one another. She knew he'd get the Jeep from wherever he'd parked and follow the cab that would take her home.

As she sat in the back of the cab she replayed the night in her mind in excruciating detail. On the surface, he'd been every woman's dream man...attentive, pleasant and charming.

She thought about the following night still to play out. Special fruity drinks, that's what he'd offered her. She knew from her research on GHB that it was often added to fruit drinks because it had a slightly salty taste. The fruit masked that distinctive taste. If she'd had any doubt what he intended, the mention of those special fruity drinks wiped the doubt away.

At least he'd said that tomorrow night they'd be all alone. She and Luke wouldn't have to worry about two additional men who were paid to keep Willowby safe.

Everything was falling into place. By this time tomorrow night she and Luke should be on the jet with Willowby in tow, headed back to the States where Willowby could begin serving his sentence.

She had no idea how things would stand between her and Luke when they got back to the States. He was impossible to predict, and she wasn't sure what she wanted to happen.

When she got back home she had another item on her plate to be taken care of: the little problem of Mundy's boys trying to kill her.

She needed to figure out what she was going to do about it. She didn't want to live the rest of her life looking over her shoulder, afraid of who might be around the next corner.

She dismissed this problem from her mind as the cab pulled up in front of the hotel. She got out, paid the driver, then headed for the elevator. Before the elevator could arrive to whisk her up to her floor, Luke joined her.

Two other people got into the elevator with them, making any talk between them impossible. Luke looked pissed and she wondered if something had happened on his drive back to the hotel.

They had just stepped into their room when he grabbed her and pulled her tight against him, so close she could feel the beat of his heart against her chest.

"The most difficult thing I've ever done in my life is sit and watch that scum touch you," he said. He didn't give her an opportunity to reply, but kissed her with a determined intent that instantly set her on fire.

"I hated it," she gasped when the kiss finally ended. "I hated the touch of him on my skin. I hated having to be nice to him, to pretend to be interested in him."

"Every time he touched you I wanted to punch him out. I wanted to slap my cuffs on him and take him to the floor, to hell with the consequences." He took her mouth again in a kiss that enflamed her.

Within seconds they were both out of their clothes and in the bed. She welcomed his kisses, his touch, the very scent of his skin, eager to banish any and all thought and feel of Willowby.

There wasn't a moment to think, she could only survive the explosion of raw desire that possessed them both. There was no need for foreplay. She was wet and ready for him when she got on top of him and guided him into her.

He gripped her buttocks and as she moved her hips his fingers clenched tightly into her skin. His eyes blazed as he held her gaze. She moved against him in a frenzy, falling onto his chest as the tension inside her wrapped tighter and tighter.

She nearly sobbed with the force of her climax. It washed over her in wave after wave of pleasure. At the same time she was vaguely aware of him crying out her name as he found his own release.

She slumped on his chest and after a moment he rubbed her back with one hand, then nuzzled her shoulder with a gentleness that squeezed at her heart.

She rolled off him and to his side and at that moment realized that there had been no time, no thought of a condom. "That was foolish," she said.

He leaned up and gazed at her. "Foolish?"

"Unprotected sex isn't smart."

"True," he agreed and reached out to run a hand over the curve of her shoulder. "That's the problem with you. You make me forget to be smart. You don't have to worry about me. I'm clean."

"So am I...and I'm on the pill so we don't have to worry about any little Crazy Colemans coming from this moment." She ran a finger over his shoulder where the tattoo felt slightly rough beneath her fingertips. "Is there a story behind this?" she asked.

"Typical tattoo story." He stared up at the ceiling. "It was weeks after Seth's death and one night I got rip-roaring drunk and stupid and decided to have some schmuck poke inked needles into my arm."

"Why an eagle?"

"Why not? An eagle is proud and free and I thought it looked a little more respectable than a naked lady or a hula dancer."

"And you were worried about respectability?"

"Of course not," he said with a laugh. "I just liked the eagle."

There was something intimate about lying in bed with a man and sharing laughter...almost as intimate as sharing sex. Chantal would have liked to linger in the bed for hours, for days, and just listen to Luke laugh and that's exactly why she excused herself, slid out of the bed and headed into the bathroom.

She cleaned up and pulled on her robe, avoiding her reflection in the mirror. She didn't want to see herself with her cheeks flushed and her hair mussed from their lovemaking.

Jeez, they'd fallen on each other like a couple of animals. She hadn't even had an opportunity to tell him all that had transpired between herself and Marcus.

She returned to the bedroom where Luke was propped up with pillows behind his back. She sat at the table rather than climbing into the bed beside him. They had things to talk about and she was afraid that if she got back into bed with him they might not talk.

"We've got him," she said with suppressed excitement. "I've been invited to his bungalow tomorrow night for drinks. He's promised me it will just be the two of us, so we're set to take him down tomorrow night."

Luke frowned and got out of bed. He grabbed his slacks and pulled them on, then joined her at the table. "Chantal, I know I initially agreed to this plan, but I've got to tell you, I don't feel good about this."

"Don't you back out on me now, Luke," she exclaimed. "It's all set up. It's going to happen whether you like it or not."

He shook his head. "I just don't like it. Too many things could go wrong."

"If you don't want a part of it, then just stay out of my way and let me do what I need to do." She leaned back in her chair and sighed. "Look, I know getting Willowby into custody isn't going to magically fix my friend's life. I also know that it won't completely take away the guilt I do feel about the night Willowby raped her, but I need to do this. I'd like to do it with your help."

He rubbed the center of his forehead where a frown line cut deep across his skin. He dropped his hand, his eyes dark and troubled. "All right. You've got my help. But we're not going to sleep until we sit here and address every potential problem that might arise, make sure there's as little risk to you as possible."

"Sounds like a plan to me," she agreed. She wasn't about to admit to him that for some reason she had a bad feeling about the next night as well.

Chapter 14

The bad feeling Chantal had felt the night before when she and Luke had hashed out their plan only intensified the next evening as she prepared for her date with Willowby.

Nerves, she told herself as she pulled on the red sleeveless dress. Surely it's just a bad case of nerves. Anyone would have a bad feeling knowing they were going into the lair of a monster.

At least Luke wasn't there to complain about what she was wearing or to glare at her with those dark, compelling eyes. He'd left the hotel room an hour before to check things out at the bungalow and find a position where he could safely peek into the windows without being seen.

They were counting on the fact that the bodyguards would be nowhere around, counting on the
fact that Willowby would stay true to his pattern and
want to be alone when he indulged in his perverted
activities.

She left the hotel room, nerves twisting in her
stomach as she rode the elevator down to the lobby.
Her high spike heels clicked on the lobby floor, a
staccato beat that had nothing on the frantic beating
of her heart.

This was it. If they were successful, then by the end
of the night Willowby would be in custody. If they were
not successful and something went wrong there could
be disastrous results.

A screw-up could warn Willowby and he'd escape
again, this time to where nobody would ever find him.
A screw-up could end in her being another victim in a
long line of victims. A misstep could see both her and
Luke behind bars. They had no jurisdiction in Mexico
and Willowby could claim to be a victim of kidnapping.

As she waited for the cab that would take her to the
bungalow, she went over the plan she and Luke had
come up with the night before.

It was relatively straightforward. She would lull Willowby, pretend to drink his "special fruity drink" and
also pretend to fall unconscious. That was when Luke
was to burst in and take Willowby down.

It was strange that a week ago the last man she would
have expected to watch her back, the last man she would
have trusted to be her partner in any way, shape or form

was Crazy Luke Coleman. And now, she couldn't imagine trusting anyone else. Crazy Luke Coleman wasn't crazy at all. He was one of the sanest men she knew.

He was the only man in her recent dating history who wasn't a diamond between the sheets and a lump of useless coal when out of bed. He was the only man in a long time whom she not only liked but respected, and who seemed to reciprocate those feelings.

"Tiaras, New York City, hot fudge sundaes," she muttered under her breath. "Cruises, body wraps, Luke's eyes…"

She had no time to wonder how Luke had made it into her list of favorite things for at that moment the cab pulled up before her.

As she got settled in the back of the cab she shoved thoughts of Luke to the back of her mind. She needed to focus on only one thing at the moment and that was the date that was about to begin.

Luke had parked the Jeep down the street from the row of bungalows and now sat behind the wheel, watching the front of Willowby's bungalow.

He'd wait in the Jeep until darkness began to fall, then he'd get closer to the house, close enough to peek through the window and keep an eye on what was happening inside.

He tried to ignore the feeling of impending doom that he'd awakened with that morning, a feeling that had lingered throughout the long day as they'd waited for this time to arrive.

They'd gone over things a million times the night before, trying to identify any potential problems that might arise. He'd felt as confident about their plan as he could feel, so why did he now feel as if it might all come crashing down around their heads?

Since he'd parked there had been no sign of any activity from the bungalow and, he noted thankfully, no sign of the two men who had trailed after Willowby whenever he made a public appearance.

Luke had enough to worry about without thinking about tangling with two men each the size of a tow truck. If they showed up, then the odds definitely changed in Willowby's favor.

Never in his life had he felt such nervous anxiety. He'd done a hundred more dangerous things in his lifetime, but never had his stomach twisted so tight, never had he broken out into the kind of cold sweat that plagued him now.

What in the hell was wrong with him? He'd faced far more dangerous men when he'd been working as a bouncer in a bar. Working for Big Joey, he'd brought in mean sons of bitches who would just as soon knife you as look at you.

So, why did this particular job feel different? Why was he sweating this so much? The answer came to him in one word. *Chantal.*

If it were only his own safety at stake, he wouldn't be as concerned. He was accustomed to taking risks, to living life on the edge. But, this wasn't about him. This was about Chantal and that made everything different.

If that asshole touched her, Luke might forget about getting Willowby to the States and would instead execute his own brand of justice. He placed a hand on the gun next to him on the seat. He hoped he wouldn't have to use it.

In the years that he'd been bounty hunting he'd never had to use his gun. He preferred to control the situation enough that the show of firepower wasn't necessary. But, if he had to use it to save Chantal, he would, without any guilt, without any self-recriminations.

As far as Luke was concerned there were only two things worse than a rapist—a murderer and a pedophile. But Luke thought there must be a special place in hell for people who preyed on children and men who preyed on helpless women.

He raked a hand over his jaw, where a five o'clock shadow had appeared. His thoughts returned to the woman who had insisted on being bait for a rapist.

Chantal Worthington.

She was different than he'd expected her to be. Oh, he'd expected her to be hard-headed and she was. He'd anticipated that she'd want to do things her way, would feel the need to be in control.

What he hadn't expected was the softness beneath her steel. He hadn't expected her sharp intelligence or wit, her willingness to compromise and her passion. He definitely hadn't expected her passion.

Even now, just thinking about sex with Chantal stirred him up. She was a lusty lover with just enough inhibition to be tantalizing. She gave as easily, as freely as she received and had stirred a seemingly insatiable hunger in him.

He sat up straighter in his seat as the approach of a cab signaled the arrival of Chantal to the bungalow. The knots in his stomach twisted even tighter as he watched her get out of the cab and head toward the front door.

The short red dress she wore only increased his nervous tension. Her bare, tanned legs looked long and sleek, but he cursed beneath his breath as he spied her red spike heels. If the night went bad how was she going to be able to run in those things?

Why had she chosen such a short dress? She looked good. She looked too damned good.

Luke grabbed the gun and shoved it into his waistband. His job was to make certain things didn't go wrong, that she wouldn't have to run in that short dress or those damned sexy high heels.

Willowby greeted her at the front door and Chantal disappeared inside. Time to move, Luke thought.

"Nice place," Chantal said as Marcus led her into the living room. It was a traditional beach house with rattan furniture and brightly colored cushions. The floor was tiled for easy clean-up of sand and water and bamboo slatted shades hung at the windows flanking a door that led outside to the back of the house.

"It's all right for now," he said. "If I decide to stay here in Tamillo long-term I'll be in the market to buy something instead of just renting. Please, make yourself at home," he gestured toward the sofa.

Marcus was dressed in a pair of casual black slacks and a short-sleeved blue-and-black shirt. The dark colors complemented his blond hair and blue eyes, and again she recognized he was a very handsome man…a very handsome pervert, she thought.

Instead of sitting she moved to the bank of windows and opened the slats, exposing a gorgeous view of the water in the distance. "It's beautiful here. This view would be hard to give up for another place."

He came to stand behind her, close enough that she could smell his expensive cologne, but not so close as to be creepy.

"It is something, isn't it? That's what drew me to these bungalows in the first place." He stepped back from her.

"Can I get you something to drink?"

"No, thanks." She turned to face him and smiled. "I'm fine for now." She wanted to give Luke plenty of time to get into position. "Why don't you show me the rest of this place." She flashed him her most charming smile. "I've never been in a real beach bungalow before."

She wanted to see all of the place, she needed to know the surroundings and she needed to assure herself that they were really all alone. She had to make note of windows and doors in case she needed to beat a hasty retreat.

He returned her smile, as if he found her request charming. "I'm afraid you'll be underwhelmed. This is casual living at its best."

For the next few minutes Marcus showed her around

the bungalow, which included two bedrooms, a bathroom and the kitchen. She was glad that they were, indeed, alone in the place.

When they returned to the living room he opened the door that led out onto a large patio. "I spend a lot of my time sitting out here," he said.

"I can understand why." Together they stepped out onto the porch. Dusk had fallen and the beach in the near distance was practically empty of people. The evening air smelled sweet, with just enough salt to be invigorating.

She had no idea where Luke might be, but she knew he was near, knew he was probably watching her and Willowby at this very moment. Even though she felt confident that if push came to shove she could subdue Willowby by herself, there was still a certain amount of comfort knowing Luke was near.

She'd had a single, sole purpose for going out on the patio and that was to make sure the patio door remained unlocked when they went back inside. She didn't want Luke to have to break through a locked door when the time came for him to make an appearance.

When they went back into the house she sat on the sofa and crossed her legs. He sat next to her and his gaze lingered for a moment on the length of her bare leg.

She felt his gaze as potent, as repulsive as an unwanted touch. "So, tell me something about yourself, Mark. I don't even know what you do for a living."

"To be honest, I don't do much of anything." He leaned back against the sofa cushions. "A year ago my parents died and they left behind a life insurance policy that has allowed me not to have to worry about working for the time being."

She thought about the worry, the love that had shone from Rebecca Willowby's eyes when she'd talked about her son. How would Rebecca feel knowing her son had just killed her off for a good story?

"I'm sorry about your parents," she murmured.

He nodded, his features radiating sadness. "Thanks, but I guess it's part of life…you know, that you bury your parents."

Yeah, she thought, but most people don't bury them until they're really dead.

For the next hour they talked. Chantal was amazed at the lies that fell so effortlessly from Willowby's lips and at that moment she recognized that the man was truly a sociopath. He had no conscience and she knew this was a man incapable of loving, incapable of feeling anything for another human being.

He talked to her about a middle-class existence in a small town in Kansas. With a pained expression he shared the story of a high-school sweetheart who had broken his heart and a dog he'd had who had also died in the past year.

Every lie he told was designed to make him look like a warm and caring man, a man who would never harm anyone. The man was definitely some piece of work and once again she recognized that she had no idea what he might really be capable of, had no idea how far he'd go, what action he'd take to save his own skin.

If she hadn't known his history, if she wasn't privy to the real facts about what kind of man he was, she might have fallen for his lies, for the sincere charm he oozed.

After talking with him at length, it was much easier to understand why the two young women had felt comfortable going to his condo for drinks. First and foremost they must have assumed that there would be safety in numbers, but secondly she had no doubt in her mind that they had been lulled by Marcus's charm, comforted by his act of warmth and sincerity.

The boy next door. He'd perfected that particular act. It would be difficult for even a smart woman to see beneath the veneer to the animal contained deep inside.

It chilled her to know that he would have continued to get away with his crimes if he hadn't replaced one of the victim's panties inside out or if he hadn't spilled a drop of semen on those panties. And thankfully the police had taken the two young women seriously and the search warrant for Willowby's place had yielded the damning video tape.

She'd been there a little more than an hour when Marcus once again offered her a drink. "That sounds great," she agreed. "With all this talking I think I've worked up a thirst."

When Marcus disappeared into the kitchen, she got up from the sofa and returned to the window that faced the back of the bungalow. Night had fallen. In the distance the moonlight splashed the water with silver rays and the beach appeared deserted.

She hoped that someplace out there in the dark Luke

was watching everything taking place inside, that he knew the time was drawing near to take down their man. Her heart stepped up its rhythm as she anticipated the takedown.

She knew in her gut that the special drink Willowby was making for her would have the drug GHB in it. She also knew that within minutes she was going to have to give a performance fit for an Academy Award…for Belinda, for all the women he had victimized in the past, and for all the women he hoped to prey upon in his future.

She had told Luke that she wanted to capture Willowby when he was most vulnerable, when he'd think himself safe to indulge in his perversion.

She'd said that she wanted Willowby's pants down around his ankles when Luke burst in, she wanted Willowby hot to trot and then she wanted to see his face when he realized what was happening.

But in order for things to unfold the way she wanted she was going to have to act as though the drugs had worked and rendered her unconscious. More important than anything, she had to make sure she didn't really drink what he fixed for her.

She turned away from the window as Marcus returned from the kitchen carrying two pink frothy drinks in tall glasses. He handed her one of them.

"They're certainly pretty," she commented. "What's in them?"

"A little strawberry, a little vodka and several very magical ingredients—a family secret. To new friends." He held up his glass for a toast.

Chantal clinked her glass against his, noting how his eyes shone with the over-brightness of anticipation. What she wanted to do was pour the drink over his head, kick him in the stomach and drop him to the floor. Instead she raised the glass to her lips and pretended to take a sip.

"Hmmm, that's good," she exclaimed.

"Yeah, these drinks are always big hits when I make them," he replied. He moved toward the sofa and sat and looked at her expectantly. "Aren't you going to join me?"

"In just a minute. I need to use the ladies' room." She flashed him a smile. "I'll be right back." She hurried down the short hallway with her drink in hand.

Once in the bathroom behind a locked door she breathed a deep sigh of relief. If he'd stopped her from carrying her drink in here, she would have been in trouble. Getting the drink in the bathroom had been an integral component of her plan.

For a moment she leaned against the locked door and drew several deep, steadying breaths. Then she stood in front of the sink and poured most of the pink concoction down the drain. If by some chance the drink hadn't been drugged, then Willowby might question her response to the drink.

But, her instinct screamed that the drink was tainted and the handsome man was simply waiting for his opportunity to have sex with her when she fell unconscious.

She ran the water in the sink, washing away any trace of the pink froth, then dried her hands on the towel and stared at her reflection in the mirror.

This was it. The moment of truth. Everything she and Luke had worked toward was about to come to fruition. She smoothed a strand of her hair, aware of the trembling in her fingertips.

You can do this, she told her image. Take the bastard down. Steely resolve flooded through her. She picked up the glass once again. There was just a swallow left in the bottom of the glass. Hopefully it wouldn't be enough to knock her out.

Fifteen minutes. In about fifteen minutes she had to pretend that the drink had taken effect. Minutes after that she hoped, she prayed that Willowby would have his pants down, Luke would burst inside and the creep would be theirs.

Drawing a deep breath, she left the bathroom and returned to the living room. She hefted the glass in the air and smiled at Marcus. "This is awesome," she exclaimed. "Maybe I should have another one."

He laughed, a trace of uneasiness in the sound. "You drank that pretty fast and I should have warned you that they're really strong. Maybe you should wait a little while before having another."

"All right." She set the glass down on the coffee table and sat on the sofa next to him. "Whew, maybe you're right. I think I feel it already."

Time for her performance, she thought.

From his position at one of the back windows Luke saw Chantal go to the bathroom, then return with an empty glass. Thank God, it was going just as they'd planned. She'd managed to dump the drink without having to consume any.

If he had his way he'd go inside now and get Willowby into cuffs. But, Chantal had insisted that she wanted the drama to play out to its fullest. She wanted Willowby half-naked when Luke went in.

He suspected that she wanted him not only captured but humiliated as well. Payback for what Willowby had done to Chantal's friend.

Every muscle in his body tensed as he prepared to spring into action. He wondered if Willowby would try to rape her right there on the sofa or if he would carry her to his bedroom? Did he already have a video camera in place? Luke balled his fists at his sides. Sick son of a bitch, he thought.

Either place, it didn't matter. Luke intended to get inside before things got dicey for Chantal. There was no way he was going to let anything happen to her.

He leaned closer to the window and at that moment something hard came down on the back of his head. He had a moment to think Oh shit before blackness descended.

Chapter 15

Chantal slumped back against the sofa, as if she was too drunk to hold herself upright. She allowed her eyelids to drift down to half-mast as Marcus continued to drone on and spin lies about his childhood.

"Hey, Carol, are you all right?" he asked suddenly.

"I'm fantastic," she muttered, slurring the words together as she willed her body to go completely limp and she closed her eyes. Let him buy it, she thought fervently. Please, let him buy the act.

"Carol?" He grabbed her hand and shook it. "Carol? Are you okay?"

She didn't move a muscle, willed herself to breath deeply and evenly as if she were unconscious. He chuckled, a low, wicked sound that chilled her blood. "I warned you that the drink was strong."

She sensed him moving closer to her, so close she could feel the warmth of his sour breath on her face. "Carol, are you in there?"

The most difficult thing she'd ever done in her life was to remain unmoving. She wanted to spit in his face, she wanted to claw at his handsome features and mark him, make him as ugly on the outside as he was on the inside.

Again she focused on keeping her breathing slow and steady, not wanting him to have a clue that she was conscious and her heart pounded so fast it felt as if it might explode out of her chest.

Minutes, she reminded herself. Within minutes it would all be over. Willowby would be in custody. Luke had her back, the jet was on standby and everything was coming together just as they'd planned.

Chocolate fondue...Swarovski crystals...silk night-gowns, she mentally began her mantra as her nerves screamed in anticipation of what was to come.

"Carol? Didn't anyone ever tell you it was risky to go to a stranger's house for a drink that you didn't watch him prepare?" He laughed again, a low deep sound of extreme pleasure. "That was not smart, Carol. That was not smart at all."

If she had any doubt as to whether he'd spiked the drink or not, these words confirmed it to her. Bastard, she thought. He was the worst kind of predator.

Then he touched her breast.

It was a light skim over the top of her dress, but it

burned the skin beneath her clothes and made her want to throw up. His breath on her face was shuddery, as if he was already in the throes of some sick desire.

Oh God, she didn't know if she could follow through on this or not. His breath, his touch filled her with revulsion.

Stay calm, she told herself. Luke is just outside watching all this and should be coming through the door at any minute.

She fought an impulse to gasp as Marcus reached an arm beneath her and with a grunt of effort scooped her up and stood.

She kept herself limp as he carried her down the hall and into the spare bedroom where he tossed her on the bed. She sprawled inelegantly, but remained unmoving as he left her there.

She waited a long moment, then another, then she cracked open one eye just enough to see him setting up a tripod with a video camera at the foot of the bed.

He was not only intending to rape her, but he also intended to memorialize the occasion. He seemed to be in no hurry as he set the camera and focused it. GHB usually rendered the victim unconscious for six hours or so. She was sure he figured he had plenty of time.

He fiddled with the camera for several minutes. "You're going to be a movie star, Carol. Well, actually I'm the star, you're just a prop, but a very important one."

Was that the way he saw his victims, as nothing more than props? The police had only found one movie that he had made with the two women who had brought charges against him. But, Chantal was certain that somewhere Willowby had a whole stash of videos depicting him as a "star."

"We're going to have a good time, Carol," he said as he kicked off his shoes and sat on the edge of the bed to remove his socks.

Any time now, Luke, she thought. Even though she'd told Luke that she wanted Willowby half-naked and panting when they took him down, she now found herself wanting it not to go any further. She wanted it over now.

When he stood and unzipped his pants, Chantal thought she was going to throw up. Urgency filled her. Come on, Luke, she thought frantically as Willowby returned to the bed clad only in a pair of boxers.

Once again she felt his breath, hot and labored against her face as he pressed his length against her side. He was fully aroused. What kind of a man found an unconscious, unresponsive woman a turn-on?

She nearly stopped breathing as his fingers fumbled with the tiny buttons on her front of her dress. His fingers trembled and his panting breaths filled the silence of the room. He unbuttoned half the buttons then stopped and she could tell by the movement of his body against hers that he was rubbing himself.

"Oh, baby, have I got something for you." He moaned, then placed his hand back on her dress.

Where are you, Luke? God, why wasn't he in here yet? Willowby had his pants off, it was time for Luke to burst into the room and stop everything from progressing further.

Was this what Belinda had felt? A sickness in her soul as she stood frozen in terror and Willowby touched her, violated her? Belinda had been helpless to save herself, inert with fear, with shock.

He straddled her and leaned forward. "You're going to have the best time of your life tonight," he breathed into her ear. "Unfortunately, you won't remember a thing about it in the morning." Once again his hand raked over one of her breasts, this time with only the barrier of her wispy bra between his hand and her flesh.

Unexpectedly she felt the burn of hot tears at her eyes. No more. She couldn't allow him to touch her any more intimately than he already had. She was going to be sick if she didn't stop him now.

She couldn't wait for Luke, couldn't imagine what he was waiting for. But she had to act now.

As Willowby tried to pull her dress from her shoulders, she snapped open her eyes and shoved at his chest with a force that sent him backward and off her.

"What the hell?" He jumped off the bed, a look of complete shock on his face as she scrambled to her feet and faced him. "What in the hell is going on? Who the hell are you?"

"I'm your nightmare…a woman who is conscious and can fight back. You bastard! I'm here to take you into custody and get you back to face the justice you've escaped for too many years."

Willowby's eyes narrowed. "What are you? You aren't a cop. Are you some kind of bounty hunter? I'll pay you twice the fee you'd get for bringing me in if you forget you found me here."

Damn it, where was Luke? Chantal had no weapon. She didn't even have her cuffs. They were in her purse in the living room.

"You can't pay me enough money to forget I found you," she replied as she stepped closer to him. There was no way she was leaving this room without him in tow. She'd use whatever means necessary.

"This is personal, Willowby," she exclaimed. "You raped my friend ten years ago at a party at your house. Now I'm taking you in."

His eyes narrowed once again as he stared at her. "Your friend?" She could almost see the wheels turning in his head. "Worthington…Chantal Worthington. I knew you looked familiar." The features that had looked so handsome, so elegant earlier in the evening now twisted into something ugly, something evil. "I'm not going anywhere with you and I sure as hell am not going to allow you to take me anywhere."

"That's where you're wrong. We can do this easy or we can do it the hard way." Chantal hoped the years of soft living had taken a toll on him and that her months in the gym sparring and playing with the big boys had worked to her advantage.

At that moment there was a deep male cry from someplace outside the window. Willowby looked toward the window and Chantal took that opportunity to charge him. She lowered her head like a charging bull and hit him square in the midsection.

He careened backward, hitting the wall at the same time his fingers tangled in her hair. He yanked her hair and she cried out with pain, gripping his wrists in an attempt to get him to release his hold.

Tears sprang to her eyes as he yanked harder on her hair. It felt as if he were pulling it out by the roots. She released his wrists and instead reached for his face, scratching her sculptured nails down his cheeks.

He screamed, a sound almost inhuman, and let go of her hair, but he wrapped his hands around her neck and squeezed. "You bitch. I'll make sure they never find your body," he said between clenched teeth. Blood welled up in the scratches that now adorned his face and his eyes held the murderous rage of the devil.

If Chantal had any questions about just how dangerous Willowby might be, his words answered them as did the painful pressure of suffocation.

His hands squeezed, cutting off her oxygen. At that moment she wasn't just in a fight for a fugitive, she was in a fight for her life.

She was vaguely aware of the sound of more men shouting outside the bungalow as she frantically tried to get air. She grabbed at his hands, but her strength ebbed and darkness grew closer.

Help me. The words flashed in her head, but she knew no help would arrive. She had no idea what had happened to Luke, but it was obvious she was on her own.

Air. She needed air. She didn't want to die. Not here.

Not now. And especially not at the hands of a creep like Willowby.

"Die, bitch," Willowby cried, his features contorted with rage.

Panic seared through her. She had no weapon and within seconds she knew she'd be unconscious. She'd be dead.

A spark of survival lit inside her. She did have a weapon, she suddenly thought in a moment of startling clarity.

She slammed her spike heel into the top of his bare foot. Thank God, Gucci made strong shoes.

He roared in pain and released her. She coughed and gasped in relief as air flooded her lungs. He sank to the floor and grabbed his bloody foot, moaning in pain as she sucked in deep breaths of sweet air.

At that moment a gunshot resounded from someplace outside, followed quickly by the sound of sirens in the distance.

Luke exploded into the room from the hallway, his chest heaving as his gaze shot from Chantal to Willowby. "Where the hell have you been?" she asked.

"Tangling with his hired help. The police are going to be here any minute. You need to get out of here," he said. He grabbed her arm as if in an effort to propel her out of the house.

In a split second, she considered their options. She jerked away from his grip. "I'm not going anywhere," she exclaimed. "You go, get out of here."

"Damn it, Chantal, get the hell out of here right now,"

he yelled, his features alarmed. "This isn't the time to be hard-headed. You don't want to spend a minute in a Mexican jail."

"And you do?" she retorted. "I'm not leaving, Luke. There's no way I'm going to let this creep out of my sight. You get out of here. It won't do any good for both of us to be in jail."

Luke released a stream of curses at the same time they heard the sound of cars squealing to a halt at the front of the house.

"Go, Luke. I'll tell them he tried to rape me. I'll be fine," she said. "It's better this way."

He held her gaze for a single long moment, then turned and left. A moment later, three armed policemen burst into the room, guns drawn and their expressions fierce.

"*¡Policia! ¡Policia!*" they cried. They screamed in rapid-fire Spanish making it impossible for Chantal to understand what they were saying. However, she easily understood the universal body language that told her to hold up her arms in a gesture of surrender.

"She attacked me," Marcus cried. He struggled to his feet. "I demand you arrest her."

Minutes later, cuffed and in the back of a police car, Chantal realized she was in deep trouble. She'd heard stories about Mexican jails and her blood ran cold as she contemplated what might lie ahead.

The only comfort she had was that Willowby was cuffed and in the back of another police car. Maybe she'd been a fool not to run when Luke had given her the opportunity, but she'd been afraid that somehow

Willowby would escape. She'd needed to see this through to the end.

Damn it, they'd been so close to success. Apparently Willowby had lied when he'd told her they would be alone. The two bodyguards must have shown up to keep an eye on the place. She wondered if they were in a police car being taken away? She wondered if Luke had been forced to kill them both?

Somebody had apparently heard the melee and had called the authorities. Their plan for a quiet, controlled take-down had been blown out of the water.

She tried to talk to the two officers in the front seat, but they either didn't understand English or her butchered Spanish, or they simply refused to talk to her. She suspected the latter.

The only thing she could hope was that when they got to the station somebody in charge would listen to her, preferably somebody who spoke perfect English.

She suspected Willowby had entered Mexico with a fake passport and if that was true, then she could only hope they would deport him back to the United States.

She tried not to panic as they reached the flat, adobe building that apparently served as the area police headquarters. She had no idea what to expect once they all got inside.

The officers weren't gentle as they pulled her from the back seat and led her into the building. She saw no sign of Willowby.

If that bastard had somehow talked his way out of custody, she'd be more pissed than she was now.

"Hey, take it easy," she exclaimed as one of the officers shoved her in the back to move her across the large office area and through a doorway that led to a large cell.

"Hey, wait a minute, don't I get a phone call?" she asked.

The guard ignored her and poked her in the back once again.

She couldn't even summon her mantra as she stared into the cell. It was filled with women and it didn't take a rocket scientist to guess that most of them were hookers.

They all wore the evidence of hard lives, destroyed dreams and a street toughness that didn't bode well for Chantal.

These were women who knew how to take care of themselves, women for whom each and every day would be a struggle for survival.

And she was the outsider…a minnow in a pond of sharks.

The officer opened the cell door and unceremoniously shoved Chantal inside. The clank of the door closing behind her sent a new icy chill through her veins.

She was definitely sorry she hadn't taken Luke's advice and run. She had a feeling it was going to be a long night.

It took her only one minute of sizing up the crowd to recognize who was boss. The woman was beautiful, of indeterminate age, with glossy black hair that hung halfway down her back.

She sat in the only chair the cell had to offer and the others clustered around her like ladies in waiting.

When the officer disappeared she rose regally and approached Chantal, her full upper lip raised at one corner in a sneer.

"Filthy American *puta,*" she said, then spat at Chantal's feet.

Chantal sighed in resignation. Her Spanish wasn't great but it was good enough to know a challenge had just been thrown down and if she didn't rise to it, her time in the cell would be hell.

"Oh no, I know you didn't just call me a whore," she said and took a step toward the woman.

"No. I call you a filthy American whore," the woman replied, her dark eyes flashing. Without warning her hand shot out and long fingernails raked down Chantal's cheek.

Without thought, Chantal bitch-slapped the woman.

There was a collective gasp from the other women as Chantal and the boss lady stood toe to toe.

Chantal's strength had never been physical. Her mind worked to find a solution that would allow this woman to maintain her dignity yet wouldn't be a show of weakness on Chantal's part.

There was a universal language among women, and although she was taking a chance, she decided to try to speak it. She managed to grab hold of the woman's long hair.

"You've got beautiful hair, ever tried to French braid it?" she asked.

The woman stared at Chantal. "French braid? What is that?"

In those simple words Chantal knew she'd won this battle with only a scratched cheek as an injury.

Chapter 16

Luke leaned against the side of the Jeep and stared at the front door of the police station, every muscle in his body painfully tense.

The early-morning sun had peeked up over the horizon only an hour or so before, but already the rays were hot and the ever-present humidity seemed closer, almost suffocating.

He'd never experienced a night like the one he'd just passed. He'd seen Chantal and Willowby taken away by the officials and had followed so he'd know where she was being held.

Once he knew where they'd been taken he'd returned to the hotel. He'd packed their bags, checked out and had come back here, this time armed with her identification and whatever cash he'd been able to rustle up.

The idea of Chantal behind bars in a Mexican jail terrified him. He knew what could happen to a beautiful woman like her and the thought of any harm coming to her made him sick.

He stretched with arms overhead then leaned against the side of the Jeep and stared at the door leading into the police station.

He'd been a fool to get involved in this, a bigger fool to get involved with her. He'd had a bad feeling from the moment she'd come up with her plan. No, that wasn't exactly true. He'd had a bad feeling from the moment they'd first made love.

Everything would have been less complicated if she'd been a pretentious socialite playing at real life. Everything would have been so much easier if he hadn't come to respect her and to like her.

It would have been so much simpler had he been able to dismiss her as a fashion-wearing, jet-setting, bubble-headed woman.

He'd spent the night trying to find somebody with the power to release her. He'd spoken to half a dozen officials and had explained the entire situation over and over again. But, it wasn't until thirty minutes before that he'd finally gotten to speak with the *capitan*. He'd explained, cajoled and finally bribed the man to release both Chantal and Willowby.

The *capitan* had stared intently with his enigmatic black eyes, slid the envelope of money into his top

desk drawer, then had indicated Luke should go outside and wait.

Wait for what? Wait for the realization that he'd just
given up a huge amount of cash to a man who didn't
intend to release anyone? Wait for word to trickle outside that the American woman had been beaten to a pulp
and raped by every man in the station?

Damn it. Instead of getting on that plane with her,
he should have locked her in her house when he'd seen
the ticket to Mexico on her kitchen counter. If he'd
done that then they wouldn't have made love, she would
have hated him forever, but at least she would have
been safe.

A trickle of sweat worked down his spine. Hell, what
did she know about surviving in jail? She probably
couldn't even survive a night in a budget motel. And
with that smart mouth of hers she'd be eaten alive by
real criminals.

His heart was a tight ball of pressure, so tight he
found breathing difficult. The last time he'd felt like this
he'd been sitting in a hospital waiting room, waiting to
see if his brother would survive the gunshot wounds
from a robbery.

At that time his heart had felt the same way, as if it
had turned to a block of concrete too heavy for his chest
to bear.

How had this happened? He'd vowed to himself in
those two days with Seth that he'd never, ever feel that
way again, that he'd never, ever allow anyone to get
close enough that he would care.

So, how had it happened that he now stood in the hot Mexican sun, worrying about a woman he'd hardly known a week before?

With each minute that ticked by, his fear increased. Maybe the *capitan* had no intention of releasing her. The moment the *capitan* had slid the envelope of money into his desk drawer, Luke had thought they'd reached a gentleman's agreement. But, how in the hell was he to know if the *capitan* was a gentleman? A gentleman who could be bribed? Now that was a contradiction in terms, he thought worriedly.

He was just about to storm inside once again when the front door of the building opened and Chantal stepped outside, the sunshine sparkling on her hair.

His heart crashed to his feet at the sight of her.

She no longer wore the red dress that she'd been wearing when she'd been taken into custody. Nor did she have on her killer high heels. She was clad in a long black skirt with multicolored embroidery around the hemline, and a peasant blouse that looked about three sizes too big. Cheap black flip-flops adorned her feet.

Why didn't she have on her own clothes? What had happened to her in there? He'd believed he couldn't get any sicker than he already was, but as he thought of all the reasons why she wouldn't be wearing her own clothing, a new wave of sickness swept over him.

The second thing he saw as she drew closer were scratches down one of her cheeks.

He was enraged at her for not running when he'd told

her to, for not letting him go to jail instead of her. He was enraged at the authorities, who would allow heinous behavior in the confines of a jail cell.

He didn't wait for her to reach him, but rather raced toward her and met her halfway. Without saying a word he reached for her and pulled her tight against him.

His pain was too great for words. His fear for her kept him silent. At least she was alive. For a long moment she leaned into him and he could feel the beating of her heart against his.

But he couldn't hold on to her forever and reluctantly he dropped his arms from around her and stepped back. To his surprise her eyes were clear and sparkling with their usual life and humor. The tight pressure in his chest eased somewhat.

"How'd you get me out of there?" she asked as together they walked toward the Jeep.

"I greased a few palms and did a lot of double-talking," he replied. "What happened to your face?" Again tension balled in his chest, making it difficult for him to draw a deep breath.

She reached a hand up and touched the scratches. "It's nothing, just a little misunderstanding with one of my fellow inmates."

"Where are your clothes? Why are you dressed in those things?"

"Me and my girls did some bartering."

"You and your girls?" They stopped at the back of the Jeep and he stared at her.

"Me and my new hooker girlfriends. I've spent the

last ten hours French-braiding hair, giving beauty advice and bartering my clothes and shoes for a cot and extra food."

He stared at her in disbelief. He'd had the worst night of his life worrying about her and she'd spent the night giving hookers beauty tips. Thank God. He had definitely underestimated Chantal's resourcefulness.

"Are we getting out of here, or what?" she asked.

"We need to sit tight for a little while and see if anyone else is released."

She shot him a sharp gaze. "You think they might release Willowby?" Energy vibrated from her despite the fact he now saw faint smudges of exhaustion beneath her eyes.

"I don't know if he'll be released or not although I told the *capitan* it would be in everyone's best interest if they'd allow us to take Willowby back to the States. I explained to him that I didn't think Tamillo needed a sick twist as one of their citizens."

"What did he say?"

Luke frowned. "Nothing."

Chantal leaned against the side of the Jeep, her gaze going from him to the building where she'd spent the night. She moved a hand up to rub her throat.

"He would have killed me last night. I'd wondered before coming here what he might be capable of, and last night he proved to me that he's capable of murder."

"I figured that out when one of his goons hit me over the head and knocked me cold. I was only out for a minute or two but when I came to the two men were carrying me to the water's edge. I'm assuming they intended to drown me."

He frowned, remembering that moment when he'd come to, the moment he realized Chantal was inside the house without backup. He'd been frantic to get inside to her.

He shouldn't be surprised that she'd managed to take care of herself, and he took back every concern he'd had about her working in this business.

"What happened to the goons?" she asked.

"I managed to get away from them and took a couple of shots at one. I'm pretty sure I missed him. Anyway, when they heard the sirens they ran like cockroaches at daybreak. That's when I got inside the house to warn you. You should have listened to me and run."

She shook her head. "I wasn't going to leave him, Luke. I told you before, right or wrong, I needed to take responsibility for Willowby." She frowned and rubbed her forehead. "In any case, it all might have been for nothing as long as we're out here and Willowby is in there. If we've lost him this time we won't get another chance."

Luke threw an arm over her shoulder but said nothing. She was right and she wouldn't appreciate him giving her platitudes. In fact it would be disrespectful of the honest and open relationship they'd shared to this point.

"How long do we wait?" she asked softly.

"As long as you want to," he replied.

She leaned against him and they remained like that for several minutes before the door of the building opened and Marcus Willowby limped out into the brilliant morning sunshine.

Luke dropped his arm from her shoulder, pulled his cuffs from his belt and handed them to Chantal.

"Go make your collar," he said.

If he'd handed her a twenty-karat perfectly cut princess diamond she couldn't have been happier. Chantal took the cuffs from him and flashed him a grateful smile.

As she approached Willowby his face twisted into a mask of rage. "Get away from me, you crazy bitch. You crippled me. I'll have you arrested on assault charges." He glanced back at the building, as if seeking somebody in authority to come to his aid. But there was nobody around.

"Shut up, Willowby," she replied. As she stepped closer to him, he balled his hands into fists, obviously preparing to fight her if necessary. "I've got handcuffs, and my partner over there has a gun."

She gestured back to Luke, who leaned against the side of the Jeep, his relaxed posture deceptive. "Nobody is coming to your rescue, Marcus. They let you out of there knowing we were out here waiting for you. You might as well just let me do what I need to do."

His eyes shifted from left to right, as if assessing his options. His eyes narrowed as he realized he had none. "This isn't over," he said as he held out his hands.

She cuffed one of his hands then pulled it behind him so he would be handcuffed with his hands behind his back. "Trust me, it's over," she replied.

As she led him to the Jeep a wave of euphoria swept through her. They'd done it. Within hours Willowby would be back in the States to face the justice he'd tried to escape.

Luke smiled at her as they loaded Willowby in the back seat. "Satisfied?"

"Not quite," she replied. "I'm an insatiable kind of woman."

"I know." His gaze lingered on her, suddenly hot and hungry.

"I'm not talking about that," she said, surprised to feel her cheeks flame with warmth. "I won't be satisfied until he's living in a prison cell and my friend is well and I've dealt with Mundy's boys so I can get my life back." She looked at her watch. "If we can get clearance to leave the airport quickly then we should be back in Kansas City in time for dinner."

An hour later they were seated in the private jet, Willowby cuffed to his chair and Luke and Chantal seated opposite each other at a teakwood table. They had been cleared for takeoff and had begun the taxi to the runway.

She was conscious of Willowby's gaze on her and she turned to look at him. He grinned, the smile not remotely pleasant. "Chantal Worthington, bounty hunting." He shook his head and released a low chuckle. "I'd say I was surprised but I'm not. We're alike, Chantal. You and me, we're cut from the same cloth."

"Shut up, Willowby," Luke said, his voice low and ominous.

"It's all right, Luke. Let him talk," she replied.

Willowby grinned again. "Deep inside, deep in our souls, we're just alike."

"Don't be ridiculous. We're nothing alike," she replied.

Willowby leaned forward as far as the cuffs would allow him and his eyes glittered with a darkness that sent a chill up Chantal's spine. "People like us, Chantal, there's nothing we can't buy, no place we can't go. Last night you would have killed me. I saw it in your eyes. You're just like me, Chantal, bored and jaded and looking for the ultimate rush."

Suddenly she didn't want to listen to him as his words found purchase in her soul, in a dark place where she'd wondered why she'd chosen this particular path.

"That's enough," Luke said roughly. "Shut up or I'll shut you up."

Willowby merely smiled, then leaned back in his seat and closed his eyes. Chantal was aware of Luke's gaze on her, dark and questioning, but at that moment the engines whined and the jet roared down the runway and took to the sky.

The flight was a quiet one. Within minutes Luke's eyes drifted closed and Chantal was left alone with her thoughts, which were unsettling at best.

She'd had no sleep the night before and now felt the drain of any lingering adrenaline and heard Willowby's final words echoing in her ears.

She'd wondered what had driven him to commit his crimes. Was it possible that it had been nothing more than a need for a kick? Was it possible he'd been handed so much, things had been so incredibly easy for him that he'd had to resort to raping women to feel truly alive?

Was it possible she had become as jaded as him? Had been given too much too soon and had been drawn to the violence, the danger of bounty hunting because life held no real surprises for her anymore?

She raised a hand to her throat, thinking of those moments when his hands had choked her, when she'd thought death was imminent. Was Willowby right about her? Was it the ultimate thrill of life and death that drew her to this business?

She turned her attention to Luke. Exhaustion lined his face. Even though she'd been frightened in that jail cell there had been a bit of relief knowing Luke was on the outside and would do whatever he could to get her out.

The minute she'd stepped out of the building and seen him standing there, she'd been stunned by the frantic worry on his face. When he'd wrapped his arms around her and held her in a near death grip she'd felt the crashing of his heartbeat and knew his night had been every bit as difficult as hers.

Where did the two of them go from here? She hated to admit it, but Luke had gotten to her as no man had before. For the first time in a very long time she'd met a man who intrigued her, one who promised all kinds of possibilities, and she didn't know what to expect from him, if anything.

For all she knew, Luke was finished with her. He'd mixed business with pleasure, but now that their business together was at an end, so was the pleasure.

He'd certainly given her no indication that he was a man seeking any real, meaningful relationship. In fact, he'd intimated just the opposite. He'd told her more than once that when he felt somebody getting too close he packed up and left the area.

She leaned her head back against the seat and stared out the window to where nothing was visible but blue sky. She'd known Luke was dangerous to her, had somehow known on some instinctive level that making love with him would complicate her emotions where he was concerned.

She sighed and once again looked at Willowby. He was awake and gazed at her with an unblinking stare and a small curve to his lips.

Despite what he faced when he got back to the States, he looked smug, as if he knew his words had bothered her and was delighted with that fact.

She returned his smile with a smug one of her own and thought of how Belinda would react to the news that the man who had raped her was now in custody.

Luke had made her recognize that getting Willowby into custody wouldn't magically fix Belinda's life. He'd also made Chantal realize that it wasn't her fault that Belinda had been raped. She'd carried the weight of that guilt around for a very long time, but now felt its absence in her heart.

We got him, girlfriend, she thought. He'll never have the opportunity to rape another woman. He was going to spend a very long time in jail and pretty boys like Marcus Willowby didn't have an easy time behind bars. In all probability he'd learn the horrors of rape firsthand.

It was at that moment that she realized how to solve her problem with Mundy and the bounty on her head.

It was dusk when Chantal and Luke left the police station in downtown Kansas City. The transfer of their prisoner had been smooth and without fanfare.

Chantal and Luke had encouraged the authorities to keep their names out of the press and the authorities were all too eager to take credit for the bust.

Chantal had arranged for a private car to be waiting at the Kansas City International Airport when they'd landed. It had taken them less than half an hour to clear customs and then they'd gone directly to the police station.

The hot night air wrapped around her and she was suddenly overwhelmed by exhaustion. It had been over twenty-four hours since she'd slept and the adrenaline that had kept her functioning ebbed away, leaving her beyond tired.

"I guess that's it," she said as they stood on the sidewalk just outside the building. "This partnership is now officially over."

His features were inscrutable in the dying light of day. "Come on, I'll give you a ride home." He gestured toward the lot where she was surprised to see his truck parked.

"How did you manage that?" she asked.

"I had a friend drop it off for me while we were inside getting Willowby squared away. I had him transfer our luggage from the car to the truck. I didn't know how long we'd be tied up inside and figured it was better if I had my own wheels."

A moment later she sank onto the passenger seat and tried to ignore the fact that the interior of the truck smelled like Luke, a clean, masculine scent she'd come to love.

Funny, that she should feel euphoric about Willowby being in custody, yet oddly disappointed that the whole adventure was now behind her, oddly disappointed that she had a feeling that now they were back in the States it would be business as usual between her and Luke.

She mentally shook herself. Of course things would go back to business as usual. They were competitors, not lovers and she was certain all she was feeling at the moment was the result of too little sleep.

She leaned her head back and closed her eyes as Luke got into the truck and started the engine. "It's always a come-down, isn't it?" he said.

She opened her eyes and looked at him. "I guess with the success of a collar comes the crash of the fall. And, of course, it doesn't help that I spent last night in a jail cell afraid to close my eyes."

"If it's any consolation at all, I didn't close my eyes while you were in that jail cell."

She smiled. "I didn't really thank you for getting me out of there. Whatever bribe you had to make, I'll gladly reimburse you."

"Don't worry about it. What kind of a man would I be if I left my partner to fend on her own? While we were in the police station I found out some other information you might find interesting."

"What's that?"

"The two punks who tried to shoot you at Danny's

pleaded guilty to attempted armed robbery and cut a deal with the DA. They're both going to serve time so you don't have to worry about them anymore."

"I guess copping a plea to attempted armed robbery is better than being charged with attempted murder." Again weariness tugged at her. "So, I don't have to worry about those two but I wonder how many other punks are in Mundy's little gang?"

"Maybe you need to talk to the police about getting some protection for a while?"

"You know as well as I that the police have better things to do with their time. No, I think I've got a plan brewing in my mind that will take care of Mundy and any threat he or his friends might have in mind."

"Is there anything I can do to help?" He released a low, dry laugh. "I figured I'd offer even though I know you're independent and stubborn enough to tell me you can handle it yourself."

She flashed him a tired smile. "I *can* handle it myself. I need to handle it myself. If I intend to be in this business for a long time, then I have to learn to take care of myself."

"You don't seem to have any problems there," he replied.

He drove in silence for several moments and she closed her eyes once again.

"Chantal?" he spoke her name softly and she opened her eyes and looked at him once again. "That crap that Willowby said to you on the plane…about you and him being alike. You didn't take any of that seriously, did you?"

She wanted to laugh it off, tell him that of course she hadn't taken it to heart, but she was too tired to lie convincingly. "I don't know. Sometimes I worry about what drew me to this particular line of work."

She sighed and focused her attention out the window, unwilling to look at him while she went to the dark thoughts that haunted her soul. "He was right about us coming from the same kind of background. Maybe I am as jaded, as bored as he is and that's why when I'm hunting a skip or closing in to make a collar, I get a tremendous kick of adrenaline. And I wonder if somehow that makes me like Willowby."

"The businessman who gets a rush when he closes a big deal, the stockbroker who gets a high when he reads the market right, are those men like Willowby?" He didn't give her an opportunity to answer, but continued, "The cops who get a rush when they catch a murderer, the firemen who get pumped about putting out a fire, are those people like Willowby?"

With each word he spoke something in her chest, a pressure that had ached for a long time, broke loose. "Of course not," she whispered.

"Chantal, on your worst day, in the foulest mood you could ever be in, you're nothing like Willowby. Willowby wouldn't have the compassion to worry about a friend's well-being. He'd never feel the guilt over something that happened that was beyond his control. Willowby doesn't have the empathy to feel for other people. You do."

"Thank you. I needed to hear that and you're right."

She grinned. "Besides, I still get a kick when I find the perfect pair of shoes or see a perfect sunset. I get a buzz when I spend a great evening with my mom or listen to good music." She wasn't like Willowby at all. She found great joy in living. She got an adrenaline rush from all kinds of simple things, including a kiss from the man seated next to her.

"And you bounty hunt because you're good at it," he said. "And you're doing something good." He pulled up in her driveway, cut the engine, then turned to look at her, his expression inscrutable. "You need to get a good night's sleep."

She nodded. "I could say the same to you." For the first time since they'd been together the air between them was strained.

If she had her way she'd invite him in, sleep the night away in his arms as she had during their time together in Tamillo. But, there was a distance in his eyes, a remoteness in his expression that kept her from making the offer.

"I'll get your suitcases," he said and got out of the truck. Chantal got out as well and watched as he grabbed her two suitcases from the back of the truck.

She followed just behind him as he carried them to her front door. As she dug in her purse for her keys, he dropped the suitcases and shoved his hands in his pockets.

She'd had uncomfortable morning-afters before, but nothing that compared to the strain she felt coming off him. Was he afraid that she'd demand he declare undying love for her? Afraid that she might expect some kind of commitment?

He obviously believed what had happened in Tamillo stayed in Tamillo and she wasn't the type of woman to pursue a man who didn't want to be pursued.

She unlocked her front door then turned to look at him. Luke, with his handsome, chiseled features and beautiful dark eyes. Luke, with that sexy grin that stirred her in a million ways. It was time to say goodbye.

"Thanks, Luke. It was fun." She forced a carefree smile to her lips.

"Yeah, it was all good." He started to pick up her bags, but she stopped him.

"I can get it from here."

"You sure?"

She nodded. "Go home, get some sleep and I'll see you on the streets."

"Good night, Chantal." He didn't wait for her reply, but rather turned on his heels and strode toward his truck without a backward glance.

She watched until his truck disappeared from her view, then carried her suitcases into the foyer one at a time. She should unpack, but the weariness that had swept over her when she'd stepped out of the police station now nearly consumed her.

As she locked the door behind her she heard a loud meow and turned to see Sam padding toward her. In uncharacteristic affection he coiled around her legs as if she were his best friend.

"Hi, Sam." She picked him up in her arms and he purred with pleasure. "I guess it's true, absence does make the heart grow fonder," she said to the cat.

She hugged the furry warmth against her chest, hoping to banish the ache of loneliness that assailed her, a loneliness that was both unexpected and unwanted and had Luke Coleman's name written all over it.

Chapter 17

Dust motes danced in the early-morning sunshine that streamed through the bank of windows at the Kansas City International Airport.

Chantal, Harrah and Belinda stood just outside the secured area, saying a final goodbye to each other.

Chantal had been home from Tamillo for two days. She'd slept the first day away. Yesterday she'd spent some time with her mother, stopped into her hair salon and had her hair color returned to its normal blond, then last night she and Harrah had staged an intervention with Belinda.

Chantal had come to Belinda's house armed with phone numbers and contacts to the most successful private rehab centers in the country. And she'd come with the single-minded purpose of seeing that the friend she loved got help.

She'd come to terms with the fact that Belinda needed help, more than the help of a good friend and the crutch of her pills, booze and men.

It had been a long night filled with angry outbursts, sharp denials and tears. Ultimately Belinda had agreed that she needed help for her addictions, for her fears and for the post-traumatic stress of the rape she'd suffered so many years before.

She'd chosen a facility in southern California and the arrangements had been made for her to check in upon her arrival.

"You'll come and visit me?" she now said to Chantal.

"The minute you're allowed visitors," Chantal replied. "I'm so proud of you for doing this."

Belinda smiled. "I've needed to do this for a long time, but I didn't want to face it." She raised her chin. "I'm proud of myself. I haven't felt good about me for a very long time."

"There will be no living with her when she gets home," Harrah teased.

Belinda grabbed Harrah and Chantal's hands and squeezed tightly. "I'm scared to death," she confessed.

"I'd worry about you if you weren't," Chantal replied. "But you'll be fine. You're stronger than you think you are, Belinda."

"I know and I know this is the right thing to do," she replied.

At that moment an announcer came over the loudspeaker indicating that Belinda's flight had begun to board. "I need to go. I guess this is goodbye." She hugged Harrah, then turned to Chantal.

"Thank you for getting tough with me," she said and hugged Chantal tightly. "You're the best friend a person could ever have."

"You promise me that when you get off the plane you'll go straight to Rolling Rivers," Chantal said.

Belinda released her and smiled. "Pinky swear."

Harrah and Chantal watched as Belinda went through security, then they waved goodbye as Belinda disappeared down the hallway that would take her to her flight.

"She'll be all right," Harrah said as she and Chantal turned to exit the airport.

"I know. Thanks for your help in getting her on the plane."

Harrah flashed her beautiful smile. "It wasn't all that much work. I think she wanted to go. She knew her life was going nowhere, that she needed help."

Chantal nodded, her thoughts already moving forward to the next item on her agenda for the day. "Did you talk to Jimmy?" she asked, referring to Harrah's brother.

"I did. He's all set."

"Good," Chantal replied, hoping her plan to neutralize Mundy worked.

Minutes later the two women were in Chantal's car. It was a twenty-minute drive from the airport to the small town of Lansing, Kansas, where both Mundy and Jimmy were inmates in the prison.

"You haven't said much about your time in Mexico,"

Harrah said as she flipped the passenger visor down against the bright sunshine.

"There's not much to tell," Chantal replied.

"You must have been terrified, going up against Willowby all alone."

Chantal flashed her assistant a quick glance. "I wasn't exactly all alone. Luke Coleman was with me."

Harrah raised a dark eyebrow. "Really? How did that happen?"

Briefly Chantal told her about Luke seeing the ticket and showing up on the plane to Tamillo. She didn't mention that they'd played the role of honeymooning couple but she felt Harrah's keen gaze lingering on her and her cheeks warmed.

"You and that hunky man kicked it while you were south of the border, didn't you?"

Chantal thought about lying, but knew she was awful at it and Harrah would see right through her. Instead she nodded. "Yeah, it was no big deal. You know, two strangers in a strange land...yada, yada, yada. It was great and now it's done and it's life back to usual."

"And you're okay with that?"

"Sure. It was just a mutual case of lust, nothing more." Chantal forced an easy laugh. "You know all about lust, it's good and strong for a little while, but it never lasts for long."

"Don't I know," Harrah exclaimed. "Before Lena and I got together I had a few lust-based relationships myself."

Chantal was relieved when Harrah began talking about her latest jewelry creations. She didn't want to think about Luke Coleman. She didn't want to examine her feelings for the man who was obviously gone from her life. It irritated her that he'd occupied her thoughts far too often in the past two days.

She assumed he was back to business as usual, working the streets as he had been before the trip to Mexico, but she hadn't been to Big Joey's so hadn't seen him since her return home.

She had consciously stayed away from Big Joey's, knowing that her week in Mexico probably hadn't cooled Mundy's goons. She was hoping her little visit to the prison today would solve that problem.

It was going to be weird, seeing Luke again. She only hoped they could both be adults and their time together in Mexico wouldn't even be mentioned.

The Lansing Correctional Facility was the state's largest complex for detention of adult male felony offenders. Chantal knew from her research that the prison had four custody levels, special management, maximum, medium and minimum.

Both Harrah's brother, Jimmy, and Perry Mundy were considered medium-security risks and were housed in the same population, which served Chantal's plan perfectly.

The women arrived five minutes before visiting hours would begin. Outside the prison entrance, inmates clad in prison blue worked on the lawn, clipping bushes and watering flowers.

Several guards stood nearby, their armed status a reminder that the men might be tending nature, but their natures weren't particularly tender.

It took nearly twenty minutes for them to go through the security process. A guard explained the rules to them, no touching, no passing of notes or items between inmates and visitors. The guard then preceded them down a hallway that led to the interior of the prison. He unlocked a metal door and ushered them into the visiting area.

The room contained tables and chairs set some distance apart. Vending machines stood against one wall and armed guards in all four corners of the room stood on elevated platforms to afford them a view of the entire area.

There were already several inmates and visitors there, chatting quietly across from each other. Chantal sat at one of the empty tables, Harrah at another nearby.

Chantal had decided the only way to deal with Mundy's threats was to fight fire with fire and that's what she intended to do. He wanted to play tough guy… she could get tough right back.

As she waited for him to appear, she wondered if this was where Willowby would spend the rest of his natural life? His lawyer had already begun the appeal process, but Chantal felt confident the original sentence would stand. Now he had the additional charge of fleeing to contend with.

She watched as Harrah's brother, Jimmy, appeared in the doorway. Jimmy was a huge man. He stood well over six feet tall and had the bulk of a bodybuilder. Harrah referred to him as a gentle giant.

His eyes met Chantal's and he nodded shyly to her as he beelined to where his sister awaited him. He joined her at the table and the two began to talk in almost-whispers.

As Chantal waited for Mundy to appear she found her gaze going to Harrah and Jimmy. She knew how much Harrah adored her brother and it was obvious he cared deeply about his sister as well. Their mutual affection was evident in their body language as they leaned forward to speak to each other.

Thank God for friends, she thought as she stared down at the table in front of her. This whole plan wouldn't work without the friendship of Harrah and her relationship with her brother.

The door to the visiting room opened and Mundy appeared. Perry Mundy was not an attractive young man. His skin was scarred with acne and he was thin to the point of emaciation, but that wasn't what made him unpleasant to look at.

There was a sneakiness in his eyes, an arrogance in his walk and a sneer to his thin lips that defined him as punk bad-ass.

He looked around the room in confusion and when his gaze fell on her, he couldn't hide his surprise. He recovered quickly, sauntered to the table and sprawled in the seat across from her.

"Well, well, if it isn't the bitch who put me in this place," he said.

"Ah, Perry, you give me far too much credit," she replied easily. "You put yourself here by breaking the law, but I'm not here to talk to you about your past crimes. We need to talk about the fact that you've had some of your buddies looking for me."

He stared at her in mock innocence. "I don't know

what you're talking about." His lips held just enough of a smirk to let her know that he knew exactly what she was talking about.

"You're complicating my life, Perry, and I don't like it. I don't like it one little bit." She leaned back in her chair and smiled at him. "So, I've decided to complicate your life."

The smile worried him. The smirk fell away and he eyed her warily. "What are you talking about?"

"You have friends on the outside? I have friends on the inside." She waited a moment to let him digest her words, then she gestured toward Jimmy, who turned and stared at Mundy.

Any resemblance Chantal thought Jimmy had to a cuddly bear was gone. His thick black eyebrows pulled together in a frown that radiated a threatening menace. His hands balled into fists on the top of the table as he continued to glare at Mundy.

"Call off your boys, Perry," Chantal said softly. "Call off your boys or your life in here isn't worth a plugged nickel. Jimmy's my friend and he has friends."

Fear darkened Mundy's eyes as he looked at Chantal. He raked a hand through his greasy dark hair, then smiled uncertainly. "I told you I don't know what you're talking about."

"Then I guess we're done here." She nodded to Jimmy, then started to rise from the table.

"Wait," Mundy exclaimed and she sank back down. He shot another glance at Jimmy who still stared at him with gleaming dark eyes that promised a particular brand of hell. "Okay…all right. I'll make some phone calls."

Chantal leaned forward. "You'd better make them quickly. Anything happens to me on the streets and your life will be miserable. I walk out of here and get a hangnail, Jimmy and his friends are going to come looking for you."

"All right," he said, fear evident on his weasel features. "I said I'd take care of it."

"Today, Mundy. I want this issue taken care of today, otherwise you'd better sleep tonight with both eyes open." This time he didn't stop her when she stood. He looked at Jimmy for a third time, then looked back at her and nodded.

Chantal left the waiting room, confident that she'd gotten her life back.

"What did you do? Piss off Coleman?" Joey asked Chantal two nights later as she sat in his office.

"What do you mean?" she asked.

"He hasn't been in since you two went to Mexico for Willowby. He called and told me to hold his check, that he'd contact me later about where to send it."

So, he was gone. She wasn't surprised at the information, but she was surprised at the wave of disappointment that swept through her.

"I didn't piss him off. Maybe he just figured it was time to move on."

Joey frowned and shook his head. "Damn shame. He was my most productive." His frown disappeared and he grinned at Chantal. "But I have a feeling if you stay in this business long enough you'll rival his skills."

"I'm not going anywhere," Chantal replied.

"You took care of your little problem with Mundy?"

She smiled. "Word on the street is that anyone harms a hair on my head they'll have Mundy's boys to deal with."

Joey shot her a look filled with respect. "I gotta hand it to you, I had my doubts when I hired you, but I'm thinking it was the best damn business decision I've ever made."

His words filled her with pride. She knew Joey wasn't a man who gave his respect easily, but she also knew she'd earned that respect.

"I'm going to get out of here," she said. "It's getting late and the forecast is for a storm and there are a couple places I want to check out before I call it a night."

Minutes later, as lightning streaked across the night skies, Chantal drove toward the west side of town where she hoped to catch sight of one Phillip Browning who had skipped out on bail a week before.

As she drove, she went over the case in her mind. Phillip Browning had been arrested for a string of traffic violations. Joey had posted the bond and Phillip had neglected to show up in court.

She wasn't expecting trouble. Other than the fact that Browning liked to collect speeding tickets then not pay the fines, he had no history of other criminal activity or violent behavior.

It was the kind of case that most bounty hunters rarely concerned themselves with because of the small recovery fee. But Chantal was bored and there was nothing else on the skip board to interest her.

Luke was gone.

She wondered where he'd run, how far he'd gone to start a new life? Had she threatened him in some way? She'd tried so hard to hide her feelings for him, to make him think what they'd shared in Tamillo had been nothing of consequence to her.

Maybe she was being completely egotistical to believe that his moving on had anything to do with her. Maybe he'd just decided it was time.

She'd just pulled up in front of Phillip Browning's darkened house when the rain began. It was a summer deluge, complete with roaring thunder and whips of wind.

No way, she thought. No way she was going to ruin her clothes by getting out in this storm. Browning would have to wait…she had her priorities.

A half an hour later she pulled into her garage. The storm that the weathermen had said would be quick-moving and brief had apparently stalled overhead.

Nothing better than sleeping with the sound of thunder and the patter of rain, she thought as she got out of her car and went through the door that led into her kitchen.

Sam hissed and spat from his perch on top of the refrigerator. The cat had reverted to his natural cranky character in the last couple of days.

"Just my luck," she muttered as she walked down the hallway to her bedroom. Two men in her life, one a cranky cat and the other gone with the wind.

Within minutes she was in a silk nightgown and matching robe and at the computer writing Belinda a letter. Belinda wasn't allowed phone privileges yet, but Chantal had gotten a letter the day before from her saying that things were going as well as could be expected. She was working the program and felt positive about her life.

Chantal had just finished her letter and shut off the computer when her doorbell rang. She frowned and glanced at a nearby clock.

After ten. Who would be at her door at this time of night in the middle of a storm? She was certain it wasn't the Avon lady.

She grabbed her gun from her desk drawer. Even though she believed Mundy had been effectively neutralized, she wasn't taking any chances.

Flipping off the gun's safety, she walked toward the front door. A boom of thunder was followed by a rapid knock. She peered out the peephole and gasped in shock.

Luke stood on the porch, drenched to the bone. She couldn't help the way her heart jumped at the sight of him. She set the gun on the table in the foyer, then fumbled with the door locks.

"Can I come in?" he said without preamble as he strode past her and into the living room. "We need to talk."

She steeled herself. The last time he'd said those words he'd told her about Mundy's price on her head. Whatever he had to discuss didn't appear to be pleasant, as his mouth was set in a grim line and tension radiated from him.

"Talk about what?" she asked. Even soaking wet the man looked awesome. His shirt clung to his chest, defining the muscles beneath. Droplets of rain sparkled in his dark hair and as usual he looked as if he could use a shave.

He stared at her for a long moment without speaking. He drew a deep breath, then expelled it. "Cold beer…pepperoni pizza…Chiefs' football games…" he muttered.

She narrowed her gaze. "Are you making fun of me?"

"Not at all. You said it worked for you when you were feeling nervous and anxious. I thought I'd give it a try." He jammed his hands into his pockets, looking as uncomfortable as she'd ever seen him.

"Luke, what's going on?" Luke's nervousness made her nervous.

He walked over to the bank of windows and stared out, his back rigidly straight. For a long moment he remained silent, the quiet broken only by a rumble of thunder and the patter of rain against the glass panes.

"For the last thirteen years, since my parents' and Seth's deaths, I haven't allowed anyone to get close," he finally said. "If I felt myself drawn to a woman, felt like my emotions might get all tangled up, I ran."

He turned back to gaze at her, his eyes as dark as she'd ever seen them. "I came back from Mexico and had decided it was time to move on. I've spent the last couple of days thinking about where I'd land, what kind of a job I'd get. But for the first time in thirteen years I let somebody get close and I don't want to run."

Chantal's heart stuttered as he took three steps toward her and placed his hands on her shoulders. He smelled like the night…hot and wet and there was something wild, something hungry in his eyes.

"Hell on heels…I knew you were trouble the first time I saw you." His hands moved slightly on her shoulders, caressing the silk of her robe. "Look, I know we come from two different worlds. You have a private jet at your disposal, about all I could manage would be a private horse-drawn carriage for a ride in the park."

He dropped his hands, but didn't step back from her. "I came here tonight because I couldn't stand it anymore. I need to know if Tamillo was just a one-week fling to you or if it was something more?"

They had begun something in Tamillo and only time would tell where it would lead, but as she looked at him and saw the need in his eyes and felt a responding need in her, she knew she was in for the ride.

"I've always loved carriage rides in the park," she said.

He smiled then for the first time since he'd come into the house. It was that sexy half smile that sent her pulse pounding. "What do you say we recreate our roles as honeymooners?" Her reply must have been on her face for he scooped her up in his arms.

She'd known this man was dangerous to her from the instant she'd laid eyes on him. He came to her with no pronouncement of undying love, no promises for any lasting commitment. She wouldn't have believed him if he had.

The future would take care of itself. They had plenty of time. For the moment it was enough that he was here with her now.

She leaned her head against his chest. "Prada handbags…sushi…Crazy Luke Coleman," she murmured as he carried her down the hallway to the bedroom.

Turn the page for an exclusive extract from
Ruth Wind's
Juliet's Law
which is out in Mills & Boon Intrigue
next month!

Juliet's Law by Ruth Wind

"Ready?" her sister asked, putting sunglasses on her head.

"I am."

A woman in a yellow jacket moved by the table and gave Desi a long, hard glare. Desi stared right back. When the woman continued toward the cash register, Desi and rolled her eyes at Juliet. "The dentist's wife," she said when the woman had gone outside. "She hates my guts."

"Because?"

"Because she's one of Claude's groupies, and in their eyes, I'm just a mean woman who doesn't understand him."

"Yeah," Josh said, behind them, "you old meanie, you."

Desi grinned, her eyes flashing in a way that made her sister wonder what had forged the bond between these two.

And was there something romantic brewing? "You better believe it, mister."

Did her sister have feelings for this man? He was sort of her type, after all, a rugged Native American, an outdoorsman. He had that adorable daughter who needed a mother.

Josh laughed softly, and Juliet felt the sound run down her neck like warm fingers. She resisted looking up at him, getting caught again in that dark, patient gaze. But even as she resisted, she felt the steady presence of him at her back, solid, steady, calm, and she couldn't help the wave of yearning it kindled in her. It had been a long time since Juliet had felt safe—if she ever had.

Scott was a good man—smart, supportive, ambitious—but she'd never felt sheltered by him. Josh, on the other hand—

With a popping little shock, she heard her thoughts. *Stop it!* She was engaged! It was one thing to admire the long, sturdy thighs of a man, or the grace of his hands. A woman had eyes, after all….

But it was something else again to be thinking of resting against that broad shoulder, to imagine taking a deep breath of relief as that deep laughter rang into the room.

Disloyal. In two directions if Desi was attracted to him, too.

Blindly, Juliet stood and walked towards the door, grabbing a green-and-brown-wrapped mint from a bowl on the counter. "I'll be right outside," she called back. Without waiting for a reply, she rushed out.

The door was in a little foyer with racks of newspapers and tourist brochures on one side. As Juliet rushed through, a man was coming in, and Juliet stepped aside, and—

Slammed squarely into her demons. She was never quite sure what happened, why she was flung back in time, but suddenly, she smelled a musky aftershave and margaritas, and there was a swooshing of all sound, as if her ears were covered. In real time, she ducked her head and managed to stumble around the man coming in the door, ignoring him when he said, "Miss, are you all right?" and got out to the sunshine in the street. Sweat poured down the back of her neck.

But even in the bright sunshine and open air, her throat felt constricted, and her breath came in ragged, tearing gasps. The worst was the sense of mindless panic urging her to *flee! flee! flee!* Her legs burned with the need, her lungs felt as if they would explode. With as much control as she could muster, she grabbed the stone corner of the building and leaned on it, trying not to fight the sensations nor give into them.

A heavy hand fell on her shoulder. "Hey, Juliet, are you—"

She screamed, slammed the hand away. Tried to back off, bumped into the wall.

Saw that it was Josh, and wanted to burst into tears.

He held his hands up, palm out to show he wouldn't hurt her. "Hey, hey, hey," he said. That rich gentle voice splashed into her panic, coating it like chocolate.

And just as suddenly as she'd been sucked into the flashback, she fell back out. With a soft noise, Juliet pitched forward, instinctively reaching for the sturdiness of his big, strong shoulders. Her head landed against his sternum, and she could smell the clean freshness of clothes hung out to dry on a line, and something deeper, his flesh. A gentle light hand smoothed her hair.

"You're okay," he said. "You're okay."

And it was true. After a moment, the dark memories retreated, and she could take a long, slow breath. Raise her head. Only then did she realize how close they were. Embarrassed, she tried to take a step back, and bumped into the wall at her back. "I'm sorry," she said, trying to duck to her left, afraid to look at him.

"Easy." He moved his big hand up and down her arm. "You don't have to go anywhere. Your sister will be here in a hot second."

"I'm—this is…oh, I'm embarrassed." She bent her head. "Thanks. I'm sorry."

"You don't have to apologize." His rumbling voice again rolled down her spine, easing the tension there, and his hands kept moving on her arms in a most soothing way. Steady. Gentle. "You don't have to say anything at all."

Juliet bent her head. He wore dark brown leather hiking boots, sturdy-looking with laces and hooks and eyes and a sole that looked as if it could withstand six inches of ice. Her feet in their thin California boots looked insubstantial, tiny even, and with a glimmer of pleasure, she thought one of the reasons to like a man so big was so that you could feel small next to him. And she was not normally a small woman.

She wanted to offer an explanation, to say something to excuse her weird behavior. The flashbacks were hateful, like a scar, and it made her feel overwhelmed to imagine telling him. Where to start? "Thanks," was all she said.

He released her and in the next instant, Desi came out, offering breath mints to everyone. Juliet moved away, vaguely aware of him watching her. "We'd better get to the courthouse," she said. "Get this taken care of."

"Yep. Let's do it. "

Juliet glanced up at Josh. "See you later."

His eyes were steady and sober and saw far more than she wished. "Right."

MILLS & BOON

INTRIGUE
On sale 19th October 2007

COVERT MAKEOVER
by Mallory Kane

Undercover agent Sophie Brooks is good at her job.
Love is another story. So when she crosses paths with
Sean Majors while trailing a kidnapper, it's just not Sophie's
life that's in grave danger…

DARK REVELATIONS
by Lorna Tedder

Trapped into becoming an antiquities thief, Aubrey De Lune
has given up everything. But after stealing a sacred
manuscript, Aubrey discovers a secret – the key to her
heritage, her power…and getting her life back.

THE LOST PRINCE
by Cindy Dees

Overthrown in a coup d'état, the future king of Baraq runs
to the only woman who can help him. Now Katy McMann must
risk her life and her heart to save a crumbling nation.

SPIN CONTROL
by Kate Donovan

With FBI agent Justin Russo refusing to be straight with
her, how could lawyer Suzannah Ryder prove him innocent
as the evidence piled up against him?

A SEARCH FOR SURVIVORS BECOMES A RACE AGAINST TIME – AND A KILLER

When a plane goes down in the Appalachian mountains, rescue teams start looking for the survivors and discover that a five-year-old boy and a woman are missing. Twenty miles from the crash site, Deborah Sanborn has a vision of two survivors, and she senses these strangers are in terrible danger.

With the snow coming down, not only are they racing against time and the elements – they're up against a killer desperate to silence his only living witness to murder.

Available 21st September 2007

4 FREE

BOOKS AND A SURPRISE GIFT!

We would like to take this opportunity to thank you for reading this Mills & Boon® book by offering you the chance to take FOUR more specially selected titles from the Intrigue series absolutely FREE! We're also making this offer to introduce you to the benefits of the Mills & Boon® Reader Service™—

- ★ **FREE home delivery**
- ★ **FREE gifts and competitions**
- ★ **FREE monthly Newsletter**
- ★ **Exclusive Reader Service offers**
- ★ **Books available before they're in the shops**

Accepting these FREE books and gift places you under no obligation to buy, you may cancel at any time, even after receiving your free shipment. Simply complete your details below and return the entire page to the address below. You don't even need a stamp!

YES! Please send me 4 free Intrigue books and a surprise gift. I understand that unless you hear from me, I will receive 6 superb new titles every month for just £3.10 each, postage and packing free. I am under no obligation to purchase any books and may cancel my subscription at any time. The free books and gift will be mine to keep in any case.

I7ZED

Ms/Mrs/Miss/Mr ....Initials ....
BLOCK CAPITALS PLEASE

Surname ....

Address ....

....

....Postcode..

Send this whole page to:
UK: FREEPOST CN81, Croydon, CR9 3WZ

Offer valid in UK only and is not available to current Mills & Boon® Reader Service™ subscribers to this series. Overseas and Eire please write for details and readers in Southern Africa write to Box 3010, Pinegowie, 2123 RSA. We reserve the right to refuse an application and applicants must be aged 18 years or over. Only one application per household. Terms and prices subject to change without notice. Offer expires 31st December 2007. As a result of this application, you may receive offers from Harlequin Mills & Boon and other carefully selected companies. If you would prefer not to share in this opportunity please write to The Data Manager, PO Box 676, Richmond, TW9 IWU.

Mills & Boon® is a registered trademark owned by Harlequin Mills & Boon Limited.
The Mills & Boon® Reader Service™ is being used as a trademark.